Fisher, Carrie

Surrender the pink

Fisher, Carrie

Surrender the
pink

DATE		ISSUED TO
DEC 2 7 1990		84-515
JAN 8 1991		83-543
JAN 1 4 1991		81-296
		84-187
JAN 1 8 1991		
FEB 2 1991		84-521

By the same author

Postcards from the Edge

CARRIE FISHER

SURRENDER THE PINK

SIMON AND SCHUSTER

*New York London Toronto Sydney
Tokyo Singapore*

Simon and Schuster
Simon & Schuster Building
Rockefeller Center
1230 Avenue of the Americas
New York, New York 10020

This book is a work of fiction. Names, characters, places and incidents
are either the product of the author's imagination or are used fictitiously.
Any resemblance to actual events or locales or person, living or dead, is
entirely coincidental.

Copyright © 1990 by Deliquesce, Inc.

All rights reserved
including the right of reproduction
in whole or in part in any form.

SIMON AND SCHUSTER and colophon are registered
trademarks of Simon & Schuster Inc.

Designed by Laurie Jewell
Manufactured in the United States of America

3   5   7   9   10   8   6   4   2

Library of Congress Cataloging in Publication Data

Fisher, Carrie.
Surrender the pink/Carrie Fisher.
p.   cm.
I.   Title.
PS3556.I8115S87   1990
813'.54—dc20   90-37077
CIP
ISBN 0-671-66640-1

Permissions can be found on page 285.

For my grandparents
Ray and Maxene Reynolds
and
for my parents

Mating is more a bitter
truce than a willful embrace.

—CHARLES DARWIN

Man's love is of man's life a
        thing apart,
'Tis woman's whole existence.

—BYRON

Love in action is a harsh and
dreadful thing compared to
love in dreams.

—FYODOR DOSTOYEVSKI
Brothers Karamazov

Love is a long, long road.

—TOM PETTY

—1—

Dinah Kaufman lost her virginity a total of three times. Not because it was so large that it took three times to knock it out, but because she thought losing your virginity was supposed to mean something and it took her three strikes to feel that she was even remotely in the meaning ball game. It seemed that all her trouble showed up in sex, that alleged road to love. In almost every other situation you could hardly tell that there was anything wrong with her; she just seemed to have too much personality for one person and not quite enough for two. But in romance—BOOM—you'd know right away.

Dinah couldn't remember how she'd first learned about sex. She remembered coming home from school one day—she must've been about seven—and telling her mother that she had seen the word *fuck* written on the handball court. "What does it mean?" she'd asked as their white station wagon headed toward home. Her mother had hesitated and said, "I'll have to tell you later, when I can draw you diagrams." She never did tell her later, but Dinah didn't really mind missing the telling so much as she minded missing those diagrams. Somehow she had a feeling that they would have come in pretty handy from time to time.

When she was ten, she got ahold of a book called *For Girls Only* which had in it, among such things as "Your Menstrual Cycle," how a man and a woman make a baby. The man puts his penis in the woman's vagina and rubs it in and out till he spills billions and billions of spermy seeds. From this Dinah deduced that while the lower half of the body was engaged in this magic weirdness, the upper half of the body discussed what to name the baby. "Should we name it Robert?" he says, thrusting himself gently inside her once again. "How about Helene?" she muses, with a wince. Dinah had a friend in school, Laura Avchen, who, after discovering the whole penis-into-the-vagina business, wanted to know, "Do the balls wait outside, or go in with the penis?"

One thing Dinah did remember clearly from when she was little was that she *knew* that she would grow up and know exactly what to do, that things would just somehow fall into place, guided by some inner Homo sapien rhythm code. She had watched grown-ups standing and talking among themselves at her mother's parties with drinks in their hands, chuckling confidently and looking as though they knew exactly what they were doing and why.

Dinah put up with a lot as a child and then as an adolescent because she assumed that, at the end of these ordeals, she would be rewarded with the unearthly calm and confidence that adulthood would surely bring. She would get out of school, get a job, meet a man, get married, have children, and grow older, all in relatively smooth, easy motions.

She was partly right. She did get out of school.

Dinah's mother brought her up to be a virgin. As though it were a high-paying job. "Men want one thing and one thing only. Once you give them that, they walk

11

right out of your life and take your self-respect with them." Dinah imagined men wandering away from her with her self-esteem in little doggie bags. Holding it gingerly away from their bodies as though it stank a little. Or had melted and was leaking.

When she was sixteen, as a Christmas present, her mother bought her a vibrator. "The ideal stocking stuffer," said Dinah when she opened it in her room with her mother. "I got one for your grandmother too," Mrs. Kaufman noted, "but she won't use it. She says she's gone this long without having an orgasm—might as well go the whole way. Also, she's afraid it'll short-circuit her pacemaker."

Dinah tried the vibrator. She lay on the cold floor of her aqua-tiled bathroom with the door locked, the lights out and the water on, so no one would hear the telltale buzz. And she had enjoyed it, she really had. The trouble was, it reminded her of her mother. Her mother—who called the penis "the staff of life" and the balls "the grapes."

Dinah tried to distill the message about sex and relationships that she had gotten as a child, and then the revised, updated version she had gotten as a teenager, and she realized that, at best, it was confused, contradictory. Sex was for men, and marriage, like lifeboats, was for women and children. It seemed that men and women were at cross-purposes.

Shortly after the vibrator episode, Dinah's mother had a mild heart attack and suddenly became terrified that she was going to die. Maybe it had never occurred to her before. Or maybe that's all it had done—*occurred* to her. But now she was obsessed. She sank into a deep depression. "Don't listen to your old mother," she would wail. "Oh, Dinah, Dinah, life is so short. Time passes so quickly. Don't let life pass you by. Look at me; I've hardly done anything. I've never really lived. I've only been with two men. I've never lived anywhere but here in the Valley. Dinah, you've got to get more out of your life than I have. I've thought about it a lot, and I've decided that you shouldn't be a virgin when you get married. What's the point? Your father left me anyway. So, if there's a boy you want to go to bed with—you should just go right on ahead. I'll arrange for you to go see Dr. Semel and he can fix you up with a diaphragm or birth-control pills." She took a dramatic gulp of beer. Dinah was alarmed. She appealed to her mother's former sense of chastity.

"Ma, whoa, wait, I haven't said that I want to . . . sleep with somebody. I'm fine like I am."

"I refuse to let you have a life like mine. What's the point? I had a life like mine and look at me. I've seen you looking at that boy Mickey in your jazz class. I could arrange for the two of you to have sex and I could be nearby to supervise."

Dinah ran upstairs to her room, all the while hoping that if she moved quickly enough, nothing could catch up with her. Closing the door behind her, feeling as though she was surfing the fear. Way out on the edge of the board on a wave that simply refused to hit sand. At times like these, she would try to remind herself of some previous occasion when she felt great. Last week in the car. In the car, on the way home from school, she'd felt exhilarated. She'd gotten an A on a test and felt equal to anything. But now all her efforts to invoke this experience were futile. She had crossed over the border into depression and fear. She realized that exhilarated didn't really pay the bills here. That currency was just no good.

"Don't be so hard on yourself, dear," her mother would say to her.

"Oh, okay. Don't be? I thought that being hard on yourself was a good thing, but you say don't. Well, there you go. You learn something new every day—which means you learn three hundred and sixty-five things a year—which isn't nearly enough—so in my spare time of learning things, I've always relaxed by being hard on myself. But you say don't. So, okay, fine. I'll stop then." Her mother would give her a look. She had many looks and she wasn't stingy with any of them.

Whenever she didn't understand something that Dinah did, something that she said, a heat that she had, she blamed it on Dinah's absent father. "That's the Jewish thing, dear."

This was why Dinah was bad with men. When she was very little, about two, her father went away. She hardly ever saw him after that, maybe once a year. See, he and her mom didn't get along and, besides, he'd moved far away. Anyway, after he left, she waited for him to come back. She made herself wonderful for his return. And whenever she saw him on his once-a-year visits, she'd put on her best behavior so he'd love her. Because she hardly ever saw him, he grew daily in her mind, a paternal tumor on her imagination. She loved—she worshiped —the father she made up in her mind. The father she created in fantasy grew more intricate with each passing day, until finally she had created two monsters—the father she had never had—and the daughter he should never have left.

So, this is why the bad things with men happen. She puts on her best behavior whenever they visit so they'll love her, and she can't possibly know who they are, for all that she needs them to be, all that she imagines they are in their absence. In a nutshell, monsters. These strangers that are her father. And if they're not leaving, she'll push them so she can try to get them to return. And if they're not leaving, she'll leave, because she doesn't know how to be with them for long. She only knows how to try to get them back. She loves them until

14

they love her. She yearns for them. This was why Dinah was bad with men.

The first time Dinah met Rudy was at her boss Charlotte's fifty-fifth birthday party, about a month after she began working on *Heart's Desire,* a new soap opera that had just started the year before, in New York. Charlotte's apartment was a huge loft off Hudson Street.

"Don't leave me," Dinah said, clutching Connie's arm as they stepped off the elevator and into a well-lit hall. Connie Sorkin was thirty-seven years old and married to her second husband, with one grown son. She had streaked-blond shoulder-length hair and dark-blue eyes. She was an abrupt, loyal woman who was good at her job and talked eternally about her menstrual problems. The frantic murmur of a party in full swing threatened and hummed from beyond the door. Connie looked at Dinah in amusement. "This is so sudden," she said, ringing the doorbell. "We hardly know each other."

"Compared to the nobody at all that I'll know at this party, you're my best friend," said Dinah.

"You know Charlotte," Connie reminded her, "and Nick and Ogden and Bob."

"I've worked with them one month," Dinah all but wailed. "That doesn't count as knowing."

"You've only worked with *me* one month. Anyway, believe me, there's not much to these guys," Connie continued, as the door was opened by a thin, blond-haired man in glasses and the party was partly revealed. "One month is about all you need to really fathom their depths."

"Enter the Dragon!" welcomed the little man who had opened the door, brandishing a drink.

"Hello, Mel," said Connie, kissing him lightly on the cheek. "This is our new breakdown writer, Dinah Kaufman. Dinah, this is Mel Metcalf, in charge of business affairs. The only kind of affairs he could be in charge of with that face."

"Always a pleasure, Connie," said Mel smoothly. He had a long, pointed nose that looked as though it protected the rest of his face from attack. "Hello, there, Dinah. Aren't you pretty. I thought all of the writers had to look dried out and forgotten, like our Connie here, or resemble a small mountain, like our birthday girl." As he said the last, his nose pointed in the direction of a spot at the far end of the room containing the highest concentration of people.

Charlotte's loft was a big, bare room with strange exotic plants and lit with soft, lonely lighting. A life-sized ceramic acrobat hung from a rope above a room choked with people and the Rolling Stones blared from strategically placed speakers. "I been walkin' Central Park, singin' after dark. People think I'm craaazy."

Connie and Dinah slowly made their way through the merrymakers toward Charlotte and the bar. Dinah decided halfway to the bar that she was going to drink. Or, at least, she finalized the decision. She had never been a good drinker, tending to get drunk too quickly, and had occasionally even been known to black out—which was a tragedy considering her fondness for blunting and blurring. But she would fall back on drinking for certain emergencies on the off chance that this time it would be different. And this party, filled to the limit with people she didn't know, seemed to her to be definitely on the emergency side.

Charlotte was standing talking to an intense-looking man wearing jeans and a dark-blue sweater. What struck Dinah immediately were his eyes. They were a pale, far-away blue. For some reason they reminded her of the eyes of an eagle. Alert. Cool. Practically extinct. The light-pastel color surrounding a pin-point of a pupil. Eyes that not only undressed you unblinkingly, but shaved your head, called your parents, and refused to refinance your house. And then there was something about him that looked to Dinah like Dinah. Like a distant relative complete with distant unrelated eyes. Attractive, painfully thin, *certain.*

Charlotte was a fairly large woman. She looked as though she might've landed a job as a linebacker if she hadn't gotten into soaps. When their director Nick wanted to annoy her, he would call her "Tuna Neck," which he had done twice that first week. But for all of Charlotte's vastness, this man that she was talking to seemed to tower over her.

Charlotte was talking in an animated way, while the dark-haired man stood observing her steadily, with his arms crossed protectively in front of him, wearing an expression only a cello could play.

"Connie! Dinah! There you are! Connie, you've met Rudy Gendler, haven't you?"

"I don't believe I have," Connie said, extending her hand. "It's a great pleasure, Mr. Gendler. I'm a big fan."

Rudy turned politely toward Connie. "Not so big, surely," he said, almost smiling. Charlotte laughed. "I'm the big fan," she said, patting her stomach. "Connie here is just a regular-sized fan."

Rudy nodded his head at Connie. "Connie," said Rudy. He said her name almost like a question, his blue eyes narrowing.

"And this is Dinah Kaufman, the newest recruit to our breakdown writing troupe." Charlotte indicated Dinah proudly. Dinah ran her hand nervously over her closely cropped red hair, her tongue over her dry lips. She felt the full force of Rudy's eyes, looking over the gaping chessboard at her, wordlessly saying, "Your move." Looking at her as though he had ordered something different and she came instead. . . .

Or did she imagine this?

She ducked her head. "Mr. Gendler," she said, the proverbial schoolgirl. Rudy raised his eyebrows slightly.

"Mister—why is everybody calling me mister tonight?" He regarded Dinah casually. The room felt hot to her; her hair felt as though it were humming.

"Just showing a little respect for your position as a lauded and respected playwright," Charlotte said, putting her arm around Dinah protectively. "Aren't we, Dinah?"

"Uh-huh. . . . He has a 'mister' quality," she said to no one in particular, running screaming down the hallways of her mind, searching for something to say, for someone to be. *Where is that file?* she thought frantically. *That party file? My new-people file. There should be something on men, for Chrissakes!* People moved past them, talking, laughing.

Rudy considered her carefully. "Thank you," he said. Then: "I think." He sipped his drink thoughtfully, regarding her closely from over the rim of his plastic glass.

"Let's get you two a drink," said Charlotte, steering Dinah and Connie toward the bar.

"Nice meeting you," Dinah said in Rudy's direction as they completed their less-than-sparkling first interaction.

"Yeah," he must've said.

When she reached the bar, she ordered the equivalent of a small safe to be dropped on her head.

She was lying on Charlotte's bed with all the coats, waiting to feel like returning to the party. But it was so nice there, stretched out, listening to the music and the hum of voices from just beyond the partition. Like when she used to fall asleep in the backseat, listening to her mother and stepfather talking on a late-night, lulling drive home. She imagined that all the people in the next

18

room had interesting lives. It was a soothing and disconcerting thought. She smiled and shifted.

The coats smelled of dust and perfume, a warm, comfortable smell. Someone sat down next to her. She opened her eyes reluctantly.

"Mr. Gendler," she murmured.

"Don't get up," said Rudy.

"No, I don't," she said, smiling. "Did they break the piñata yet?"

"I don't think so," said Rudy patiently, crossing his legs. "What's a piñata?"

"Those Mexican things you hit with a bat and candy and toys come out," she explained. "I used to like to think of my head as a piñata; crack it open and . . ."

". . . Toys and candy," finished Rudy, nodding slightly. "You're not from New York. Where are you from?"

"Well, not just toys and candy," she said, slightly defensive. "But . . ." she sighed, "Los Angeles."

"Ah yes. That accounts for the Mexican thing . . . allusion," Rudy said. "The Mexican Allusion," he repeated thoughtfully to himself, for Dinah's benefit. "That might be a good title for something."

There was a beat. The Bee Gees sang in it somewhere. Rudy coughed.

"What would come out of your head?" Dinah asked Rudy. She sat up on one elbow, her head tilted to one side, looking at him with what she had left of her vision.

"When?"

"When I cracked it open," she said.

"This is a charming conversation," Rudy said, looking at the wall. "Well, it depends which side you hit on. The left side, math; the right side, a big white bunny. How much have you had to drink?" he continued.

"I'll answer your question if you'll answer mine," she said.

Rudy looked at her. "I just answered yours."

Dinah sighed. "With me, almost any amount is too much," she admitted finally.

"So, why do you . . ."

"It generally seems like a good idea at the time."

"C'mon, I'll take you home," he said, helping her to her feet, which seemed much farther down her body than she remembered them.

"You don't know where I live."

"You'll tell me." Rudy led her from the room with polite force, a reluctant convalescent. She tried to find Charlotte or Connie to wave good-bye to as she and Rudy crossed to the front door, but found herself waiting for the elevator without having said good-bye to anyone. She followed Rudy into the street like a dutiful squaw, where someone opened a door to a limousine.

"You have a limousine," she said matter-of-factly.

"I'm afraid so," he said, motioning her inside.

She told Rudy her address and he gave it to the driver. They both sat back as the car headed uptown.

"How old are you?" asked Rudy.

"Twenty," she said.

"You shouldn't drink if you know that it doesn't agree with you."

"You can tell all that from just my age?" she asked. Then she crossed her legs and smoothed her skirt over them. "I just figured since it was a party . . ."

"A party filled with people you just began a working relationship with," he said.

"Yeah . . ." she said, now totally embarrassed and slightly more alert. Her mouth was dry, her brow furrowed. "I didn't do anything really awful, though, did I?" A feeling of panic seized her as it occurred to her that maybe she had been actually worse than what she was dimly aware of.

Rudy cleared his throat, his hand over his mouth in

20

a fist. "All I was saying is that you should be more careful," he said.

"I will," she vowed. Rudy seemed to her somehow to have so much self-assurance that it had become something else. Something beyond assurance that Dinah could never hope to attain.

They sat in silence for several blocks. Rudy cleared his throat again.

"How old are *you?*" she asked him finally.

Rudy looked at her. "Thirty-four," he said.

"Thirty-four," she repeated, as though that explained something to her once and for all. She repeated the number, this time more softly, looking out the window as the limousine sped through the park.

"I like your plays. When I was in school, I acted in *Aspects of Ezra or the Despair of Possibility.*"

"Not one of my favorites," he said. "What part did you play?"

"I played the ghost," she said.

"Really? The ghost? I wouldn't have cast you as that," he said thoughtfully, his hand over the back of the seat behind her now, staring straight ahead, shaking his head slightly. His eyes were stony and aloof, sparkling with the keen light of the fanatic. Dinah was compelled rather than charmed, compelled by her seeming inability to charm him. He looked back over at her and she looked away shyly.

"Well, I wasn't supposed to be in it anyway," she said quickly. "I was working in the art department on sets, and the girl who was supposed to play the sofa got sick, so . . ." She shrugged. "This isn't a great story. They were desperate; I was awful. Well, not awful, 'cause you can't really be bad in something that's that well-written. Still . . ."

"I'm sure you were better than you think."

She looked at him. "Don't be so sure," she said.

21

"Sorry," he said. "It's a habit."

"Certainty?"

"Certainly."

They both smiled. A flash, like a vividly felt or remembered thing, darted out of his eyes. Dinah looked back out the window, her heart pounding. Rudy turned on the radio. Steve Martin sang "King Tut." They were almost at her apartment house now.

"My favorite play of yours was *The Innocent Savage.* I *loved* that."

Rudy nodded politely, acknowledging the compliment.

"Charlotte told me that you were a good writer," he said.

"Oh yes," she said. "My samples for writing soap-opera plots are appearing this week in *The New Yorker.*"

"No, she said that you wrote something else, something about your moods," he said.

"She told you about that?" Dinah flushed. "Why did she tell you that? What did she say?"

"I asked her about you and she told me," he said simply.

"You asked her about me?"

"She said that you had names for your moods. Pam? Pam and . . ." he began.

"Roy," she said curtly. "Pam and Roy. Roy is rollicking Roy the wild ride of a mood, and Pam is sediment Pam who stands on the shore and sobs. One mood is the meal, the next mood is the check." She recited this hurriedly, staring at her hands in her lap. "Sometimes I get so depressed, I can't remember who I know," she said quietly, looking out the window. Somewhere in the night, an ambulance wailed. Dinah followed the sound; it dragged her mind with it for several blocks.

This was just sometimes, though, not all the time. This was when Pam, her sad mood, was upon her, when everything would seem far too complicated and hardly worth the effort. With Pam, she would get a kind of emotional flu. Her liquid confidence would ebb, then run dry. Her desolation class had begun and she would simply have to wait for the bell. Maybe this time, she would *learn* something, her professorial mood would sniff, as class started and she couldn't imagine doing anything ever again. The facts of her life were the same, just the fiction that she made up about it changed. This fiction said none of it was possible—the other fiction said it largely was. (And what wasn't possible was at least *interesting*.) This fiction said that not only wasn't it possible —it was frightening, it was lonely, it was *strange*. She'd missed her turn and soon the skin under her eyes would wrinkle, puff, and sag. (Three of the seven dwarfs of aging.) This was the fiction of existential pain and horror, the other fiction was a lighthearted read, a book called *Isn't It Darling to Be Human—How Exciting to Be Alive!* Of the two fictions, Roy and Pam, she obviously loved Roy, her up mood, best. But she'd sit through the Pam class, a dutiful student, waiting for the bell to ring, the Roy to sound, then she'd slam her head shut and race into the hall, ready to greet her facts armed with her preferred fiction.

"There's probably more of a Roy thing happening this evening," she said, laughing, sheepish. "With every possibility of Pam for tomorrow."

"Why is that?" Rudy shifted and turned to look at her again.

Dinah ran her hand nervously over her head, over what was left of her recently shorn hair. "Oh, potential hangover. Thinking I made a fool of myself," she said, laughing. "Actually making a fool of myself." The car pulled up in front of her building.

"You think you've made a fool of yourself this evening?"

23

"Well, yes. I mean, lying down with all the coats and everything." Her skin glowed softly in the streetlight that shone in through the car window. Rudy smiled.

"That wasn't foolish so much as inappropriate."

"How do you learn the difference?" she asked.

Rudy turned and faced her. His eyes looked grave and preoccupied, with the light of amusement flashing in them somewhere, like promising light glowing from under a door. He leaned toward her, just inches from her face.

"We'll talk about it in the car," he said softly and then kissed her a great big Saturday-night kiss, her head pressed back against the rough dark-blue velvet of the car seat. She felt the kiss everywhere, glowing like a big, bright candle. He pulled back just a little. She felt his breath on her face, his hands on her shoulders. She looked at his eyes, so near her own.

"You really *are* a good playwright," she said, smiling gently, camped out in his thrall.

"You're just saying that," he said.

Dinah straightened her skirt and pulled the strap of her purse back up over her shoulder. "Not *just* saying it, but . . . yes. Saying it all the same." She opened the door. Rudy took her elbow too late, in some belated attempt to help her out of the car.

They were standing on the street now, looking at each other. Rudy's driver stood at the back of the car, staring discretely across the street, away from Rudy and Dinah.

"Well . . ." she began, "good luck with *The Mexican Allusion.*"

Rudy seemed confused. "The *what?*" he said.

"Your new play," she reminded him.

"Oh yes," he said nodding, vaguely remembering. "Good luck with your moods. With Roy and Pam." She realized that she was waiting for him to ask for her number and that he wasn't going to. She backed toward her apartment house. Rudy stood with the door of the limousine open behind him. He'd thrown down the gauntlet of his indifference and now Dinah picked it up. She raised her hand in a wave.

"Don't be a stranger," she called with mock gaiety. "Don't be Albert Camus."

Rudy smiled. *"The Outsider,"* he called, correcting her. Dinah flushed.

"Don't be either of them. Don't be anyone if you can help it," she said, disappearing into her building. Suddenly her head popped back around the corner. "Actually, it can be either one," she said hurriedly. "I think it depends on the translation." She smiled her best enigmatic smile at him and was gone again. Rudy watched the space where she had been for a brief moment, smiled to himself, and then was willingly reabsorbed into his car.

With most species of fish, there is little or no contact between the male and the female. The male merely deposits the sperm over the eggs after they've been released by the female. After that brief interlude, the lovers may go their separate ways, never to meet again.

—2—

Most mornings Dinah would wake up feeling completely disoriented, thinking not only, Where am I, but *who, what?* And just plain am I? And then it would all come flooding back, crashing down on her in a bewildering heap. Oh, *yeah,* she'd think, remembering. And then she would set about mustering some kind of perky resignation to propel her out of bed. Oh, well, she'd think then. Here we go again. And then, My *God.*

She felt herself to be a sort of renegade member of the Homo sapien gang. All of them huddled together while the world turned them gently toward death. A big, bouncing ball of dying things, with her off to one side like salad. Her life somehow didn't seem to belong to her. She could feel herself trying to get close to people. Relating ostensibly personal information about her life as barter for something. For alliance in her war to gain possession of an acceptable self-image. Coming into her life required no great talent or skill. People seemed to come into her life all the time and just sort of mill around in it. One could easily wade into the shallow end of the whom she offered up as herself; the trouble was getting in over your head. Over her head.

Sometimes she'd just walk around the city alone. Watch the people, smell the food, the bus exhaust, the smoke coming up through the grating. She'd feel protected somehow, found a sense of belonging in the hectic sprawl. And the next minute she'd feel like the one who couldn't break the code, hit the right stride, catch the wave. Potholes and traffic and bums, oh my. With all the honking and the hum of movement, the living, breathing blur of noise gently pressing in on her, the great purr of the Metropolitan Cat turning into a dull roar. She'd feel so silent on the inside, her head as quiet as a stretch of sand, a cathedral silently worshiping the life that was all around her, storing it up for later when she needed some "too much" to draw upon.

Her skull runneth over.

The fall in New York had been beautiful. But then winter had come and it was brutal. Dinah's roommate Ingrid came into her room one morning and woke her, shaking her gently into the now. "Mr. Blizzard is out in the yard," Ingrid said. Dinah stumbled out of bed and followed Ingrid out into their living room and there on their little terrace was as much snow as Dinah had ever seen. Mounds of it lay over everything: their two chairs and small table and their one lone, bare tree.

"See," said Ingrid proudly, as if it were somehow all her doing, as if she were the Snow Queen and this her new domain. The wind was whipping around the windows of their corner apartment. Creating an eerie, wailing sound. A wind that had traveled across the world and now howled with longing for its ancestral cave.

"Wow," said Dinah, her first word of the day. She was deeply impressed. Snow never ceased to amaze her. She thought it the most interesting climate trick going.

Growing up in California, the weather can be fairly one-dimensional, but with snow, Dinah felt herself slip into the historic world of 3D. "Now we're talking weather," she said, following Ingrid to the window. They both watched the weather wordlessly for a moment.

"On the radio there are warnings not to go out unless it's an emergency." Ingrid looked at Dinah and added, "Especially not to drive."

Dinah smiled and said, "Let's go."

Outside, it was beautiful and white, hushed and waiting as they burst from their building, pushing against the wind toward Dinah's car. They were wearing so many sweaters under their coats, so many T-shirts under their sweaters that their arms stood slightly out from their sides, like gingerbread girls. Their breath came out in great white puffs, each instantly swept away by the strong wind.

The girls huddled together, eyes tearing from the cold, from laughter. The streets were empty of cars, sparsely dotted with huddled people. They stopped at Broadway, breathing hard, squinting against the wind. "It looks like it must've looked at the turn of the century," Dinah breathed.

Broadway was covered with a white, glaring blanket of snow as far as they could see. Children's laughter cut through the stillness like wild birds. "Winter Wonderland," sighed Ingrid. They watched her sigh evaporate into the wind and smiled.

They drove the car out of the Eighty-fourth Street parking lot, having explained to the attendant that it was an emergency. "She has to have some fluid drained off her brain," said Dinah solemnly. He brought the car. "We'll bring you some if there's extra," called Ingrid gaily as they drove up the ramp and spun through a bank of snow. "It's great on ice!" she said, squinting her eyes as she peered through the now icy windshield. "Yahoo," she continued cautiously as they approached the corner, their wheels crunching and sliding.

"You're the only person who can make 'yahoo' sound like 'uh-oh,' " observed Dinah wryly.

"There's no way we can die, right?" Ingrid said. "I have a show tomorrow night."

"Well, that cinches it then. We might've died if you were free tomorrow night, but . . ." The rear of the car lurched and sashayed. Ingrid screamed as Dinah fell silent, maneuvering the car. When the car was back under control, Dinah said, "Hey, this was your idea."

"Was it?" Ingrid seemed doubtful as Dinah turned the car gingerly down Broadway. "Geez," she continued as they swerved slowly into the middle of the empty street.

"The Great White Way." Dinah grinned.

The buildings stood at either side of the vast expanse of snow leading downtown. People were shoveling pathways to their stores, their homes, their cars; a bulldozer churned somewhere in the distance. The wind whistled into the car, carrying a light, icy, stinging snow. "No skies of gray on the Great White Way," sang Ingrid. "That's the Broadway Melody."

Dinah chimed in, "Though you may roam to distant shores, your heart's at home on Broadway. Each night I dream that I'm still there . . ." They forgot the words but they sang on, making up what they forgot, bellowing out proudly what they remembered, as they huffed and puffed and blew toward Lincoln Center.

Theirs was one of about five cars that they spotted along the way, pressing along, skidding a bit, bumping over the newly fallen snow. Two boys of about nine ran over to the car and demanded a ride, hopping onto the hood. They bounced along for a couple of blocks before Ingrid stopped the car and told them to get off. "This is *not* a taxi service," Ingrid called through the partly open window, and then closing it as they started their slow, moseying drive once again. A snowball landed *THUMP* on the back window after half a block.

"What if it *is* a taxi service?" Dinah said, the fire of good samaritanism burning in her breast. Ingrid looked at her. "We're one of the few cars out here," Dinah said. "We'll be helping people. We'll become known for it all over the world. The Ice Maidens—sweeping down on people through the snow, providing temporary shelter and shuttle services for the windblown and snowbound."

Ingrid looked out the window, tempted. Considering. Finally, she said, "All right—but only older people. We can only pick up people over fifty, who are truly struggling in the snow."

Dinah banged the wheel with enthusiasm. "Yes," she crowed. "Oh yes." And they stole along listening to the radio blare "Blue Christmas."

"If we get killed, though," Ingrid cautioned over the music, "I'll kill you."

"Fair enough," replied Dinah. And the Ice Maiden Patrol made its way slowly downtown. Children waved at them, threw snowballs, cheering them along.

"It's as if they've never seen a car before," Ingrid commented.

"Africa in the snow," said Dinah.

"What?" said Ingrid. But, before Dinah could explain, Ingrid pointed suddenly out the window. "Look! Senior citizen at three o'clock." Ingrid's father was in the army.

"Where's three o'clock?" Dinah asked. "Talk American."

"Over there," Ingrid said, pointing to an older gentleman creeping along the icy sidewalk with a cane. She rolled down her window. "Hello!" she called. "Sir?" The man slowly turned his white head around and looked cautiously for the source of the call. "Over here!" cried Ingrid. "In the car!" The man saw them and looked confused, worried. He pointed to himself with his free, cane-less hand. Dinah now rolled down her window, letting in a blast of icy, stinging wind.

"Can we give you a lift?" she called, snow on her face now, her eyelashes and hair. The man timidly approached the car. "We're headed downtown," she continued, "providing an emergency carpool for people such as yourself." He was next to the car now, standing awkwardly at Dinah's window.

"You're not a murderer, are you?" piped Ingrid across Dinah to the old gentleman.

"Eh?" he said, removing his glasses and wiping the snow from them with his sleeve. He was quite a small man and most likely thin under his big black coat. He wore a gray scarf wrapped around his head in a stranglehold and carried the Sunday paper in one of his dark-gloved hands. "Girls," he said as though identifying a type of amoeba under a microscope, "this is not a day for driving."

"It's not really a day for walking either," Dinah said. "Can we drop you anywhere?"

"We're the Ice Maidens," added Ingrid. Dinah got out and stood in front of him like a royal attendant, indicating with pomp and flourish that he should enter the car.

"At your service, sir," she said proudly. "Frigid, but mobile." The old man hesitated, then bent and stiffly climbed into the car. "Offering service during this cab famine," Dinah concluded.

"I was just going home," he explained almost sadly.

"Well, we'll take you," said Ingrid. "Welcome to our anecdote." Dinah climbed in after him.

"Don't mind if I do, girls, don't mind if I do." His red nose practically glowed as he settled into the backseat. They recommended singing "The Broadway Melody" as they ferried their passenger the long two blocks to home.

"Bye!" the girls called after him as he ambled slowly

to his building. "Bye, bye," they continued sadly as he disappeared through his door, a bottle bulging in his coat pocket. They sat for a thoughtful moment. "I'm going to miss that guy," said Dinah.

"At least he didn't murder us," mumbled Ingrid.

"Speak for yourself," said Dinah, shifting into Drive.

There was a tap at the window. Ingrid nudged Dinah, who looked up and saw Rudy Gendler through the fine, twinkling snow. "Do you remember me?" he called through the glass.

Something in Rudy's face, in his presence, infused Dinah with feelings of longing and a sort of hope. His certainty shone through the snow. Maybe no man is an island, but some sure look like them. All safe and dry and looming on her horizon. As she rolled down the window, she thought, if only *she* could be that certain, that safe, that dry, that *apart*. He became not, in that instant, so much her ideal mate, as her ideal. She wanted to become this person. If only she might cast her lot in with his and one day find their two lots inextricably confused. Dinah Kaufman *is* Rudy Gendler. She smiled up at him through the window, wishing she'd worn more makeup, glad her skin was relatively clear. She nodded; of course she remembered him, how could she forget The Outsider, The Stranger, The Man with the Waiting Limousine? She would love this man, she thought. He would save her from herself. What she never considered was: Who would then save her from her savior?

He asked Dinah for her number and she wrote it on an old receipt with an eyebrow pencil of Ingrid's and passed it to him. The snowflakes were falling slower now, larger. Rudy slipped the number into his pant pocket, nodded to Ingrid and to Dinah, then strolled off through the swirling snow. An explorer in this metropolitan wilderness. It had taken a blizzard to bring Rudy back into Dinah's life; Lord knew what it would take to pry him out.

When the female elephant comes into estrus, she selects a mate. This marks the beginning of a very close, affectionate relationship. At first, she's very coy and flirtatious, alternately inviting the bull's advances and then running away from him. During the courtship of several months, they're inseparable. Playing, touching, stroking, petting and mooing. The male displays remarkable restraint and only at the end of the long courtship—and only at the female's invitation—does he consummate the relationship in copulation.

Rudy and Dinah sat across from one another in an Italian restaurant in SoHo, surrounded by plastic foliage draped along the tops of walls twinkling with Christmas light. He was once more in dark blue, his hands folded before him. Dinah's chest was tight with what to say, what she was saying.

"I have too much energy."

Rudy smiled as he signaled the waiter. Dinah bit into a breadstick. "Maybe you have some of mine," he said.

She laughed, the center finger of her left hand rhythmically picking at her thumb; the other thumb sporting a fresh bandage. "Anytime you want some of it back," she said grimly.

It turned out the restaurant served no alcohol, and though they both claimed it was probably just as well, Rudy ran across the street and bought some wine. He returned flushed, his eyes sparkling, and sat across from her slightly out of breath. "Why are you so smart?" he asked as the cork popped and the wine was poured, the grease for the wheels that would turn them toward each other, drive them increasingly together, and eventually roll over them.

Dinah shrugged and held her glass as the red liquid filled it. "My mother was pretty and I knew I didn't look like her—I remember thinking I looked like a toe—so I figured that I'd better develop some compensating feature. So I . . . I don't know . . ." She shrugged. "I smartened up, I guess. Why are *you* so smart?" she asked back at him, popping the last bit of breadstick in her mouth.

Rudy sipped his wine and looked thoughtful. "Because your mother was pretty," he said.

"What a coincidence!" Dinah laughed.

Rudy raised his glass and Dinah clinked hers to it. "To your mother." They both drank. "And good genes," he added.

They drained their glasses and Rudy refilled them. The waiter arrived with their appetizers, placing them before each with a slight flourish. Neither ate much, warmed now by the wine and the possibility of who the other person might turn out to be—Dinah dreamed of her life working out, Rudy dreamed of his night working out. Basking in the warmth of foregone conclusion, of mutual appreciation, of eventual contact.

"I think I'm basically an introvert," Dinah was telling him. Dinah was telling him everything now, dragging out all of her best stuff from the shadow of her skull and into the bright sunlight of this new boy, this interesting man. "My extroversion is a way of managing my introversion, but I'm sort of back down behind it all, waiting for the apparent me to end and the essential me to begin."

"Run that by me again," he said, holding his wine in front of him with both hands.

Dinah leaned back and laughed. "If you call in advance, I come with Cliff Notes."

Rudy smiled and emptied the bottle into his glass. "I'll remember that." Dinah leaned forward on her elbows, her face radiant from the wine.

"We haven't touched our food," she pointed out to him sheepishly.

"Fuck touching it," he said. "I'll touch it; I just don't want to have to eat it."

They got into their overcoats, Dinah almost losing her balance in the process. "I may have some of your energy," she said happily, "but I think you've got all of my . . . what do you call it . . . *poise.*"

"I never call it poise," he said, putting down some money for the meal and walking away from the table. "Let's go." He headed through the door, which was also surrounded by colored lights and holly.

"I'm your geisha," Dinah said, following him into the cold winter night. It was a promise she inevitably failed to keep.

They were in the car headed uptown.

"Where to, sir?" said the driver. Rudy looked at Dinah; she colored and gave the driver her address. They sat in silence for a moment, faced with the possible enormity of what was to come. Finally, she spoke, picking invisible lint off her black coat with her gloved hand.

"Why didn't you ask for my number that first night?" she asked casually, concentrating on the lint.

Rudy cleared his throat, looked out the window briefly and then at her. "I was living with someone at the time," he explained. "It was in its final . . . whatever . . . throes and . . . that party I met you at pushed it over the edge. Me not taking her, I mean." He stopped talking abruptly. Dinah watched the side of his face expectantly. New York swept by the window in a blur. The car halted at a stoplight, silhouetting him briefly against a tenement or a town house. Pedestrians crossed the street huddled against the cold.

"Just don't let it happen again," Dinah said with mock gravity.

"What about you?" he said.

"What about me?"

"Why aren't you with anyone?"

She considered saying, "I'm with you," then checked herself and sighed from the effort of self-censorship. "I was going to marry someone, but then . . . I didn't." The light changed and the car lurched forward. Rudy continued watching her, so she continued, "He wanted me to get used to how he brushed his teeth."

"How awful."

"No, you know what I mean. He was—"

"Dull."

Dinah tilted her head to one side, considering, and then shook it slowly from side to side, sadly. "But he was so nice."

"Too nice?"

"How can that be?"

Rudy shrugged. "*I* don't know. He was *your* fiancé."

Dinah went back to working on her lint. "What was the matter with your girlfriend?"

Rudy folded his arms and squinted. "Vicki was very . . . God, I don't know. She was very attractive and certainly . . . a good person. But I just felt so *confined.*"

"Uh-huh."

"Also, she was an actress, and every time I didn't put her in one of my plays, it was an ordeal." He cleared his throat. "Also, she shopped all the time."

"What'd she buy?"

"Shoes."

"Well, there you have it."

They were silent for several blocks, illuminated briefly by the drive under streetlights, then swept back into shadow. Rudy leaned forward and turned on the radio. Peter Gabriel sang "Solsbury Hill." He sat back.

"Also, in the end, she was a little bit of a ball buster."

Dinah laughed. "My friend Connie says there are no ball breakers, just breakable balls."

The car rounded a corner sharply, sending Dinah

smack up against Rudy, who was, in turn, pressed up against the door. Rudy put his arm around Dinah as the car righted itself, her gloved hand pressed into the center of his chest. They found themselves inches from each other's faces, eyes wide, mouths closed. Dinah gave a nervous laugh, pulling back slightly.

"Of course," she continued, "by the same token, you could say there are no heartbreakers, just breakable hearts, no homewreckers . . ."

"Do you ever not talk?" he asked quietly, so close now to her, their faces once again illuminated by streetlight as they stopped in the middle of a line of cars headed across Central Park South.

"Sure," she said, her smile softening.

"When?" he said.

Dinah looked at him, near, then nearer. "Soon, I guess," she half-whispered. Their mouths pressed together in a kiss.

A chill ran down her spine on twinkling little feet. Cities have been built up around less, she thought, feeling the world of *him*, just over the wall. The soft ghost rope of his voice, drawn through his throat and wound around words. What world is this? What language is spoken?

The kiss broke; they pulled back, breathless. Dinah's expression was solemn. "I've been thinking about it a lot," she said, "and I think we should start seeing other people."

The rank or pecking order is of great importance to the raven. When a dominant female, high in the ranking order of the group, pairs with a submissive low-ranking male, she will adopt male behavior—even taking the superior position during copulation. In such a relationship, the male accepts the submissive role along with other female behavior patterns.

—4—

Dinah was on her way back to her office from the gynecologist. She walked slightly more slowly than usual—
the Pyridium and sulfa pills she had so recently taken for
her latest bout of cystitis had yet to take effect. Charlotte
met her coming down the hall.

"Just the little lady I'm looking for," she said,
her blue eyes twinkling somewhere in her large
face. "How're you feeling?" Charlotte put her arm
around Dinah, navigating her down the hall toward her
office.

"Better," said Dinah bravely. "I'll be better soon."

Charlotte patted her roughly on the arm as they
squeezed through the door to her office and she sat Dinah
in a chair facing her desk. "Connie says you've got female trouble," said Charlotte, sitting behind her desk;
Dinah sat pale and stiff in her chair.

Dinah shrugged and shifted uncomfortably, looking
toward the bookshelf lined with scripts and videos.

Charlotte leaned back and crossed her large legs.
"Cystitis," she said disapprovingly. "No excuse for it. I
went with a guy who I swear gave it to me on purpose. It
was like some sort of proof of his virility. The doctor said

he'd never seen a case so bad. And when I told that to Doc—my boyfriend's was Doc for some reason—I could swear he was *proud*. It was some sort of trophy awarded to his—awarded to his—"

"Charlotte, I appreciate your concern, but I hope everyone hasn't been informed of my . . . complaint."

Charlotte waved Dinah's concern away with a plump pink hand. "No, no, no—I was just looking for you earlier and Connie told me where you were. Busy-body that I am, I asked her why. And that's all there is to it."

Dinah looked at Charlotte gratefully. "Sorry," she began, "I just—"

"No need, no need—just make sure you use more lubricant next time and drink plenty of cranberry juice. Now, here's why I was looking for you. I read those plot outlines of yours with your two new characters, Blaine and . . . uh . . ."

"Rose," Dinah reminded her.

"Rose, that's it. And I gotta tell you, it's good. I like it. The point is, I'd like you to block out some more. Take them further along. Work on it with Connie if need be. I'd like to send them to the network as soon as pos-sible."

Dinah was dumbfounded. "Gee, Charlotte, that's great. . . ."

Now Charlotte stood, the meeting apparently at an end. "Good stuff, good stuff," she was saying, coming around her desk, leading Dinah away. "Especially the stuff about the difference between foolish and inap-propriate. Oh, and the Camus material. It may be a little highbrow for the sponsors, but I'll fight the good fight."

They stood in the doorway, Charlotte as large as many lives and twice as beaming. "Good work, little lady," she said in closing. "You'll make head writer before long if you keep this up," she said. "Who knows, someday you may even have my job. Now scoot on back and get to work. And don't forget about the lubricant."

She slapped Dinah rowdily on the back, then went back into her office and closed the door.

———

Two women stand in front of a door. Party noises can be heard from beyond it. One of the women, the lovelier of the two, clutches the other smaller, darker woman by the hand. "Don't leave me, Margie."

Margie looks scornful. "Oh, Rose, it's just a party. Relax."

Rose reaches into her handbag and removes a compact. She opens it and passes the powder puff over her nose and chin, examining her face gravely when she finishes.

Margie laughs. "Don't you love how we look at ourselves in mirrors, with expressions we never use in the real world? If I were smart, I'd talk while I applied my war paint."

The door swings open and the party is revealed. "Charge," says Rose weakly, snapping her compact closed and returning it to her bag.

"Welcome, ladies," says a tall, thin man with a face like a chicken hawk. "Kenneth O'Connor."

"Rose Chassay."

Kenneth regards Rose. "Chassay. What a lovely name. It sounds like dancing."

"Yeah," says Margie, steering Rose toward the bar. "Allemande left and a do-si-do."

"Yes sir, yes sir, three bags full," responds Rose automatically.

The two women make their way through the crowd to the bar. "Two margaritas, please," says Margie. Rose surveys the room. People are talking, drinking, dancing.

Suddenly she sees a man at the far end of the room talking to a fat woman. Rose nudges Margie.

"Hey—who's that with Ruth?" Margie peers across the room to where Rose is looking. "Don't be obvious," says Rose, turning her back.

"Sorry," says Margie. "It's a family tradition."

She sees the man, a handsome blond man with blue eyes, wearing gold wire-rimmed glasses. "Him?" Margie gratefully receives her drink from the bartender. "Why, I thought everyone knew him. Oh, I forgot, you just moved here. That's Blaine MacDonald, the most powerful lawyer in town."

Rose turns back around and discreetly surveys him over her glass. "MacDonald," she says thoughtfully. "Isn't that . . . ?"

"Yep," says Margie. "MacDonald Industries. That's his family. Rich as thieves."

Suddenly the music changes from a fast song to a slow one: "Solsbury Hill" by Peter Gabriel. A mirrored ball glitters and spins in the center of the room, bridging the gulf between Blaine and Rose. "Don't look now," says Margie in a low voice, "he's staring at you."

"Really?" says Rose, smoothing her smooth hair.

Margie smirks. "Be careful, Rosie, he's trouble," she warns. "Besides, he's practically engaged to Avery St. Claire."

"Not . . . ?" begins Rose.

Margie nods. "St. Claire Shipping."

"What does she do?"

"Do? She marries Blaine MacDonald; that's what she does."

Rose squeezes Margie's arm. "He's coming over," she says under her breath. And as Blaine approaches, everything in the room softens, practically falls away, leaving them in sharp focus. Rose no longer is aware of the music, the mirrored ball flashing. Then, they stand facing one another, silent, spellbound.

"I'm Blaine," he says finally.

"I'm Rose," she says.

We fade to commercial.

———

The male snake first rapidly flicks out his tongue while following the female around and attempting to crawl over her. The courtship behavior in many snakes is controlled by pheromones, produced by a specialized gland on the female's back. By her odor, he knows whether or not she is the correct mate. Instead of having a single penis for injection, the male has two, one on either side of the tail. They are both fully potent and barbed; however, he does not put in both penises simultaneously.

of course not.

— 5 —

The first time Dinah lost her virginity, she was almost eighteen. It happened with her friend Bud. That one time only.

She had first met him when she was fourteen. He lived two blocks away from her in North Hollywood. A handsome, hatchet-faced boy, he had jet-black hair and jet-black eyes, and was very intense, always champing at the bit, as though something at the back of him was pushing him a little too far forward. He had a tendency to look impish or sly, as though he'd just left the scene of some bad-boy behavior. He was the prince of the practical joke, the whoopee-cushion wizard, whose short-sheet, pink-belly and phony-phone-call pranks lay somewhere in his recent wake. Dinah and Bud fell into one another's company, along with Bud's best friend, Mickey, also just fourteen, a small, powerfully built, pock-faced teenager with blue beseeching eyes. The three of them would roam the streets of their sprawling neighborhood or, later, when they were older, comb Ventura Boulevard for adventure. Dinah desperately tried to be one of the boys, to be accepted, to fit in, be a musketeer or a musketette. For three years, she had a secret crush on Bud, and Mickey had a secret crush on her. But Bud loved an outsider, loved practically every older, lanky girl he saw. He had already had an affair with Suki, an older girl with a tattoo of a blue bird on her ankle and big, braless breasts, for whom he still pined. So, gradually, Dinah reabsorbed her infatuation into the pure semi-tragic energy of late adolescence.

The three of them loping along together. Each tormented by some unrequitement. Whipped up, almost formed, itching for something, for everything, together.

Then, finally, when they'd known each other for three years, they borrowed Bud's mother's Town and Country station wagon and drove to Las Vegas, each armed with new fake IDs, the radio blasting for the full six-hour drive. They flowed up the stream of red taillights to Nevada while the downstream white lights flowed gently by their side. They were almost eighteen now; they were ready to roll.

"What a groove!" whooped Dinah as the Strip twinkled into view, the sun setting behind them in the deepening desert sky. "Groove and a half à la king!" she chanted, a saying she had concocted the year before. "Groove and a half à la king!" they all crowed together as their car veered into the Strip and it pulsed and glowed before them, stretched out as far as they could see. Looking sinister and brazen, the electric leer of the neon signs was drawing them farther and farther into the bidding of this adult forbidding world. They whooped and cheered. Vegas! Wow!

Wow.

They smoldered with joy as they cruised slowly down the Strip, trying to take it all in and make it a part of them. "Hookers!" crowed Bud gleefully, his dark eyes gleaming. Mickey was howling with laughter, slapping Bud loudly on the back. This, at least, was the plan. Hookers. Well, anyway, one.

49

The plan was to get Mickey a hooker to separate him from his virginity once and for all. Bud hadn't been a virgin for ages now, if you could believe him. And now he had decided it was Mickey's turn. Time for his rite of passage. Of course, Dinah was still a virgin, but that was different; she was a girl. It didn't really count. It was more appropriate than foolish.

So the three of them had pooled their fortunes, robbed their parents, and roared off to decapitate Mickey's maidenhead.

"Hey, girls!" called Bud to two women walking down the street. The Strip. Unescorted women. Them. They both laughed and one of them called, "Hey kid, where are your parents?"

"In my pants," called Bud. "Want to see them?" And they roared off into the night, Mickey and Dinah falling back into their seats, helpless with laughter.

"Okay—this is the plan," said Bud in hushed tones. They were in a hotel now, in two small, cheap rooms. The cheapest that the Desert Sun had to offer. They had just enough money left for room service and a hundred-dollar hooker. "Why are you talking like this?" asked Dinah, mimicking his hushed tone. "Is the room bugged?" She smiled a gentle, mocking smile.

"We're underage," replied Bud in the same tone. "We're underage. This is how you talk when you're underage." He continued conspiratorially. "Now—I call the bell captain, requesting a girl for the evening. Mickey, you get ready."

"Okay," said Mickey. He looked at Dinah and shrugged, then moved into the bathroom, nervous and distracted now. Dinah stood awkwardly, looking at Bud, who was sitting on the bed holding a receiver to his ear. "I'll hold," he said into the phone in a low voice. "What do I do?" whispered Dinah, not unaware that she had a privileged position in this largely male ritual, this boy world. Bud put his hand over the mouthpiece. "You can make sure the tape recorder works right." Dinah nodded solemnly, moving to the bag that contained the recorder. She hesitated. "I still don't understand why we're taping this," she said, her brow knitted. "For *later*," hissed Bud as he removed his hand and said into the phone, "Yes, I'm here."

How did Bud know all this stuff? wondered Dinah, realizing somehow that it was his job to know. They were in Bud's domain. Part of Bud's future world.

Dinah checked the recorder. "Testing," she said, holding the machine close to her mouth. "One, two, three." Then she amended, for no one in particular, for later: "Fucking . . . one, two, three." She rewound the tape and played it back, pleased with the result. Mickey emerged from the bathroom with his hair slicked back, wearing a rumpled tie. Bud replaced the phone. "It's all set!" he announced cheerfully, then saw Mickey and laughed. "What're you—going to a prom, for Chrissakes?" Bud laughed, grabbing Mickey and yanking his tie. Mickey pulled away and blushed, embarrassed. "You told me to get ready," he mumbled in explanation. Bud jumped on the bed, and bounced there several times in excitement.

"Not for a *date*, asshole," he said, continuing to bounce on the floral bedspread, which twisted and bunched beneath him. "For a *blow job*."

Mickey sulked, but stuck with the tie. Dinah drew the curtains and opened the sliding door, which let out onto a tiny balcony overlooking the pool through a tree. She inhaled the desert night air deeply and leaned out over the railing, feeling she had finally arrived, that she was now truly one of the boys. She walked back inside, back into the rarefied world of this inner sanctum, and curled up catlike in a fluffy blue velvet chair. Bud hopped off the bed and approached the miserable Mickey, playfully punching him, mussing his sandy hair. "Ready, pal?" he leered in a taunting voice. "It's D-Day, Mr. Hosemaster," he continued. "It's deflowerment day, Captain Thrust. Time to force the item!"

"Quit it," entreated Mickey, brushing Bud away and attempting to retuck his shirt.

There was a knock at the door. Everyone stood motionless, paralyzed, a post-pubescent tableau. Bud unfroze first. "Who is it?" he called. Mickey panicked and ran back into the bathroom to slap on more after-shave. "What are you *doing?*" hissed Bud to Mickey's back.

"Carol," called the voice from beyond the door. "The bell captain sent me."

Mickey stood ashen in the doorway of the bathroom, looking nowhere in particular, his arms dangling uselessly at his sides, stinking of Mennen After-shave.

"Just a minute!" called Bud, grabbing the tape recorder from next to Dinah. Dinah thrilled, crossing to Mickey, taking hold of his arm. He looked at her weakly.

"Do it for all of us," implored Dinah gently.

"I hope I can just do it for me," said Mickey.

Bud slapped a key and a condom into Mickey's hand. He had the tape recorder folded in a jacket to conceal it. "It's already on record, pal." He clapped him on the back. "The room is next door. We'll be right here." Mickey tried to look grateful, but only succeeded in looking sick. "Now get out there and poke some pussy, boy."

Dinah grimaced. "Bud . . . ," she said, "try not to take *all* the romance out of this."

"Hello?" Carol called from beyond the door. "Coming!" called Bud, his eyes dark and glittering. "Get it, buddy?—Coming! Now get out of here. Make me proud —make her scream."

Bud pushed Mickey to the door, Mickey with the face of a condemned man, walking the last mile. He attempted to pull himself together and opened the door.

Dinah darted into the bathroom, her hand over her mouth, holding her breath, not wanting to see this girl, this woman, not wanting this whore to see her.

Dinah waited in the fluorescent light of the bathroom, the sanitary seal still around the toilet, Mickey's after-shave uncapped over the sink, the room reeking of it. She twisted the cap back on and looked at her face in the mirror, running her hands through her hair. Her father's hazel eyes stared out at her. She passed her hand absently over her pale white skin. It was a nice-enough face, she concluded finally. She'd prefer another one, but she could work with this one. Certainly, there were worse, weren't there? She wondered what the whore looked like. She wondered how you ended up being a whore. She wished she could be a boy so she could lose her virginity with impunity, stinking of after-shave and wearing a tie. Bud tapped at the door. "The coast is clear," he informed her in his hushed underage voice. Dinah emerged. Bud stood with his ear to the wall in the semidarkness. He had turned the lights off. He motioned Dinah to join him. She stood in front of him and put her ear to the wall. It was cool. She couldn't hear anything. She held her breath. "She wasn't a dog," Bud whispered to her, his breath warm against her ear, smelling vaguely of the beer that they had gotten someone to buy them outside the town. "I asked them to send someone with nice skin," he added, emphasizing this point with a single nod of his head. Dinah nodded. There was still no sound from beyond the wall. She turned and looked at Bud, who stood behind her. Now muffled voices came through the wall. A bed squeaked.

Bud put his hand on her shoulder and pushed her to a crouched position on the floor. They faced each other now, their ears pressed to the cool wall, their eyes on one another. Hunched together, motionless, Yorkies in a basket, orphans in Mickey's approaching storm. A moan came from the room next door. Their eyes widened in surprise, then squinted in laughter. Bud motioned her to be quiet, but she continued laughing, falling back onto the white-carpeted floor, tears coming out of her eyes. Then again a sound from beyond the wall; from deep within her, Carol moaned one whole sex-response word. "Wow." Woooow. As though Mickey was doing something unimaginable to her, something altogether new. Dinah laughed harder now. Bud shook his head, went to scratch his nose and somehow made a sort of snorting, farting noise. They both laughed now, silently, breathlessly, red-faced in the dark room, tears running out of their eyes. "Shhhh," insisted Bud when he could finally get enough breath to form words. He moved to Dinah now and sat on her stomach, putting his hand over her mouth. "Shhh," he repeated, more ragged now with laughter. Another moan came from the next room. "Wooow," once again. "Wow," mimicked Dinah. Bud collapsed onto her, their laughter surged once more, rekindled by the moaning. "What's he doing to her?" Bud said, still laughing. Both were breathless now, Bud's weight pinning Dinah, pushing her down. She pushed back at him. Finally rising on his elbows, he put his face so close to hers, her tear-streaked, laughing face. His beer breath was warm on her cheek. She felt the heat and the pulse of him, of her. Bud, still smiling, kissed her, shifting his weight. The kiss deepened. She received it, him. Big clam kisses. His hands moved over her. He pushed her legs apart with his leg. The soft arctic sex ghost drifted through her hallways, rattling its chains.

Moans come from beyond the wall. Neither hears it now, neither laughs. As his mouth moves over her throat, he pulls her sweater up over her head, his tongue darting over her breast. Now hands squeezing them. Her eyes closed, head back, one hand on his hip, the other slung back over her head. His hips moving into her, pushing hard into her. He pulls her skirt up. She wonders what they're doing. The moment closes in around them, pressing them farther along. Bud pulls at her underwear, rough. Now, his fingers move over her, into her. Both breathing so hard. Now hands on his shoulders, mouth on mouth. He undoes his belt buckle, his jeans. Tears open the extra condom packet. Her legs open, skirt at her waist, his pants at his knees, his penis poised hard on her. No! she thinks, Not . . . not now . . . no. He pushes himself hard into her. She begins to squeak, a pre-scream; his hand covers her mouth. He moves into her sporadically, roughly. Her eyes wild just above his hand. A moan beyond the wall, ghostly, far away. Dinah's hands grip his arms, nails gouging them. Bud's face, concentrated. A grimace of pleasure, of what's next. Not this way, she thinks. His motion more regular now. She closes her eyes. Gives over to what's gone. His pace quickens. Face changes. She watches beyond this. Be over. Takes herself back into herself as he freezes suddenly, whimpers a small whimper. "Oh . . . oh, God," he prays. His prayer plunges in her, his body of Christ, her blood, this communion of creatures. "I'm coming . . . I'm coming." He falls on her, wet with perspiration, crammed up inside her. How could it fit there? She could barely contain herself, but herself plus a penis . . . unthinkable . . . but . . . it's happened. The sex, having come from nowhere, now goes back to the same place.

Bud sighs now. She shuts her eyes, pinned—sprawling, heart pounding, mouth dry, disappointed, disoriented. A door beyond the wall opens and shuts.

Bud sprang to life. "Jesus," he cursed. Pulled himself from her quickly. She winced. Her hair wet, matted down, brow shining. "Sorry," he offered, pulling his pants up. "They're coming," he warned her. She sat up, located her underwear well down on one leg, pulled it up, her skirt down, world-weary, girl-weary. Her sweater over her head, her hands through her hair. They heard two voices beyond the door. Mickey and the hooker, the whore, that woman, escorted now, briefly. Bud and Dinah avoided one another's eyes. Sticky between her legs, she shifted uneasily, nowhere to go. That's what it's like? "Are you okay?" he said now, not a question, wanting no answer. She nodded mutely as he buckled his belt. "We can't tell Mickey," he added now, his head down, apparently lost in the activity of buckling. "He loves you, you know. It would hurt him." At last now, he looked at Dinah, a soft look, a boy pup. "It gets better," he smiled then, more himself; Dinah still a long way off from what she had been once, earlier, long ago.

It was 2 A.M., later that night, when the three of them piled back into Bud's mother's Town and Country station wagon, heading south. None of them could sleep; they were restless and unsettled in spite of having accomplished what they set out to accomplish. They were heading home. A newly deflowered Mickey, poised, was driving, ready for the rest of life. Dinah sat in the backseat with the window open—wind on her face, ballbearings behind her eyes, dreading the rest of hers. Her two friends' heads bobbed before her as she sat with her legs crossed, panties damp. "Play the last part again," said Mickey to Bud, who held the tape recorder in his lap. "Mick, we've heard it about a thousand times," moaned Bud, looking at Dinah out of the corner of his eye. "No way," said Mickey, a new man, his pockmarked face glowing with pride. *"Twice,"* he insisted. "We've heard it *twice.* God, what's the matter with you? You wanted me to do this, for Chrissakes—you wanted to record it. What's the matter with you? All of a sudden, the both of you are so goddamn quiet. Ever since we left the hotel. *Before,"* he amended, *"before* we left."

The three of them were silent after Mickey's outburst. Dinah leaned forward and patted his shoulder. "We're all proud of you, Mick." Bud looked at Dinah briefly, quietly, then back at Mickey. "Yeah," said Bud hollowly. "Yeah," he said again. "Well, you sure don't act like it," mumbled Mickey sullenly. "If I'd known you were going to act like this, I never would've done it." Bud pushed the rewind button on the tape. "C'mon, we'll listen to it again," he said valiantly, not looking at Dinah, shifting uncomfortably in his seat. "Forget it," said Mickey. "Don't do me any favors." He was in full post-coital sulk now. Bud pushed "play." "That's it," said a female voice on the recorder. "That's real good. Yeah," Carol crooned to Mickey, who moaned, "Wow."

"Turn it off," said Mickey hotly, changing lanes. A sign said: "Los Angeles—74 miles." "No, let's listen," said Bud. The three drove silently through the night to Los Angeles, listening to sex from hours before. Mickey's moans sang out of the recorder. Carol said, "Yes, oh, yes. That's real nice, isn't it?" "Yes," said Mickey. "God."

They dropped Dinah off at dawn. She raised her hand good night. She'd see them soon. She opened the front door gently, closed it behind her, crossing to her bathroom. She turned on the lights. The same face she had seen in Las Vegas stared out at her from the mirror. But, going closer, she looked carefully into her eyes, now ghoulish and matter-of-fact. It was true then, she concluded; she looked different. She was different—would everybody know? Would she be exposed to all as deflowered, a slut? She would have to swear Bud to secrecy; that was clear now. If they never did it again, she could somehow atone for it—one time against no other times would win out and she would be pure again with a potentially perfect initiation lying before her, a bright, cheery promise, an unopened letter once more now, instead of the junk mail she had overnight become. She could not rewrite the episode as romantic, with Bud falling to his knees, imploring her to marry him and swearing undying devotion. No.

Well then, she would not think of it. Ever again. She

removed her clothes, pulled her nightgown over her head, feeling all the while a funny burning and push in her loins. She hadn't really bled; what was wrong then? She sat down on the toilet and a sharp, stinging burn seared her deep inside. Agh. Dinah put her head down, brows knitted, knees together. Oh, no! A burning punishment. Fire, damnation, a burning punishment from God expressly for her . . . her what? Transgressions—what'd they call them? Loose behavior, looser morals. Oh, no. She hadn't really believed in God until the punishment came, forcing her to her knees, her hands together, her head back, face to the heavens. "Please, I'm sorry. I meant no wrong. I tried to stop him. I swear. Oh, please." The burning persisted. She ran some water, sat in the tub feeling as if she had to urinate, but no, it was just the pain, the dark hot leaden burn between her legs. Her shame, a scarlet "S" drawn on her insides with an absent, dull knife.

She finally fell asleep, but when she awoke, the pain was still there. She kept a damp washcloth in her panties all day Sunday. Listening to the sting her body sang through her, "Oh, for shame, for shame." She avoided Bud and Mickey for days after. Afraid she had God's punishing cancer, unable to ask anyone what it could be. How to cure it. Could she cure it? Would she die, feeling the sinking feeling that she had brought it all on herself 'cause she couldn't say no to Bud, couldn't risk his disfavor, his disapproval? Wanting to be one of them so much, she allowed even that, and now she had nothing left to give away. She walked through school carrying her secret God cancer, wearing her washcloth, distracted and ashamed. Gradually, over the week, the stinging subsided. No more bolting to the bathroom or praying to a wrathful, vengeful God. But her friendship with Bud and Mickey had sustained a blow from which it could not recover. It gradually toppled and fell. She extracted a promise from Bud that he would tell no one. "Not ever," she insisted. "Never," he vowed, worried, looking down at his scuffed shoes.

Years later when she discovered what she'd had was cystitis—"Honeymoon cystitis," her friend called it— she stared back down through the years to the time when she had carried the crotch cancer, and smiled to herself, shook her head. "Jesus," she said. It turned out there were pills for it, this bladder infection that comes from sudden sex, sex after a long time—a lifetime—or too much sex with too little lubrication or too little or no foreplay. She saw Bud and Mickey again, one now an agent, the other a restaurateur. But, at almost eighteen after the cystitis or her scarlet cancer, Dinah would wait awhile to lose her virginity again.

The second time Dinah lost her virginity was to Henry Stark, an associate professor in the art department. She hadn't surrendered up any other portion of her virginity since the episode with Bud. She was now eighteen and interested in having an affair, as all her friends seemed to be. She'd tussled with a few men in cars and on sofas, but she'd withheld the prize of her lagoon of mystery, as she was fond of referring to it. Her V account. The savings in her V account.

A boy in her film class was also in love with her, but there was something too frightening about the completion of that. There was nothing left for her to do. Besides, she was fairly comfortable with him and was laboring quietly under the delusion that love was an uncomfortable thing, an unnerving, upsetting thing. She thought that it meant you liked someone when you didn't quite know what to say to him.

Dinah would see Henry in the halls at school, or walking to his car. She met him in the parking lot. She had locked her keys inside her car and was trying to do something unsuccessful and silly; he approached, watching her wriggle a stick to pull up the lock, pry it up somehow through the top of the window.

"May I ask exactly what you're doing?" he asked in a serious voice. Dinah was too exasperated to be unnerved by him at that moment. "I'm cooking," she replied. "Mixing very small ingredients in my car with this stick. Would you like some?"

"No," he said, moving to the trunk of his car. "But I think I have something for the mix." He got a hanger from his trunk and opened Dinah's car door for her. He wore a light-blue shirt and tan slacks. There was a small circle of sweat under his arms. He looked stern, handsome, contained, married, with a thin gold band on the appropriate hand. "Thank you," Dinah said sweetly as he opened her door. "Has anyone ever told you that you look like the Marlboro Man?" she continued, detaining him.

He stood near her now. She looked up at him. Was he sneering? "You," he said, closer, looking down at her. Both were breathing slightly harder from their exertions. Dinah smiled down, ducking her chin. "Has anyone ever told you that you were going to have a drink with me?" he said.

He promised to get her back safely, not to worry—c'mon—almost as though he was saying something else. Appraising her, measuring her for a coffin, a coffin for the two of them, where they might lie buried together by night and haunt each other by day. She slid into the seat beside him. Somehow he had taken command. Of her. Of the entire situation. Wrapping her in the situation and sweeping her off her feet, the street, to the bar. This must be what older men are like, she thought. Married men, like kings, so confident.

They were quiet as they drove to The Elbow Room and parked. Henry looked over at her, his face so . . .

what was it? There was a smile in it somewhere. He had her. She knew he knew; the rest was just filler. They talked so much filler at the bar—their names, what he did, their ages, her studies, with her always feeling that he was saying something else. Some vaguely communicated disapproval, impatience, lust lurked just below the surface, leaking in every so often. She had a cigarette and he lit it as though he'd rather be doing almost anything else in the world. She had never met a man like this; like an animal he had stalked her, offhandedly, a sideline, ever so briefly, and now she knew he would take her. She had officially lost her vote. He took her hand almost gruffly. "You bite your nails," he said. Dinah withdrew her hand and blushed, unnerved. "Tear," she corrected him, as if this were somehow more worthy. "Not bite, tear, you know, peel—and mostly my thumbs."

"Uh-huh." His eyes held her eyes, fiercely, indifferently.

"It's true—see." She held her thumb up for him to look. He continued to watch her eyes.

"I believe you," he said. Dinah laughed, clutched her drink. "I feel like you're humoring me or laughing at me," she said. *Or fattening me up for the kill*, she thought. *Softening me up. . . .*

"Nah," he replied, leaning back in his chair, tapping back against the wall, his hands behind his head. "Why would I do that?"

Dinah didn't answer, downed her drink instead. Her second. "These are good," she said. "What are they?"

"Tequila," he answered. "The only hallucinogenic hard liquor. Comes with a worm." He signaled the waiter to pour her another and rolled himself a cigarette. Dinah felt slightly queasy.

They slid back into his car, Dinah pretty drunk now, her antidote for the unnervement, for the presence of this formidable male animal. Without speaking, he drew her to him. Her heart pounded, his mouth covered hers. He seemed so large, so overpowering. His hands went up her skirt. "Wait," she whispered breathlessly.

"I'm waiting," he replied.

So much of him, so little of her. For years she remembered the sound of her hand as it slid down the material of his shirt on his back. "Where do you live?" he asked. Dinah was now wide-eyed. Weak and wide-eyed. Helpless, helpless. "But . . ." His eyes so close now. She closed hers and told him. They drove there, his hands still on her. She put her key into the door, pushed it open. His hands on her ass, her hips, moving around to the front of her legs. She was paralyzed. He pushed up against her, pushing the door open and both of them through it, everything a metaphor now of the genitals. I'm taken, you take. Dinah reached to turn on the light; he retrieved her hand. "No." A command from her new king, his thorn pressed up against her crown, his keys near her kingdom. He shut the door hard behind them, turned, reached down and pulled her shirt up over her head.

"This is so prehistoric," she whispered.

"So, don't talk," he said, putting his large index finger over her lips. He got on his knees, pulled her skirt off and put his open mouth on her privates, breathing his hot O of breath just there.

Dinah passed out.

Henry revived her some moments later with some water. Master of the situation, the universe, her. "Drink it slowly." She obliged him, drinking slow, big gulps as he kissed his way up her legs and home.

And another coin from her V account was spent.

Who was this guy, these guys, these men? What were these men?

When the tide went out, when Henry went home, she was left beached on the silent sands of her sheets, wide awake, unable to shake herself out of the dream of him. Slammed up inside herself, trying to think herself out, remember herself before, but her head was jammed shut, rusted by wet dreams. Henry had installed himself front and center in her head. He sat high in her head and looked out of her eyes, picking out the wrong clothes for her to wear to parties so she would never meet anyone ever again but him.

She always felt confused when people consoled her sometimes by saying that something was "all in your mind." As though that were comforting. For Dinah, that was the most dangerous place in the world for anything to be. At the times when people said that, she would want to say, "Well, God, let's get it out of there then. Get me some bug spray or something."

They met every Thursday after that and had prehistoric sex in her apartment. It was exciting for her, it was lonely, it was almost out of character. Worshiping from just this side of afar, loving him to the degree that she was able, considering her background, considering she barely knew him. Wishing the infatuation would end—how could she live like this? Short of breath, raw, perpetually aroused, preoccupied, thrilled: at night praying her condition would at least lessen slightly; waking in the morning with a start—is it gone? The unbearable buoyancy of Where is he now? Wishing the madness to return. Something boiling, a buzzing in the blood and in the bones, a slow, percussive pounding—effervescent and carbonated. Alive. Alive and wishing her giddy demon back.

She didn't know what she was doing with him, but she didn't have to decide, as she was largely without him. Most of the time she either gave herself the benefit of the doubt or watched television. These were Dinah's beginnings as a polite masochist.

Every so often on a Thursday now, Dinah will remember the rolled-cigarette smell of him, the undeniable

63

fact and force of him, the cystitis and the sulfa drugs. Thursday night was bath night.

Henry somehow managed to make his silences look like a decision rather than an accident. Dinah lacked that talent. She would keep quiet because his quiet seemed so stern and final. He assumed his grown-up apathetic poker face, while she sat practicing ironic, knowing looks somewhere in his periphery.

He said once that she had the eyes of a doe and the balls of a samurai. Then there was that time in the park when they had the closest thing they ever had to a fight. That time, when they almost didn't talk in code. That time she said, "I am not a samurai."

But now he wasn't here to argue that point. Henry got a job in Chicago after about five months of Thursdays and moved away. She heard later that he had divorced his wife and married someone else. Someone he was now faithful to. Someone he shared his Thursdays with. Someone he had dragged by the hair to his cave and covered with the bearskin of his being.

This is how Dinah lost her virginity that second time.

The third and last time Dinah lost her virginity was in what would be her last year of college. She had gone back to being a virgin in her mind because the first two times she lost her virginity had been so loveless, hadn't meant what they were supposed to mean. When her friends talked about their sexual experiences, she simply didn't bring hers up. She had never told any of her friends about her trysts with Henry or her trip to Las Vegas with Bud. It was too humiliating. It hadn't gone the way it was supposed to go, so she simply decided that it hadn't happened. She air-brushed it out of her mind. Now, at nineteen, she was apparently the last of her friends to take the plunge.

Greg wore leather jackets and clogs. She would listen for the sound of his shoes coming down the hall. He had blond, messy hair, deep-green eyes, and a casual, indifferent air. They had poetry class together. Dinah read a poem in class during the first week. The assignment was to read a poem you either liked or had written.

"This is a poem I wrote when I was sixteen." She looked down at the sea of expectant faces. Why wasn't she reading someone else's poem? Someone good? Why wasn't she reading something of Anne Sexton's? She cleared her throat and looked back down at the paper. Oh, God, this was a stupid poem.

> "Don't offer me love,
> I seek disinterest and denial.
> Tenderness makes my skin crawl,
> Understanding is vile.
> When you offer me happiness
> You offer too much,
> My ideal is a long-lasting longing
> From someone whom I cannot quite touch."

She finished reading the poem and looked up, completely embarrassed. She caught Greg's detached glance, not consciously knowing that she had just given him explicit instructions on how to woo her. Greg looked down, apparently indifferent, as the class politely applauded. At that moment, Dinah began to fall in love with him.

He listened to her poem and proceeded to love her in a leaving way. "I shun affection," he told her, squinting off into the distance. He couldn't see well without his glasses. It turned out he had one green eye and one brown eye and he couldn't see out of the green one. "My grandmother was like that."

"What?"

"A hornet. She didn't let anybody near her. I'm like that. I don't let anybody near me."

"You're introspective," she ventured.

"I am not introspective," he said. "People who are introspective tend to know themselves. I don't."

"Withdrawn, then?"

"No," he said, "I'm a dullard. A frozen dullard. Frozen dullard yogurt. Frosty the Robo."

He walked as though he were fat, as though he had glue in his armpits and were balancing something very small on the top of his ass. He wore leather jackets, jeans, black T-shirts, and clogs on his feet. He rode a motorcycle. He had a police-badge collection and was obsessed with vintage cars.

She listened for the sound of his clunky footfalls all the time at school. He was one of those boys you think you've discovered. That no one else knows he's attractive, until later, when you find out that almost everyone does.

She loved the way he looked at her in that faraway, half-blind, half-hornet stare. Loved how they didn't talk well together, how unnerved she felt around him, how they had foreplay for months before she actually had sex with him. Before she relinquished the last and best third of her virginity to him. The third that had never had an orgasm. With him thinking she was a virgin, her being a virgin for him—men like that, she thought. And she loved him now.

They would kiss until that was all they knew how to do, leaving them like fish moving their lips in a half-kiss. He'd look at her, his eyes all soft and turned down at the ends. "When I die, I want them to cremate me and scatter my ashes in your hair," he would say, holding her at arm's length, with her seated on his lap. "You're a spectacular woman. I don't deserve you. No one deserves you. You're a phenomenon, a comet, a rare creature of substance and fire. I'm a manual on car engines compared to you. Marry me and divorce me for all that I've got." His leather jacket squeaked as he held her.

They decided to marry and Dinah loved him tenderly for three whole days. As though she were falling, falling . . . a haven of reciprocal love. The novelty of trust and commitment.

On the third day, as Greg was brushing his teeth, and Dinah was removing her makeup, he turned to her and said, "You'd better get used to this. You'll be watching me do this every day for the rest of our lives."

Dinah looked at him as he spit the toothpaste from his mouth. "The rest of our lives?" she thought. "What was that he said about not deserving me?" Greg finished brushing his teeth and headed for the toilet with a magazine.

Later that night when he looked at her with eyes all soft and turned down at the ends, she found herself, for the first time, steeling herself against his softness.

Dinah realized that the shared common denominator between all these men was that they were extremely uncomfortable with themselves. That there was a tight band of tension wrapped around their chests. A tension that communicated itself to her, that she vibrated with or felt responsible for. This was an extremely tense, male male. A manly man, almost a caricature. Something so vividly drawn that even she could see it. For her to be the little woman, he'd have to be a pretty big guy. Right?

The men she was attracted to tended to be quiet, introverted, shy, *other*. They were rumpled with the effects of interaction so that sex, in effect, became a sort of smoothing agent. Almost as though her feeling of being drawn to them would catapult her over the wide chasm of a foreign language, where sex becomes a relief, instead of a continuation of an existing conversation. Almost the sole means of communication. It was as if men with whom she could converse easily shared no part in an intrigue, a mystery with some sensual stigma attached. So it was the men from strange other tribes that drew her. Drew her down to her pre-verbal knees where she waited in prehistoric supplication for a bone, a crumbless way home.

Hansel the alien.

The trick was to keep men in her head, and to keep them in your head, they can't really be in your life. Oh, they can dip in every so often—imagining something better. A reality against which to measure the fantasy. A towering fantasy eclipsing your dwarfish reality. A man was sort of like heaven—and if you were a good enough girl, you'd get to go there. If only it matched up with how it was in your mind—but it never can, it never does. That's where Dinah's mind lived its most active life— between how it was and how it could be. Trying to bridge that gap, make those two friends. But they can never be friends, it can never be right, they can never love her right, that's how she picked them and then she punished them for being the way they were, for not living up to a standard she had never seen in her life.

The standard of a fantasy.

Dinah didn't want to meet a guy, she wanted to throw herself on a grenade. An act of heroism, terrorism, courage, folly, white-water, daredevil love. Her mind lay open like a half-eaten fig; see what you did? A man loose in her identity, having leaked into it when she wasn't looking. Approval, approval, an unnatural high, the subtle buzz of an indifferent fly.

The shine of plausibility seemed to have gone off all her affairs.

She heard early on that the truth hurt, so that when the hurt came, she recognized it because it felt so truthful. So the worse things were, the more authentic they seemed. That became one of the few things that she could identify as real. What could be more real than painful feelings? That accursed looking back and fearing to go forward. . . . Given all of that, who could she turn out to be? Who had she turned out to be? Sometimes she felt that she couldn't do all of this anymore, all this life stuff, that she was afraid of the next thing. The bad thing that stands up ahead and waits for her to catch up, grinning, looking over its shoulder, beckoning her forward, and she was the fool who then closed the distance. The gap. Trusting fool marching ever toward the bad thing. And doing it all wrong until then. She wanted so much to care less. It was the biggest thing that she wanted: apathetic indifference to most of her outcomes. To be carefree for her, then, was probably to be almost sleeping, with everything all blunted and blurred. She decided at some point that her skin was so smooth, so particularly polished, because she was so careworn. The doubting could be crippling. She wanted to say to people, "Remind me —who am I?"—hoping to hear some fairly acceptable version.

Before he can woo a female sparrow, a male sparrow must have a nest. It does not matter if the nest is straggly and untidy, for later the two mates can clean it up and make it more presentable. The important thing is that the male have some sort of nest. Females will have nothing to do with male sparrows without property.

—6—

Dinah and Rudy lay on the floor on a quilt from the bed. Moonlight shone in through the window onto the two of them, their nude bodies partly draped, partly revealed. He stroked her, kissed her.

"I can't stop kissing you," he said. Dinah smiled and shifted to look at him, feeling subdued, as though her central nervous system had been wrestled quietly to the ground.

"Kissing fever," she said. Rudy turned so that Dinah was beneath him, facing up to him.

"Say you love me," he said, his mouth to her cheek, his breath warm against her face. Dinah attempted to duck her chin, to get a little away.

"I could say it in another language. I could love you in Japanese or Swedish or Greek for awhile and then gradually work my way into—"

"Say it," he urged. Dinah's limbs had gone rigid. She was now truly locked in an embrace. "*You* say it," she muttered, blushing slightly. Rudy closed his eyes and put his mouth to her ear.

"I love you," he said in a low, serious voice.

There was a pause. The silence pressed in on them,

contained them. "Now you," he urged again gently. Dinah turned her face to one side, so that she looked at a desk, a chair and a waste paper basket across the room. She held her breath.

"Ay ishete imasu," she whispered softly in Japanese. "I love you," she tenderly translated, listening to hear how true it sounded. Hoping that, if she said it softly enough, the air would carry the words away before they counted, before she had to live up to their invisible contract, their dizzying, vague implications. To her "I love you" was something said instead of something done. A marker, a manipulation. Meant to reassure and guarantee. But if she accepts that Rudy loves her, then the loneliness sweeps in for all the years that he didn't—maybe no one in fact had. She could now officially feel afraid—afraid of depending on the thing he seemed to be presenting. Once she loves him out loud there is no taking it back. It's been charted, and now it cannot be removed from the maps. Oy.

Rudy kissed her, a small smile on his closed face. "I love you for your mind and you love me for my body," she said. "Oh, I like your body and you like my mind, but, overall, the percentages are off." She stopped suddenly, considering. "If you like people for their minds, how great can the sex be?"

Rudy frowned. "Well, there are several answers to that," he said. "Either not that great, or even better because it's a continuation of the conversation. The great conversation."

"Do you like me for my conversation?"

Rudy narrowed his eyes in apparent concentration. Finally, he shook his head slowly. ". . . Mmmmmm . . . not *really*," he said absently. Dinah smiled. "Sex?" she asked.

Rudy considered briefly. "Mmmmmm . . . no . . . no."

73

Dinah laughed, bouncing on him. "Well, what?" she asked. "I make you laugh?"

Rudy pursed his lips. "Well, maybe, but . . . no, not that either." Dinah hit him playfully. "You're such a girl," he said.

"In what way?"

"In the best way."

Dinah laughed, kissing him on the mouth, taking his bottom lip between hers.

"Bend down," she said, "bend down, so I can get over you."

Rudy suppressed a yawn. "What are you doing tomorrow?"

"Getting over you," she reminded him.

"After that?"

"There is no after that," she said. "What are you doing?"

"Little things to ensure your not getting over me."

She had loved him quietly for several weeks, and now, for the first time, she had loved him out loud. It would be okay. Everything would be okay now. There they lay, a whopping mix of vitality and certainty, there in the dark hum of hanging out. She'd found someone. A man to clasp her to him. His hand lay flat and warm against the small of her back, encircling her, ensnaring her. Their faces crossed and kissing, a man to hang her hopes on; here's your hopes, what's your hurry? Thrashing toward the border of just enough of him. They had fallen into step with one another in a kind of syncopated sympathy, an overlapping of empathies, a kindly, kindred kind of love.

Rudy stretched and looked up and around at his room. "I love this place," he said. "Sometimes, I feel as though all it needs are some doggie toys and some baby things. You know, the trappings of life that provide the illusion of living. Then I could just look exhausted, like

I already do, and say that the family and the pets were away for an extended weekend, giving me a much-needed rest. A tricycle in the hallway, a dog bone on the stair, the arm of a doll. The clues of a life, without the life itself."

Dinah rolled away from him and teasingly sang: "We have so much in common, it's a phenomenon. . . ."

Rudy joined in, pulling her back to him, pinning her under him. "We should start raising horses, we're nuclear forces, coming on. . . ."

"You're such an innovator," she laughed. "An innovator or an elevator; I can't remember which."

He rolled off her, smiling. Dinah ran her hands down the sides of his smooth body. Rudy pulled the covers up around them and pulled her to him, hugging her. "I want some hot chocolate," he said absently.

"I'll keep an eye out," assured Dinah. "And if that doesn't work, I'll take out a breast."

Rudy smiled, rubbed his cheek slightly against her hair. "Keep the breast out, and I'll forget about the hot chocolate," he said, his hand squeezing her shoulder for emphasis. A horn sounded from the street far below. "We agree on rhythm; that's why we get along," he continued to the ceiling, dark above him. "When people have different rhythms, they don't want to be around one another. People are offended when the rhythm is different. When you don't like somebody's rhythm . . . and taste. You have to like their taste."

"Okay," she said, suddenly matter-of-fact. "Every woman sells you a bill of goods about yourself . . . gives you back a happier, heftier version of yourself. You know, a newer, preferred version. So, what did Vicki sell you?"

"Um . . . that I was . . . that I was . . . I don't know— talented. Very talented. Brilliant. And she was also a playwright, so . . . ."

"Right. Victoria Hanover. The woman's playwright. When a woman writes plays, she writes women's plays. Men just write plays."

Rudy nodded vaguely. "Uh huh."

"And Anne? What did she sell you?"

"Uh . . . that I was a nice guy . . . and good-looking."

Dinah rolled her eyes. "And me?"

"Ummmm . . . that we're alike . . . soulmates, the same."

She punched him gently. "That's what you told *me.*" Dinah rolled onto Rudy and lay on top of him now, her head on his chest. "I have a painter friend who said this great thing to me. He said that years ago there were tribes that roamed the earth and that each tribe had a magic person. Well, now there are no more tribes, but there are still magic people, and every so often, you meet them. Every so often you meet someone from your tribe. Well, maybe we're that to each other. Maybe not magic people, but fellow tribesmen. You're my mammal. All twisted together like twins waiting to be born into a hostile world."

Rudy looked at her sternly, with his hands gripping her shoulders. "He said all that to you?" he said. "Who is this guy? Should I be worried?" Dinah laughed. She kissed him now, a shallow kiss that deepened and they moved downward into its depths, limbs entwined. "Let's get these IQ points down to room temperature where they belong," he murmured into her neck, one hand on her back, the other holding the back of her head, moving her into him, farther and farther in, till she was far from whoever she was without him.

"Ladies and gentlemen," she said to her assembled collective unconsciousness. "We have a new president."

Dictator, mumbled her superego, its evil yellow eyes leering.

"President," she said louder, doubtfully.

Dictator, ruler, boss, king, snarled the superego.

"Boyfriend?" offered Dinah demurely, timidly. And the menacing howl of her superego's laughter was heard sweeping over her hippocampus, sending the students in all directions.

We see a pale, delicate manicured hand with a gold wedding band being slipped onto the third finger by a larger, male hand. Our shot widens and we discover Blaine and Rose dressed as bride and groom. He pulls up the veil, revealing her beautiful radiant face, leans down and kisses her.

Suddenly, a shot rings out.

Rudy woke and sat up in bed.

"What's the matter?"

"I had a dream."

She snuggled up to him, yawning. "What was it?"

"I dreamed we were in a car trying to cross the bridge, the George Washington Bridge. But I didn't want to pay the thirty-nine fifty for the Shakespeare. I wanted to find another way across."

Dinah drew him down onto his back and kissed him on his hot, moist neck. "Go back to sleep," she coaxed. "You don't have to pay for the Shakespeare now. I'll pay. Go to sleep." Rudy looked unconvinced as he lay back down and allowed himself to be soothed. "I'll pay," crooned Dinah sleepily. "Sleep."

A courtroom. A judge is looking sternly at two people. An extremely attractive, awkward couple. The man is blond and blue-eyed. The woman has light red hair, almost strawberry blond, and dark-green eyes. Both stand apart, watching the judge solemnly. They do not look at one another. Two lawyers are seated at tables on opposite sides, one on the bride's, one on the groom's. The judge studies his notes over his reading glasses and then surveys the youngish couple. "It says here you were together for five years and married for one. Is this true, Mr."—the judge once again refers to his notes—"Mr. MacDonald, Blaine and Rose MacDonald." Blaine shifts slightly, his hands clasped in front of him.

"Yes, Your Honor."

The judge looks stern. "I guess the marriage spoiled the relationship, is that it, Mrs. MacDonald?" He glances again at his notes. Rose tucks the hair on the left side of her head behind her ear, watching the hands that hold the notes.

"Yes, sir," she responds, her voice soft.

"No chance at reconciliation?" he asks gruffly, laying his notes aside.

Blaine's attorney half stands and says, "We cite irreconcilable differences, Your Honor."

The judge is scornful. "Irreconcilable differences, my ass! In my day we worked out our differences. Now, it seems, they work us out—or over. Well, since I gather there's no division of property and no children, the law decrees that after one year of legal separation, you two will be officially divorced." The judge smacks down his gavel and puts Blaine and Rose's papers to one side. "Next case."

Now, for the first time, Blaine and Rose look at one another. Rose is the first to speak. "Well . . . ," she begins.

Blaine looks over his shoulder, where both of their lawyers stand, talking. Another couple approaches the judge. Blaine puts his hands in his pockets and clears his throat. "I guess we should feel relieved."

Rose laughs nervously, revealing bright, even teeth. "I'm not exactly the relieved type."

"Yeah, well . . ." Blaine touches his tie absently, almost superstitiously. "I guess we weren't from the same tribe after all."

Rose watches him go. The music surges as the camera pushes in on her luminous face. Tears quiver in her eyes.

The shot dissolves and, in its place, we see a bright red heart with an arrow through it. The words "Heart's Desire" are scrawled diagonally across it.

━━━

Dinah and Connie sat in the control booth, watching the courtroom scene on their monitors. As the scene dissolved to the red-heart logo, Connie stood and crossed to her bag, which sat on top of a small refrigerator in the corner. She removed a bottle of Motrin from its depths and took two without water. "I shouldn't have come in today," she moaned. "I've got cramps that could sink a ship."

Dinah sighed and put her hand over her eyes. "Ships don't get cramps," she explained patiently. "I believe the expression is 'cramps that could start a fire.' It's from the Dutch *'Branden tiatan met blood.'* Or the Gaelic—"

"Okay." Connie lit a cigarette and proffered the pack to Dinah. "I'll stop complaining about my period if you cheer up."

Dinah took a cigarette and lit up. "What a swap," she said, smoke issuing from her nose and mouth.

"Is it the scene that's bothering you?" Connie asked. Below, on the studio floor, the crew was striking the set and preparing for another shot.

"No, no," Dinah lied. "No more than usual. It's still cathartic in a way to see Rudy portrayed by a semi-Southern WASP and me played by this astonishingly beautiful Breck girl." She passed the hand that held the cigarette over her brow. "Does Breck still exist?" she asked vaguely as an afterthought.

"Does Rudy know he's been immortalized in soaps?"

Dinah sat back and put her feet up on the console, as co-head writers of *Heart's Desire* were wont to do. "He knows," she said simply. "His sister told him. He's never seen it, though. When we were together, he watched it a couple of times as a kind of gesture, but..." She shrugged. "He wouldn't like it no matter what. Even though Blaine has become one of the most popular characters..." She smiled to herself. "If I thought he watched the show, I could put in little things in code for him. You know, like a message in a bottle." She took one long last drag on her cigarette and then stubbed it out.

Connie watched her carefully. "Are you going to call him when you go to New York?"

Dinah looked exasperated. "What are you, the CIA?" She looked up at the monitor. "They're ready," she said, indicating the scene on the floor. She pushed a button on a panel in front of her. "Let's see a rehearsal," she said. A man below gave a thumbs-up gesture in the direction of the booth. Without taking her eyes off the monitor, Dinah said to Connie, "I am not going to call him next week. I have more self-control than that. I haven't seen him since his play opened here over a year ago, and you remember what a mistake that was. If I do call him, that's all I'll do. I won't see him. Or, if I do see him, I won't see him at night. I'll see him in some neutral day environment. And I *definitely* won't fuck him; that would be fatal." She pushed the button before her once more. "Action," she said.

Connie smiled, lit another cigarette and watched the monitor.

———

Blaine stands pounding at a door.

"Rose!" he calls. There is no reply. He bangs again.

80

"Rose, I know you're in there—open up!" A window opens from above and Rose's lovely face appears.

"Go away, Blaine," says Rose tremulously. "We agreed not to see each other."

"I want to talk," insists Blaine, his golden hair catching the light, his blue eyes flashing.

"You don't want to talk; you want to—"

"Let me in!" roars Blaine, ramming the door with his shoulder. It gives way and a hand-held camera follows Blaine into Rose's house. Rose backs into a corner.

"Look, Blaine, it's taken me this long to get my feelings for you down to a dull roar." He comes nearer; she continues to back away. "I guess I'll always love you, but my goal is to love you like people love their country." He is almost on her now. Rose is against a wall, her arms outstretched in an effort to keep him at arm's length. "And I don't mean my own country. No, no. I mean like part of Scandinavia maybe." Blaine finds her now, his arms encircling her, her arms pushing him back, resisting him, then giving in. "Or Pakistan," she says with a sigh, as his mouth covers hers.

The music swells as they sink to the floor. "Well, make up your mind," Blaine says in a low voice just out of frame. "Is it Pakistan or Scandinavia?"

The shot dissolves on a globe sitting on a piano.

———

81

The polecat places his paws on the female's shoulder and bites her neck, inducing for fifteen minutes a condition of muscular paralysis.

7

Dinah," said a voice, followed by a nervous cough. Something horrible inside her shimmered and moved. She stiffened. "It's Rudy," he said.

"Rudy," she repeated, as though loosely translating.

"Rudy," he said again. "Rudy Gendler? From the late seventies to the mid-eighties?"

"Oh, *that* Rudy Gendler." She laughed a nervous laugh. "You know, you meet so many Rudy Gendlers these days. Where are you?"

"Here."

"Which here?"

"Your here."

"L.A.?" she gasped. "But you *hate* L.A.!"

"So do you, deep down," he said. "It's a company town. You told me so yourself. In New York at night, you can feel that everyone is off somewhere having a great time. In L.A., you know they're all home in bed. There's something too sweet about the life out here or something."

"I *work* here."

"How *is* work?"

"Writers' strike," she said by way of an answer.

"Writing soap operas counts as writing?" he exclaimed ironically. "What will they think of next?"

"Everybody can't be a great artist like yourself."

"Even me," he said. "Even I can't be a great artist like myself."

"Don't you miss these enlivening conversations?"

"Actually," he said absently, "I do. I have to admit I do."

In fact, Rudy said almost everything absently, as though being himself didn't deserve his entire attention. Interaction was a sort of hobby of his, a mildly interesting hobby he engaged in from time to time. He spoke softly but with authority, and he didn't have a wide range of expressions. His speech was muted. Smoky. Convalescent, almost, as if recovering from the ordeal of personality. As if carrying his weighty words from far away. As if the sound of his measured voice might wake him from his sleep of self. A kiss might turn the frog of his attention into a prince. Might . . .

"So . . ." she began awkwardly.

"So . . ." he echoed. "No soap—writers' strike."

"No soap radio," she said distractedly, a bad imitation of him. Dinah's voice, though, is like a bell ringing in her mouth, her throat calling you in for the supper of her person.

"No soap radio . . ." he repeated. "What is that?"

"Nothing," she assured him. "Just a punch line to an old joke I knew in high school."

" 'No soap radio' is a punch line?" he mused, turning the phrase over in his mind like a stone.

Dinah sighed. "Two elephants are taking a bath and one elephant says to the other one, 'Pass the soap,' and the other elephant says, 'No soap radio.' "

"I don't get it," said Rudy patiently.

"You're not supposed to," she explained reluctantly. "It's a mean joke. You're supposed to tell it to several people who know the joke and someone who doesn't. Then, when you say the punch line, 'no soap radio,' everyone hopefully, including the person who doesn't know the joke, laughs and you . . . oh, forget it. It's stupid. All I meant to tell you was that there was a writer's strike."

"No, no, no, I get it," he said. "If he laughs, then he's an asshole. Right?"

"Right. And everyone makes him feel bad for pretending to get it."

"Attack him for his blatant need for acceptance," Rudy said thoughtfully.

"I guess," she said. Now Dinah was nervous. Rudy could really make her nervous.

"That's awful," said Rudy appreciatively.

"Well, see, another reason why you should be glad we're not together and you don't live in L.A."

Rudy coughed his cough. Dinah put her head down and shut her eyes, waiting.

"Di——" he began.

"Yeah," she said softly, in someone else's voice. Someone younger and not as defensive.

"Wanna have dinner?"

"I can't have dinner with you, Rudy," she said heroically.

"Sure you can," he countered. "Why can't you?"

"Same reason as before."

"We had lunch before," he reminded her needlessly.

"That was over a year ago and it was *lunch*—which is a far less dangerous meal. You're asking for dinner. You know what'll happen if we have dinner."

"Remind me," he said.

She sighed. "I still have a romantic fantasy about you," she said in a low, even voice. "And I can't see you till it's over."

"It'll never be over entirely," he informed her. "Besides, I have a fantasy about *you*." He cleared his dusty throat. "And the worst thing we can do with a fantasy is feed it. The fantasy will only increase if we don't see each other. But if we dose ourselves with a little reality, we'll *demystify* the whole thing. We'll become more real to one another."

"I don't see how we could be more real to one another," she mumbled.

"Dinah, I'm talking about demystification," he said. "I'm talking about dinner."

There was a long, familiar pause, with the two of them in it, the pause holding them like its little friends.

When she arrived at his hotel, she called him from the lobby. "I'll be right down," he said.

So she stood there, trying to look casual, trying not to feel so afraid. Oh, who cares? So I'm afraid, she thought. He's probably changed his shirt a couple of times himself.

Then there he was. Rudy didn't look as though he smiled much, but if he did, he did it somehow without smiling. A cool flame, he burned indifferently.

They looked at each other, then looked away. "Well," he offered. "It'll loosen up. It's the first couple of minutes." She watched the side of his face as he said this; it looked blank. She guessed that he was containing himself. It was as though he was hermetically sealed—water-resistant. Dinah—she was leaking all over the place. She couldn't contain herself. Rudy—that was all he did.

Since she didn't have much of a relationship with her father, Rudy was the most vivid male relationship she had in the world. He was more familiar to her than any other man. When he walked in, it was as though the world had finally arrived. An arrow appeared over her head that said YOU ARE HERE. He was her reference point. When she was with him, she was with him. When she wasn't with him, she was NOT WITH RUDY. It was just as specific, required just as much of her. Almost.

"You're at your low weight," he said mildly as they got into her car.

"Really?" she said and frowned. "I think that you just remember me fatter than I am. Also, it's night. Everyone seems thinner at night."

Rudy practically smiled. "I'm glad you're here to tell me these things. Imagine living all these years and not knowing that people seem thinner at night."

Dinah colored. "You know what I mean." She opened the car door and got in, reminding herself to breathe. She started the car, they fastened their seat belts, and Rudy handed her several envelopes. "What's this?"

"They came for you," he said.

Dinah took the letters. "Recently?" she said.

"Yup. You don't see Vicki Hanover, I guess," he said.

"Your ex-girlfriend, Vicki Hanover?" She laughed, starting the car. "Not really." The radio blared violently —Los Lobos singing "Let's Say Goodnight." She turned it down quickly. "Why?"

"I got a couple of letters for her too," he said, looking out the window as they drove out of the hotel parking lot and into the L.A. night.

"Where do you want to eat?" she asked him, checking her rearview mirror, wondering if she should have dressed more casually so he wouldn't know that she cared. Oh, fuck it; he knew that she cared.

"Oh, anywhere," he said, studying her profile.

"You're the guy," she reminded him. "You decide."

"I'm the *guest*."

"Right. Okay. What do you like? Italian, right?"

"Sure, Italian's good. Or Japanese."

"Right, right," she said, remembering. "California Rolls."

"There you go. One of the main things I like about California. Their rolls. How's Kevin?"

Dinah laughed. "There's a segue—California Rolls to Kevin."

"Actually, if you think about it, there's a connection."

"Kevin and I had a fight," she said, ignoring his remark. "We had a fight."

"A bad one?"

She looked at him. "A bad one."

"That's too bad," he said, smiling.

"Yeah. Well, relationships are tough. Like my grandpa says, 'They're tough enough when they're clipping right along.' "

"Yeah, they're tough," Rudy sighed. "How *are* your grandparents?"

"Speaking of tough relationships?" she laughed. "He's okay. She had a stroke."

"I'm sorry."

"Yeah, well . . . she still has enough personality to be mean with."

"That's good."

"So, which is it?" she said. "Japanese or Italian?"

"I don't care. Whatever. Japanese."

"Japanese," she repeated, making a sudden turn up Coldwater, heading over the hill. The lights of the Valley shone below, spread to the San Bernardino Mountains.

"Unless you don't want Japanese," he added. "Wait a minute. You don't really like Japanese, do you?"

"If they have Yakitori, I do."

"Right, right, Yakitori. You're the girl that likes Yakitori. So . . . what was the fight about?"

"The fight?"

"The Kevin fight."

"Ah yes, the Kevin fight," she began. "Well . . . you really want to hear this?"

"Sure I want to hear it."

"Okay, I came home from this seminar . . ."

"You're still doing seminars?"

"Yes," she said defensively. "I'm still doing seminars. Anyway, I came home from this thing and Kevin was waiting for me in my room, watching TV . . ."

"You guys were living together?"

"No, no, he just knew my alarm combination and he was waiting for me. He didn't like to go out with me, which I should have seen as a sign right away. I mean, in all the time I was with him, he only met two of my friends. And that was by accident. I never met *any* of his friends."

"Yes, but Di—"

"Never say Di."

"You're an extremely social person. You know, this is not dissimilar to one of the problems you and I had."

"Oh, come on, what is this, male bonding in absentia?"

"Di, you always had hundreds of people calling, people were over all the time. Sometimes I felt like I had to make an appointment. And I was living with you, for God's sakes—"

"I thought you wanted to know about Kevin."

"I do."

"Well, then let me finish my story."

"Sure, go ahead."

"Unless you feel that it's gonna sidetrack you into a sense-memory descent into the hell that was us," she said.

"No, no, go ahead. I'm sorry that I interrupted."

"Okay." She thought for a moment. "Where was I?"

"Uh . . . you never met any of his friends."

"Right. I never met any of his friends or family or anything. Which is kind of weird if you think about it. I mean, we were together for over six months. Anyway, I come in after this seminar and he's sitting there on the bed, watching TV. . . ."

"I don't know if I want to hear all of this."

"No, no, it wasn't like that. There's no nudity in this story. He was sitting on the bed, fully clothed, with just his boots off, watching TV, and Tony, my puppy—I had gotten a new puppy that week—was on the floor, crying, yelping, howling. It was awful. It was so annoying and he'd been doing it all week. So I sit down on the bed, the TV is on, Tony is screaming—I don't know. Maybe, *maybe* I wasn't paying enough attention to him. Anyway, Tony's screaming and I turn and scream TONY! at the top of my lungs—and you know how loud I am just regular, in the middle of my lungs—and Kevin just kind of stiffens and leans back and I think uh-oh, we have an incident on our hands. So I say, 'What?' and he looks at me funny and says, 'Nothing . . . I just don't like screaming, that's all.' And I say, 'Well, I don't either, but he's been doing that all week and I wasn't screaming at you.' And then he just jumps off the bed and grabs his boots and says, 'I'm not having a good time,' and walks out of the house and drives away."

"Uh-huh, drives away. You don't like that," Rudy remarked. "You never liked it when I wanted to go for a walk to cool down during an argument. I don't know how you could go out with someone named Kevin anyway. It sounds like an Osmond."

"Can I finish my story?" Dinah asked.

"Yeah," he said.

"Oh, I don't know, it sort of ends after that anyway," she said. "He called me from his car phone . . ."

"He has a car phone?" Rudy interrupted. "Well, there you go, right there."

"He didn't have it when I first met him," she said defensively. "He had just gotten it. It was new."

"Well, that's almost all right then," he said, "from your point of view."

"Thanks," she said. "So he calls and says, 'What

does somebody have to do to get your attention? Wrap a bullwhip around your neck?' So I say, 'How dare you!' He said later that I called him a cunt—it's entirely possible—anyway, he says, 'How dare I?' and hangs up on me."

"Yeah," said Rudy, "then what happened?"

"Well, I was very upset," she said.

"I can imagine," he said. "That can't possibly be the whole story."

"No," she said thoughtfully. "Well, sort of. There isn't much more. I called his machine after he hung up on me, knowing that he wouldn't be home and that I could just leave him a message. I don't really remember the message, but the gist of it was, 'I don't know what happened, but I don't see the need to be *Sicilian* about this.' I was very upset. Anyway, then he didn't call me for four days and I knew that it was over. I knew that I'd never be able to understand what happened—it was almost a cultural thing. I should have known that you can't go out with a guy who talks about himself like he's in the next room."

"What does that mean?"

"Oh, nothing. You know, he would compliment himself like he was someone else who was in the next room," she replied. "Like: 'A lot of people might condemn me, but I'm an honest person, no matter what the situation, and I'm devoted to my family.' "

"He actually said that?"

"Not exactly *that*," she answered. "But like that. Like he was this secret perfect American and he was sharing his secret with me. It was like being with a brochure."

"Well . . ." Rudy began, "what did this guy do, again?"

"Lawyer," she said. "Show-business lawyer."

Rudy sighed. "It doesn't surprise me so much that

you dated a lawyer," he said. "It's that you admit it so readily."

"I guess," she said. "I thought that I was semi-safe, though. A lawyer is almost a normal job."

"Not at all," Rudy said. "They're predators. They use the truth like a lie. Finally, he's in *show business*, in the non-creative end of show business, which is as off-center a place as you can be. Those people are always frustrated and end up venting their frustrations on you. That's where they get creative. And he's not Jewish— that's where your cultural problem lies."

"How do you know he's not Jewish?" she asked. "I don't remember telling you that."

"His name is Kevin," Rudy explained simply. "There are no Jews named Kevin. Although I must admit the car phone did throw me for a moment."

"Get over yourself!" she exclaimed, smiling. "I'm not really Jewish either, you know."

"You might as well be," he said.

"I Marcus Welby," she said.

"I think of you as Jewish," he said. "Who is Marcus Welby?"

"He's that doctor on TV that Robert Young used to play," she replied. "Get out of here. You know who Marcus Welby is, you just pretend that you don't know TV things so that people think you only read plays and poetry all the time."

"Right," said Rudy. "And you know me best. You know that I actually *wrote* some episodes of *Marcus Wellman* on brain tumors."

"*Marcus Welby*," she corrected him.

"I said that," Rudy said. "Welby."

"No, you didn't," she said. "You said Wellman. If you're going to make patronizing TV jokes, at least get the character names right."

"This is like bad Pinter," Rudy remarked.

"No, it isn't," she said. "Pinter is interesting without leading up to something—we're not that interesting and we are leading up to something—dinner. We're having dinner."

"Di, only you could take TV things personally. Identifying yourself with a medium."

"Only you could compare us to bad Pinter," she sulked. "Here we are." She turned off Ventura Boulevard into the parking lot of Teru Sushi and put the car in park. Rudy looked at her.

"You're not *mad*, are you?"

"No," she reassured him, "I'm not. I'm really not. I'm just hungry. I was nervous to see you and, on top of that, I'm hungry."

"Great," Rudy said. "Let's eat."

It was a warm spring California night. A soft wind blew. Several motorcycles rolled down Ventura Boulevard. She took a ticket from the attendant and followed Rudy into the restaurant, a detective and her clue.

It's not that Dinah was afraid of Rudy per se—afraid of what he would do to her. It was herself that she was afraid of. Afraid of what she might do with what he did or didn't do to her, what she would do to herself in his name. But then, maybe it was him too. Anyway, it was one or both of them, enough of a reason for her to avoid him or the combination of him and her.

"You want sake?" Rudy asked innocently.

"You know what'll happen if I drink sake," Dinah said, as much to herself as to anybody else.

Rudy just looked at her.

"I get very drunk on sake," she said in a low voice, leaning toward him. "Remember that time at Sean's birthday when I got into the Japanese garden in the middle of the restaurant and pretended to be a man peeing? And then the thing where you wake up in the middle of the night all dehydrated and with palpitations and everything?"

"Hon, if you don't want it, fine," he said, "but don't spoil it for the rest of us."

"You should have some!" she said cheerfully. "You're always greatly improved by alcohol. It relaxes you."

"I am relaxed," Rudy said irritably.

"You never seem relaxed."

"Neither do you. Shall we order?"

Dinah talks in explicit code—it's a neurosis that ultimately fails. The code is never so secret it can't be deciphered. A diaphanous stronghold, a chiffon wall.

Here is her personality: it is a pack of wild dogs on a leash, dragging her around . . . dogs rabid for conversation; it is an eleven-year-old loose in a toy store pulling his father through the fun-packed aisles searching for treasure. Her voice is a brass band parading through her throat. Squeezing her personality, a giant thing, through a tiny throatish hole, working its way back to you, babe, clear and singing. An express train to your ears. She was dropped into the center of her personality decades ago and has been trying to crawl to the edge of it ever since. Either there is no edge or it's all edge, endless stretches of edge flat on its back and sunning in the heat of who she is. She's dreaming that she is herself and she can't wake up, can't come to the surface, world without end, word without end. It's aerobic to be her.

"How is that?" he asked, nodding his head in the direction of her food.

"How could it be?" she replied with her mouth full. "It's yakitori, chicken on a stick. How's yours?"

He shrugged and bit into some square sushi thing. She stared at his second sake. Tom Scott's saxophone crooned softly over the speakers.

"You know what I thought after the fight with Kevin?" she asked Rudy's sake bottle.

"Hmmmmmmmm?" grunted Rudy, chewing.

"I thought, If relationships are going to be stressful, I should've just stayed with you. At least I know you."

"Uh-huh," nodded Rudy. "Relationships needn't be stressful, you know."

"Well, I'm sure I wouldn't know," she said. "They've kind of had their way with me. I mean, cut off my head and count the rings. What relationships have you had that aren't stressful? Certainly not Vicki or Lauren or Anne. Those are all your relationships prior to me. And you never indicated that they were anything but stressful."

Rudy cleared his throat. "I'm in a situation now that's very different from my previous . . . relationships."

Dinah's heart stopped. She stared at Rudy. It had never occurred to her that he would have another relationship. Particularly a successful one. That is, during her lifetime.

"What?" she said faintly.

"I'm seeing someone now who's wholly unlike anyone I've ever known before," he explained calmly. "I mean, we started out as friends and it's gradually matured into a very . . . nurturing situation. I don't know quite how to describe it except that"—he looked to the corner of the restaurant almost wistfully—"she's so kind to me."

"Why shouldn't she be?" Dinah said tensely, baring her teeth in what she hoped would pass for a smile. She signaled the waiter. "Could I have some sake, please?" She turned back to Rudy. Her heart was pounding. "When did you start seeing this person? What is her name?"

"Lindsay," he said. "Well, let's see . . . when did we have lunch?"

"Um . . . about a year ago," she offered.

"Yeah . . . that sounds about right," he said, putting

his hands together and narrowing his eyes slightly. "That's when you told me about you and Kevin. You were still very angry at me."

"Yeah . . . well," she began as her sake arrived and she poured herself a cute little cup and downed it, screwing up her face as its bitter taste passed down her throat, "I was more afraid than mad. Disappointed."

"Well, you seemed mad," he said as she poured herself another sake and drank it dutifully. "I thought you weren't going to drink," he continued mildly.

"I'm not going to," she said cheerfully. "So, what does Leslie do?"

"Lindsay," he corrected her. "She's an interior decorator."

"Really? Lindsay," she said, her eyebrows slightly raised. "How did you meet her?"

"At a party, actually," he said as the waiter cleared away their dishes. "We were both there with other people. Later on I found out who she was and got her number."

"Great," she said, filling up her sake cup again. "So you've been together, what, like a year?"

"Not quite," said Rudy, smiling slightly. "I mean, at first I was very reluctant to get into anything with anyone after our whole disaster. I mean, I have to say I was pretty devastated. I now think that I . . . had kind of a breakdown." He laughed to himself. "I was a shell of a man because of you. If you put your head against me, you could hear the ocean roar."

Dinah tried to look civilized and nonchalant as she finished off the sake. "Yeah, well, we both got beat up pretty badly," she said generously.

"Exactly my point," Rudy said. "Which is precisely why I would be so reluctant to, you know, involve myself with anyone for quite some time." He stared off into the handy corner of the restaurant again. "But Lindsay makes it . . . pretty easy. She basically wants for me . . . I don't know how to say it. She's completely undemanding somehow."

Dinah shook her head in wonderment. "How can you respect that?"

Rudy shrugged and smiled a small, mysterious smile. "Why do I have to respect it? I enjoy it." Dinah glared at him. "C'mon, Di . . . what's the big deal? I don't know, it's not really as much about what I want as . . . how little I have to give. Not really that, but . . . she's just on my side . . . on the team," he said. "Which, if you think about it, is a very touching gesture."

"Doesn't she have a life?" she asked.

"That's not the point," he said, looking at the check and counting out the money to pay. "The point is, she cares about me enough to want to see me happy. That actually makes her happy."

"Well, that's very . . . touching. In an archaic sort of way," she said as they both rose and she followed him miserably out of the restaurant and back into the parking lot.

"Just because it's not an impulse of yours doesn't mean that it's archaic," Rudy said mildly, with his hands in his pockets as they waited for her car. "Do you know that in the eight months that I've been seeing this girl, we've only had two fights?"

"That's great," she said tightly.

"That's not great," he said as they climbed into the car. "It's a miracle."

Dinah knew at that moment, as much as she'd ever known anything, that she had to get him back.

They drove to her house in silence. He wanted to see her new gate and would get a cab home. Sure.

The radio played "I Haven't Got Time for the Pain" as they rolled over roads. Her head ached. Rudy sat with his hands folded politely in his lap, staring at the road in front of him.

"I never liked this song," he began. "It always reminded me of . . ." He looked down at his watch with a mock worried expression. "Ooooh . . . gee, I'll tell you something, I gotta run here—what's your week like? 'Cause maybe I could check back with you on this, but right now, I really haven't got time for this pain thing. What about Thursday? And that song 'You're So Vain.' 'You're so vain, you probably think this song is about you.' But it *is* about him—so, does that mean he's less vain?"

Dinah gave him a thin smile.

They drove on and arrived at her house. She parked. They both stared straight ahead. "There's the gate," she said, pointing vaguely.

"Uh-huh," he said. "Nice."

She was feeling the sake. She was feeling sorry for herself and lonely. The thundering hooves of tender feelings—historic feelings—stampeded across her psyche. She had lost Rudy forever to a Girl Scout, a cheerleader, a nice girl. She could not have predicted how much this would affect her.

Rudy coughed. "Do you want to come up?" Dinah said with her hand on the door.

He paused. "Okay."

Oh, come on. This was what this was all for, wasn't it, she thought. Why was she doing this? Oh, why not, what did she have to lose. It had been over for two years, and now it was really and truly over. It was over with Kevin and over with Rudy. She was alone. She would die an old maid. Or she would live a long, long time an old maid, have a stroke, drool and nod and no one would be there to take care of her. While somewhere across the world, Lindsay would ladle soup into Rudy's crumbling, happy old face. "Sure," she added to herself as she turned off the engine and got out of the car, "why not?"

. . .

They sat on the couch in her living room listening to the air conditioner do its job. Rudy coughed. Dinah's eyes filled with tears.

"I'm going to cry now," she announced. "I'm being visited by some unexpected emotions." Rudy continued staring straight ahead. She mopped her hazel eyes. "We can continue talking among ourselves," she tried to say brightly. "I don't know why," she continued in a softer voice. "I just feel so . . . lonely or something."

"Yeah, well . . ." he said, crossing and uncrossing his legs. He coughed with one hand over his mouth in a fist.

"Still," she said, "still it's pretty weird sitting here like this. Like we're waiting to see a doctor or something."

Rudy laughed and cleared his throat again. He twiddled his thumbs. "You can't say we didn't try. Which goes to show that sometimes there actually *can* be harm in trying," he said quietly. There was a pause.

"So, this is the demystifying process," she said.

He looked at her. He actually looked at her with his whole face. "You said that you still had a fantasy about me, about being with me." He looked away abruptly, as though he had said too much.

"And you said you still had a fantasy about me," she countered.

"Yes," he said matter-of-factly. "And by seeing each other, we make ourselves more real to one another."

"And thus we have the overall concept of Rudy Gendler's demystification process."

Rudy sighed. "Well, you didn't have to see me, you know. I think, though, to avoid one another creates another type of situation. Besides," he continued thoughtfully, "I want to know you—you know what I mean. I like to talk to you. I like you as a person."

"As opposed to what? An end table?" smiled Dinah.

100

"C'mon, Dinah."

"What about your girlfriend?"

"What about her?"

"Why don't you talk to *her?*"

"I do talk to her. That's not the point."

"What's the point?"

"Oh, Dinah, come on. What Lindsay and I have is completely different from you and me."

"Sure," Dinah said shrilly, "one relationship is about comfort, the other is about stimulation. And you're just comfortable because you're the focal point of the relationship," she finished.

"I don't know if that's necessarily so, but . . ." began Rudy, spreading his hands over his knees, "what would be wrong with that?"

"She's auditioning for the role of your wife."

"Again, Dinah, what's wrong with that? She cares about me."

"Well, it's not as though I didn't care about you."

"*Hon,* you left *me.*"

They were silent for a moment. "I had to leave. It was your apartment."

"Oh, c'mon, Dinah, let's not get into all this again. This is historically not a good conversation for us."

She laughed. "*We* are not a good conversation for *us.*"

"We're not," said Rudy. "Look," he continued, "even if Lindsay is a reaction to you, is that so bad? It's not as though we were so happy or anything."

"No," she agreed, "that's true. Not happy. We loved each other, but we weren't happy."

"No," said Rudy, still looking ahead of himself, wondering how long this was going to take, if this was a good idea at all, if her ass was still as good.

They sat like solemn bookends, with their years of history between them. As Rudy continued staring at the space before him, he reached over and touched the hand in her lap with his fingertips. She stared at their two hands together, as though trying to place them somehow, then she slowly began caressing their two hands together. They sat silently this way for some time. Considering. She brought his hand up to her mouth and pressed her lips to it. Rudy looked at her. He leaned toward her, pulling her to him as he did. He had a worried, helpless look. She felt sad and caught. Caught in the tractor beam of her old obsession. Both their expressions disappeared into one another and combined as they pressed their mouths together, pressed their history together, their long separation together.

A mesh of mouths. A mess of mouths. Deep-sea kissing. Kissing as though intent on perfecting it once and for all. Cramming for the kiss finals. The last kiss, the one that counted. Everything leads up to this one kiss, everything leads away. The wholehearted half of a kiss.

He put his hands on her breasts as though he were tuning in a message from deep space. She tried listening to her body outside of her head, watching it respond without words, unattached to anything past or present— *obedient*. A cork on the river of the world, floating. A still-life living. Then he comes preying on her obedience; she does everything in her power to take her mind away, leaving him her body in her will. She watches him, eyes closed, following the melody from memory, over the wall and into her system, a stern anchor sunk in her rowdy surf. Taking her mind away, leaving room for his body. Her body obeying him where her mind will not. Fallen down, down and out of her head. Words fail her where he is now succeeding. Her pulse quickens, her mind slows behind, falls away, until there remains but one thing of her identity: Who am I? I'm with him, that's who.

Which is just a notch up from: I wish I was with

him, that's who. Dinah, just now, was somewhere between the two. Someone between the two.

He thinks; therefore I am.

"Are we going to feel guilty about this?" whispered Rudy into her hair, inhaling her familiar scent.

"Sure," she said, biting into his lip.

"Yeah," he agreed, pulling her underneath him.

Dinah watched herself as if she were Rudy. Judging herself as he might do. It was her way of keeping him with her. Of keeping herself company. Her little friend in her mind, sometimes an unfriendly friend, admittedly, but company all the same. She looked at Rudy so close to her and thought, *I can't wait to remember this.* Until she was alone with him in her mind, where he never left her, where he watched over her, visiting her throughout the day, a thing she could refer to, return to, reminisce about, plot. A world, with him in the middle and her all around. Apparently trying to penetrate the center, the nucleus, but really quite happy to toil and spin—quietly weaving—the silent pool cleaner. To give him up would be to give up her almost constant companion—however cruel or kind his company. Reveling in the phone not ringing—striving toward eventual contact—trying to be worthy. Living a thousand lives till he called her. *I don't care, it's over, how dare he, I'm worth more, what ego, well, fuck him, it's over, I'll miss him, he can't miss, not able, so shut down, I'm better now, what's so bad, he's not so, his hands, can be so cute, but sometimes, he's so cold, that time that, and when he, he's selfish, he loved me, I blew it, he's not that, not his fault, maybe next time, maybe now he'll, soon it could be, could be different, that bastard, where is he, why can't he, I should have, it's my fault, he said so, I'm high-strung, demanding, he's quiet, I'll be good, he'll see then, I'll prove it, it's different, mustn't lose him, he'll leave me, where is he, I love him, or is it? who cares?*

Rudy was powerful because he existed in Dinah's head and had become a fundamental part of her mind, sometimes replacing focus and intelligence. All math was gone.

And then there he was, all complete against her, with her circling his mood, looking for a way in. A side door, an open pore. At times their two natures melted into one another, wound around each other and smiled. Two easily overlapping circles, round, pleased and open. Then suddenly, he was apart, his circle tight around him, hers around her, no way in. There he was, over there, a whole other person, sealed up tight. So far off, his eyes glittering in his head like a snake. Flower in my heart, snake in my head, over you.

Her feelings for him, these feelings that absorbed all other feelings into them, smiled and burped.

Ah.

They lay in bed after a nostalgic bout of sex. Rudy gazed in typical relaxed consternation at the ceiling. Dinah gazed expectantly at him. The air hung curiously around them. Finally, she spoke, shyly.

"What are you thinking about?"

"Money," he replied sadly. "I was trying to determine what effect a recession would have on the value of real estate on Long Island." Dinah felt a twinge of terror.

"Uh-huh," she responded awkwardly. "Could you move your arm a little bit? My hand fell asleep." Rudy shifted obediently as she continued. "If you're quiet, you can hear it dreaming."

Rudy looked at her out of the side of his eye, laughed and looked away. "Where do orgasms go?" he wondered with a small smile.

Dinah smiled at this seldom-seen expression. "Consciousness," she guessed, touching the side of his face.

"Don't you think that they got the idea of malls from genitals?" It sounded like a hypothesis he had come to from a great distance.

"Excuse me," she said to her side of his face.

"You know, everything in one place. I mean, you might want to make a side trip for a kiss or a breast—but otherwise, it's all there."

"Like a mall," she said thoughtfully.

"Yeah," he said.

"Kind of a capitalist view of sex," she commented.

He frowned. "Maybe." She put her arm across his chest and nuzzled her face into his shoulder.

"If you were fifteen, we could do it again," she said, smiling. Nervous. The whole evening was a tribute to the What-are-we-pretending-not-to-know? style of interaction so popular in this century.

"If I were fifteen, we'd have been finished in two minutes."

She closed her eyes and rolled onto her back. "You never seem relaxed," she sighed.

"Neither do you," he shot back lazily.

"I guess that's what bothers me," she continued to the ceiling. "You remind me of a muted version of myself. I'm nervous—the extroverted version of not relaxed. You're tense—the introverted version."

He laughed. "I don't know what you'd do without these theories of yours."

"It makes me happy to try to figure out stuff," she said. "For years, I wanted to be smart. Then I got smart —I don't mean information-smart, but . . ."

"I know what you mean," he said.

"Yeah, well, after I felt more confident about my smartness, then I wanted to be *clear*. Now, I mean, Now, I just want to be clear."

"Yeah, well . . . ," he began, "that's more complicated. Particularly if you're smart. It's very difficult, then, to be clear, because you can see both sides." He spoke slowly and deliberately.

Dinah felt as though she was pushing him up conversation hill. "I know that I'm not information-smart," she said sadly. "I have very little information. You have a lot of information."

He looked at her. "You place much too much emphasis on being smart. You're always measuring people. 'He's smarter than I—I'm not as smart as he.' You should maybe rethink the value you place on intellect."

Her eyes widened. "But it's a big deal to you too, isn't it?"

"Well, you know, it's a quality I enjoy in people," he said thoughtfully. "But not necessarily to the exclusion of other qualities. It's a gift if you're smart. Don't slam your smart into everybody's gut. With intelligence, you might find a kind of intolerance and maybe . . . a lack of compassion, I guess. The ideal combination is really intelligence combined with compassion. But a lot of the time, you find one or the other."

"Yeah, I tend to get kind of frightened around people who I think are really intelligent. Like I have to concentrate real hard to keep up."

"You gotta give yourself a break, hon. Stop keeping score so much."

"Well, yeah, sure, I'd love to do that. But it's not me so much as my brain. My brain just sits up there, reporting back to me, clicking on and on and on like ticker tape. Sometimes it feels like my brain is smarter than I am. It doesn't seem to matter what I want. My brain just goes on and on relentlessly, expanding to space."

Rudy looked at her oddly. "What must you have been like at twenty?" he said almost to himself.

"I don't know," she said shyly. "You tell me."

"I remember you had this insane energy," he said.

She smiled. "And you liked that?"

He pursed his lips. "Well, I liked the energy part."

"I didn't think you liked me in the beginning," she said. "I think I sort of counted on it. You pursued me as though you were doing something else. I could tell when other people liked me. But I couldn't tell with you."

Rudy sat up and looked at the clock by the bed. "You're a very ballsy girl," he said to the clock.

"Ballsy how?" she asked. Rudy did not lavish compliments that often. When he did, they were usually well considered.

"You're not afraid of . . ." He paused and thought. "You're not afraid of the things that you're afraid of," he said finally. "You keep coming at it. You're nervy."

"I don't feel so nervy around you," she said, drawing her knees up and pulling the blankets around her. "I feel girlie. I don't feel girlie around too many men, but I feel girlie around you."

He ran his hand through his hair. "Girlie," he repeated. "Do you mean feminine?"

She considered, femininely. "Feminine," she said. "Yeah. I guess. You know, squeezy and tilty."

"Well," he said, "I think that that's attractive. Feminine is attractive."

"I guess it's a control thing then."

"What do you mean?"

"I think of feminine as sort of coy," she said. "You know, demure and sweet."

"C'mon, Dinah," laughed Rudy. "I hardly think of you as demure and sweet."

"I'm demure and sweet compared to you," she said haughtily. "You're very male."

"You always thought I was arrogant," he said.

"Not arrogant, really," she said. "More like grand."

"Yeah, but you don't mean as in 'Thou Swell, Thou Witty,' " he said pointedly. "You don't mean that I'm like Cole Porter."

107

"Rodgers and Hart," she said, laughing.

"What?"

"Rodgers and Hart wrote 'Thou Swell, Thou Witty.' We learned it in school. I played it in the band."

"See," he said, "you *do* have information."

"Yeah. Meaningless information about Rodgers and Hart. You just seem very respectable to me."

Rudy got a wry look. "You once said I was pompous. You yelled it, actually."

Dinah's eyes widened in disbelief. "Yelled it?" she said, her eyes squinting in remembrance. "I doubt that I *yelled* it. And I certainly don't think you're *pompous*. I think you're incredibly *confident* about all of your . . . opinions and . . . beliefs and everything, but I don't think of that as pompous. Pompous to me implies some sort of an attitude with nothing behind it. You just have this incredible *certainty* that's based on . . . outcome and . . . experience and . . . everything. You're like a well-bred person. Not by background, but by yourself. Your strut is earned—not that you strut."

"I'm just trying to get the comfort out of giving up being a kid," he shrugged. "You might as well be more definite and not pretend you don't know, 'cause you do. Or that you're naive—because you're not."

"Is that why you seem distracted?" she asked.

"The distracted thing is because there's this whole other conversation happening in my head—running parallel to the one I'm actually having."

Dinah smiled at this insight.

They looked at each other, tense. "I didn't really yell that you're pompous, did I?"

Rudy pursed his lips slightly and narrowed his eyes. "Maybe you didn't. You talk pretty loudly anyway. Maybe you were being your normal self and I was just oversensitive that day. It doesn't matter," he sighed. Dinah had stopped breathing while he spoke.

"Sometimes when you talk, you sound like the mayor," she said softly to prove that she wasn't loud.

Rudy laughed and stood up. "The mayor of Eighty-first Street," he said.

"His holiness, the Chinese mayor of Eighty-first street," she added.

"Why Chinese?" he asked, walking slowly to the bathroom.

" 'Cause you're inscrutable," she said.

"I see," he said, then gestured toward the door. "I have to go to the bathroom."

"How humiliating for you," she said. Rudy laughed. "Sometimes at the end of when I see you," she called, "I want to pat you on your hand and say, 'Don't worry, you didn't give anything away.' "

There was no reply as she listened to the water running. She didn't know what had made her say that anyway. It was just the impression that she had gotten the few times that she had seen him in the two years that they had been apart. Why would he want to give anything away? And who was she? The image of emotional generosity? The emotion that she was most free with was nervous energy—high-spirited anxiety. Christ, her and her galloping gestalt.

How could he have a normal relationship? That meant that the failure of their relationship was all her fault. Because here he was having a stress-free relationship, and all she'd had was a four-month disaster with a would-be Sicilian. She should have just stayed with Rudy. Why did she have such a hard time with him? There was clearly an answer to this, but she had forgotten it in the heat of self-recrimination.

Here was what the hard time was about. She would feel unimportant, dispensable. It was those times when she'd feel him so far from her, so cool, it pained her—

how could she start a fire in him? Until, finally, she'd resort to the most accessible response, an angry one. In the face of his apparent indifference, she felt like running away. Like when she was a kid and wanted to get back at her parents. She'd imagine how they'd feel if she were hit by a bus—then they'd miss her. Regret their ill-treatment of her. She'd panic in the face of his cool when confronted with his frostiness. Well, then, she wouldn't care either. She'd hurt him back. She couldn't be caught caring more, waiting for him to want her. She'd flush out her feeling and match him shrug for shrug—we'll see, for we'll see. She would feel the urge to go away so that he might miss her. But no, he said he didn't miss anyone. Oh, early on with her, he'd craved her. Just to lie by her side brought him relief, was something. But he had re- sented her power over him. He had loved her and he was disappointed. She always had been. She had never be- lieved she would be anything but disappointed. She went into everything disappointed, so she could never be un- duly let down, could only be surprised. It was her best defense and it did not always keep her safe. She became attached in spite of herself. Something loved beyond her control, was disappointed on top of her original disap- pointment. So, to the degree that she was able, consider- ing her background, she had loved Rudy with a fury, hoping to stir some apparent response in him. She loved him with a love that would melt him, beat down his resistances, bag his demeanor, warm the chill in his eyes, waken the sleeping fantasy and bury their combined dis- appointments.

But finally she'd thought, There must be softer walls to beat my head against. And she had left.

Looking for a new, softer wall.

Missing his.

Rudy and Dinah had broken each other's hearts, a very intimate activity. Like going through the war to- gether—it binds you somehow for life. A shared, intense experience, the bad acid trip of love. And having gone through that together, having crawled to the other side of that experience, they regarded one another with fear and a kind of respect. The way you would regard a skilled assassin.

The Chinese Water Torture. The only way you can survive it is by deciding you like it.

Rudy returned from the bathroom, looking sort of offhand and cavalier.

Dinah didn't look at his penis.

"What are those animals that mate for life?" she asked, sounding like a little girl. "Is it swans?"

"Swans," he mused. "Yeah, I think so. Or wolves."

"That's what it's like with us then," she pronounced. "We're mated. Well, me, anyway. I'm your swan. Your black swan from hell."

There was an awkward pause. Then he tried to change the subject. "Dinah, I'm going to have to be—"

"No, wait," she interrupted. "I think that it's pigeons. Yeah, that's right. I remember some story about—is it homing pigeons?"

"Is what homing pigeons?" he asked patiently. "I'm not sure," he said. "I think so. Maybe."

"Yeah, yeah." She rushed along nervously. "I heard this story about how they train homing pigeons. They put them with an opposite-sex homing pigeon and get them all . . . bonded or whatever, and then they separate them. And how they get them to deliver messages is they put the love-interest pigeon where they want the other pigeon to go and then they fly there. The pigeons deliver messages in hopes that they'll see their darling again." She paused breathlessly. "But it's very sad because they never actually let the pigeons be together. They live in longing and hope—delivering messages for humans in hopes of getting a glimpse of their one true-love pigeon. They're really just slaves to love."

"I'm going to have to go soon," he said.

Dinah felt her center go cold with panic. She had allowed herself to forget that he would ever leave again and here she was being brought back to her old pal, reality. What could be more real than painful feelings? Something, she hoped. Please God, something.

"Oh, God," she said dejectedly. "I'm on a tangent, huh? I'm either yodeling at the top of my personality or resting in the valley."

"I'm kind of a valley guy myself," he commented as he stepped into his pants. She should have burned his pants and kept him with her nude until he agreed to accept her as she was and stay.

"Do you want me to drive you?" she said, watching him as though from far away. Someplace where this had already happened and she was okay. Fine really. Better than she'd expected to be. Eleanor Roosevelt. Her mind seemed to do things without her. Unfortunately, the reverse wasn't true. What was Rudy saying now?

"I called a cab from your bathroom phone."

Dinah nodded vaguely and inwardly groaned. He planned his escape. He can't wait to leave. Recidivism, that's what they call it. Visiting the scene of the crime. That irresistible urge to return and then make a clean getaway. "Why?" she found herself saying now. "Do you have to get up in the morning?"

"Sure I have to get up in the morning," he said reaching for his shirt.

Of course he has to get up in the morning, she thought to herself with a wince. I'm the only one who's never going to get up again. I'm the one who shouldn't have gotten up in the first place. She envied Rudy his detachment, his ability to see things in a way that didn't cause him pain. Tell himself a good story.

"I told Lindsay that I would call her. She gets very jealous."

Dinah nodded numbly, holding down the riot inside. "What kind of decorating does she do?" she asked sadly.

Maybe it would be an interesting story and somehow disperse some of the mattering. Mattering more than anything else in the world.

"Modern mostly," he replied as he sat on the bed and put on his socks. "It's not something that she's really interested in, finally. She may just phase it out. Which is fine with me. I realized from being with you that I don't want to be with someone with an intense career."

Dinah stared at him. Everything else and now this. "You don't want her to work," she said flatly.

"It's not that I don't want her to work," he said, tying his laces. "I mean it's not a job that she's that interested in anyway. She wants to quit and I've just encouraged her to do what she wants. She's had several career-making offers; I've simply made her aware of my take on the issue. It just doesn't work out when two people are ambitiously pursuing their careers. Everybody's revved up all the time. It's exhausting. A woman has to have a less intense job."

Dinah listened to all this as far away from caring as she could manage. She picked casually at a thumb. No big deal. "Like what?" she said.

He shrugged. "I don't know."

Dinah frowned what she hoped was a friendly frown. A come hither furrow. "Well, what do you think?"

"Hon, *I don't know.* It's not that I don't know because I don't think about it, I just don't know. Hey, look, I wish I had a less intense job, but I don't. So for me to be with someone who has an almost equally intense job . . . well, it just isn't going to work."

Dinah considered, then offered: "Who's going to mind the relationship?"

Rudy almost smiled. "Exactly."

Dinah tried to keep herself, her objectionable self, out of her voice, the room, this city. "What's she gonna do if she doesn't work?" she asked benignly.

"Well, she has other interests," he informed her, getting his jacket from the chair and standing awkwardly near the bed.

I never should've done this, thought Dinah, my mother was right—men want one thing, and when they get that—boom—bang—hit and run. She looked up at Rudy who was still answering her question, watching his lips form the words. "She likes gardening and . . . politics."

"And you," she added. And how, she thought.

"And me, yes," he said, simply. "She's interested in making me happy."

Dinah shook her head in disbelief. Happy. Happy and Rudy hand in hand heading toward the sun. "Isn't that a lot of pressure? I mean, having someone on a kind of twenty-four-hour call to make you happy? You'd let her give up her job just to sit around and garden and talk politics and make you happy? What about her—do you have to make her happy? Or is this just a one-sided thing?"

"I think about what makes her happy," he said darkly. "I think about what makes the *unit* happy. Anyway, I'm just relieved that I don't have to eat take-out Chinese all the time anymore."

"Well . . ." she said, flabbergasted.

"Well . . ." he said. There was a lonely, inevitable pause.

"Thanks for the demystification," she said.

"Listen," he said, "relationships are process-oriented and you and I are more or less goal-oriented. So I'm just trying to be more process-oriented this time is all."

Dinah smiled. "We're great at capturing the castle— we just don't know how to live in it once it's achieved."

Rudy's eyes softened slightly. "Yeah," he said. "Those suckers are a motherfucker to heat."

Neither looked at the other for a moment. Dinah's yearning could've filled stadiums.

"I think that it was good that we saw one another," he said, making an effort to sound hearty.

"I guess I'm really in pretty good shape," she said, apropos of nothing at all. Wishing . . . wishing . . . what good was it to wish.

Rudy laughed and cleared his throat. "You're the only girl I know who compliments herself."

Dinah frowned and considered. "I think it's sweet that I do it though." They looked at each other during the instant that it took to realize what she had said. They both laughed. "Well, I'd better do it, because God knows when . . . anyone else will," she said.

"You've been doing that since I met you," he said.

Their eyes held for a moment. Dinah tried to feel into him. Stir some soft into his eyes, remind him of what they, for the briefest of periods, had been. And what they, with teams of dedicated professionals, could perhaps someday be again.

"Bend down," she said finally, softly. "Bend down, so I can get over you."

Rudy leaned down and kissed her. Dinah shut her eyes, receiving the kiss like a sacrament. "I wish that I had met you now," she said softly, an incantation for the spell.

He straightened and looked at her guardedly.

"No, you don't," he said. " 'Cause if you met me now, I'd be all shut down, like I am." He stood up.

"No, you wouldn't," she assured him. " 'Cause you're all shut down now because of me, and you wouldn't have met me till now, so you wouldn't be shut down."

"I guess." He looked at her strangely for a moment. "I'll try to call you tomorrow, around two, before I leave," he said quietly, and then walked out of the room.

Dinah looked mournfully at the space he had left behind. She thought, Don't ask for more or you'll get less

115

than you have already. Don't rock the boat. But then, what boat am I on if I can't ask for anything? She considered.

The Love Boat.

She sat out at the other end of the world, his world, an outcast from loveland, an exile from loveland. Banished. She had given him up and found herself on the other side of that decision, longing to go back with him under the shade of any conditions.

After Rudy left, she turned on the television because she didn't want to listen to the sound of his not being there, the sound of her by herself after he went back to his hotel to call his jealous ... nice girlfriend. She fell asleep watching *The Great McGinty* and dreamed that Rudy was in love with a French girl and she had to pretend not to care.

In the morning, she called her friend Connie. Dinah had come to rely on Connie's advice, not so much as something to be followed, but as something to be enjoyed. She now told her about the demystification process.

"Demystification," Connie pondered. "It sounds like something they do to your car at the car wash."

"I shouldn't have slept with him. I promised myself that I wouldn't," Dinah said. "Now I'm going to feel more loony."

"Oh, please," drawled Connie. "You had no choice. You were lost as soon as he told you that he had another girlfriend. You went into shock and he revived you by slapping you in the vagina with his penis."

"Be serious, Connie," Dinah begged. "This is hard."

"Honey, everybody sleeps with their exes," Connie said soothingly. "Or, if they don't, they want to. You were with this guy forever. You were mad at him, then you were all bummed out, then you were scared of him, and now you're all three. Let's face it, Rudy is a hard act to follow."

"Part of the reason that it's a hard act to follow is that no act preceded it."

"Well now, come on, you weren't a virgin when you first hitched up with him."

"No, no," Dinah said impatiently. "Oh, I don't know. I've lost him now forever. And I thought that was a good thing. I mean, I've been better since we've not been together. I was so—we were so—oh, Connie, what am I gonna do?"

"Well, the main thing is, you don't have to decide right now. Don't just do something, stand there. Why don't we go to the health club and discuss our options?"

"Oh, Connie, you truly are a groove," Dinah said gratefully.

"So they claim," said Connie magnanimously, "so they claim."

Dinah and Connie sat in the sauna at the Korean Health Spa in downtown L.A. A television in the corner glowed, showing some Asian courtroom drama. The sound was down. Two small Korean women sat on the other end of the wooden bench, one cross-legged with a towel over her face.

"Waiting for execution," mumbled Dinah as they sat down. Connie smiled and put her head down. The towelless woman watched the courtroom drama without sound.

"So, how was the sex?" asked Connie, smoothing her towel underneath her.

"Good," answered Dinah. "Sad and good."

Connie laughed. "I used to think that sex couldn't be good unless it was a little bit sad."

"Well, this was a little bit sadder than usual for a

number of reasons," began Dinah, "not the least of which was that I locked Tony outside of the room and he's used to sleeping with me, so all through the sex, Tony sat outside the door and howled and yelped. It gave a kind of undeniably tragic underscoring to the whole thing."

"That's the first time you've had sex since you got Tony?" asked Connie. "Isn't he almost a year old?"

"Ten months," said Dinah. "I got him when he was six weeks—remember, that was when I broke up with Kevin. So that's like seven or eight months ago. Yeah, I haven't had sex for like eight months or so—is that bad? That's not so bad. Who am I gonna sleep with?"

"It's not bad, Di, it's just long," said Connie. "No wonder this episode had such an impact on you. I hope you've been masturbating or something."

"I don't masturbate."

"Ever?"

"Once," said Dinah. The Korean woman got up, wrapped a towel around her and padded out of the sauna. "I hope it wasn't something I said," said Dinah, looking after her.

"Most women in Korea masturbate at least twice before they're thirty," joked Connie.

"I see."

"I guess you must not have liked it then," said Connie.

"What?" asked Dinah. "Oh, the masturbation thing. No, that's not entirely true. I liked it all right. The trouble was that it took me like eight hours to come, and even though it was kinda great, I didn't really feel that it was worth that kind of a time commitment."

"Eight hours is too long," nodded Connie, looking at the courtroom drama continuing in the corner. "Didn't you fantasize?"

"In the beginning," said Dinah slowly. "In the beginning, I pretended I was someone else. That my hand was someone else. But in the end I realized that it was only me. Men are lucky, you know. With their penis all out there getting little erections on the bus, waking up with erections. The penis is . . . the penis is an organ. The vagina is a quasi-organ."

Connie shook her head in amazement. "Who has more fun than *people*, that's what I want to know." She rearranged her towel. "So wait, back to the Rudy report . . . ," she said.

"I shouldn't have said the thing to him about the black swan from hell," said Dinah with a slight grimace.

"Excuse me?"

"Nothing," sighed Dinah, wiping some sweat off her back. "Just some asshole thing I said to him that partly revealed my inner life."

"So you did talk about your little event?"

"Our blessed event, you mean?" said Dinah. "No, no, we didn't discuss it. And I think it's good that we didn't discuss it."

"That *is* good. It keeps the tensions alive. And you can always use more tension."

It was hot. The kind of heat you could practically hang a painting on. A small painting. The heat pressed in on Dinah and Connie.

A woman stood with her ass in Dinah's face, turning the channel on the TV. Dinah leaned over to Connie and said softly, "I think someone should introduce us."

Connie laughed. "At least."

The woman bent over farther; her ass loomed closer to Dinah's unhappy face. "And then perhaps she should meet my folks," she added.

Connie said, "When my sister goes to the gynecologist, before he actually puts anything—including himself —into her, she says, her legs spread wide, 'Doctor, could you at least kiss me?' I was just at the gyno this week

119

and got an anal exam that was so long, I could have formed a lasting relationship during it and broken up and still it would have marched on. I wanted to say, 'Hey, what is it exactly that you're looking for in there? Maybe I can help.' "

"I know," said Dinah. "At least men get to turn around. They just face the doctor for the cough part."

"While they go down the list, 'No masses in the breast, nipple coloring seems normal. How does this feel?' How could it feel? You have a metal clamp holding my vagina open and you're sticking special Q-tips deep inside me. 'Uterus seems soft and perfectly shaped, outer abdominal reflexes seem okay, external vagina seems normal.' All while you're lying there like an uncooked ham about to be baked. Like you're not present at all. As though you're in the other room having punch and cookies."

The woman's ass lumbered away.

"I can't remember," mused Dinah. "Is it big hands, big dick, or little hands, big dick?"

"Big hands."

"Are you sure?"

"I always wanted to say, small upper lip, huge balls. Or, at least, one huge ball."

"Or, no head, no dick."

"Now, that's very Zen."

"I have to get out now."

Dinah rose and pushed the wooden door open, her towel wrapped securely around her. Connie followed, her long blond hair flat against her head and neck. The main room to the bathhouse was a large room in pink tiles with maroon trim. There were three pools, each a different temperature. One hot, one very hot and one ice-cold. There were two troughs down the center of the room where women sat with scrub brushes and soap and washed themselves. Their hair, their bodies, each other.

120

In one corner were three shower stalls. In another, four massage tables were set up. On these, Korean women in bras and panties would either massage you or scrub the top layer of your skin off with loofah mitts. Then they would wash you with milk and put a mask on you. Dinah and Connie got into the regular hot pool. Another woman floated nearby, only her head above water, her eyes closed to the world.

On the wall over the jacuzzis were instructions in Korean characters: Except for the words "Culligan Water Service" and "Skin Cancer," everything was written in Korean.

"I think I must've loved Rudy more. Not in the beginning, but finally. Finally, I loved him more."

"It's not that you loved more—I think Rudy loved you just as much as you loved him. The difference is that you needed his approval and he didn't need yours."

"How could he have loved me without giving me his approval?"

"Maybe that was his hold over you. And you even wanted him to approve of the reason why you got out of the relationship. It's like people who call people and say, 'I'm gonna kill myself,' so that someone can talk them out of it. As long as he withheld his approval from you, you were transfixed. I always thought that he didn't trust you because he thought if he gave you his approval, you might leave. But I just think he's probably not capable of loving uncritically. A lot of people are like that. As long as you had his apparent ambivalence to subdue, you were transfixed. You were his curio. A curio desperately trying to become a passion."

Dinah sighed. "I see myself sitting in front of him saying, 'See how funny, see how pretty, see how smart. Like me, like me. Oh, please like me.' An organ grinder for a body and a monkey for a head."

"You're well out of it."

121

"I may be out of it, but I'm not that well." Dinah started out of the pool, then stopped and got back in. She held her breath and dunked her head under water. She re-emerged.

"So, that's it for the Rudy material?" said Connie. "You said something about swans, he told you about his girlfriend, you slept with him and called me? I'm sure there must be more to tell than that."

"What's to tell? I saw him, he told me that he has a new, perfect girlfriend. I slept with him and now he's flying back to the Hamptons to receive Little Miss Lindsay's primo focus. You should've seen his face when he told me how nice she is to him."

"They have a saying where I come from: 'If you can't be interesting, be nice,' " said Connie. "Honey, you're better off without him. Look how well your life has been going these past couple of years."

"How well has it been going?" asked Dinah. "I'm alone."

"Oh, c'mon, Dinah, that's not fair," said Connie. "Just because you haven't really been with someone doesn't mean that nothing is happening. It isn't like you haven't had any opportunity. Besides, men aren't the only thing going on."

"Don't tell any of them that," said Dinah. "What is that other saying you told me? Men get their identity from their work and women get their identity from their men?"

"I told you that about Chuck," said Connie, "when we were in a fight. Not about you and Rudy."

"Oh, these sayings of yours only apply where *you* say so?"

"They're *my* sayings," sulked Connie, sweat dripping from her nose. "Look, Dinah, you know that I like Rudy. I always have—I just don't like him for *you*. And I don't think you like him for you either; you just don't like the idea of anyone else having him. Particularly when his career is going so well."

"That's not totally so," said Dinah. "It's true that I don't like the idea of somebody else having him, but more because I haven't ever really gotten over him than just random resentment of the new girl. And his career is always going well."

"You know what I think?" said Connie.

"No, but I'm sure you're gonna tell me."

"I think that it's dangerous for you to be idle," pronounced Connie. "I think that this strike is affecting you in a very profound way. I think that your reinvention of how important Rudy is to you is largely the product of being out of work and not giving yourself anything creative to do with your time. So all your energy that you normally expend writing soaps is now free to attach itself to all sorts of wild fantasies. You have all this free time and energy to spend on creating a little drama for yourself. Why don't you do what I suggested at the beginning of the strike—finish one of your short stories, write a script—"

"I don't want to be a scab," explained Dinah.

"Dinah, everyone is writing scripts right now. Just not officially and not for any producers. Next year is going to be huge."

"I can't write scripts," said Dinah. "It's too hard. I'm not good enough."

"Then find someone to work with who's strong in your weak areas," argued Connie. "That's what Larraine and I do for each other. We've gotten an enormous amount of work done during this strike. It's dangerous to just sit around and do nothing."

"I'm not sitting around doing *nothing*," whined Dinah.

"Really?" said Connie. "What are you doing?"

"I'm . . . taking a massage course in Santa Monica

three times a week and I have Yoga and I was thinking of taking this . . . screenwriting seminar at the end of the month."

Connie just looked at Dinah. "Dinah, you know what I'm talking about," she said gently. "I think that it's good that you've got yourself a couple of activities, but none of these things seem to be absorbing-enough for you—you know what I'm saying?"

"You think that if I wrote a short story or something it would keep me out of trouble? What am I supposed to write about? My low-impact life? Crawling from one end of the day to the other like a slow fat bug?"

"So, what do you want to do—get into a little anecdotal trouble so that you have something to write about?"

"Writing from experience is always more interesting. Writing from what you know."

"What about using your imagination? Or some past experience? You think that turning your life into some laboratory to conduct your experiments of prose in is . . . ?"

"I didn't see Rudy again so I could write about it!" exclaimed Dinah. "He called me! And I don't want to write about it! I don't want to do anything. I just want to go away and read. Not write. I write for a living; why would I want to write while I'm on vacation? Or on strike or whatever?"

"Go away where?" asked Connie suspiciously. "You wouldn't, by any chance, be thinking of going east, would you?"

"No, I wouldn't," said Dinah emphatically. "And even if I would, it wouldn't necessarily be just to see Rudy, you know. I did live in the East for a long time. I could have other motives for visiting an entire coast than just one guy."

There was a pause. Connie looked at Dinah. Finally

124

Connie said, "Just promise me that you won't do anything silly without talking to me first."

"Connie, I'm not going to do anything silly."

"That's what you think," said Connie. "Just promise me, Dinah, that you'll talk to me before you do anything *large*."

Dinah shrugged noncommittally. "Okay."

"Okay what?"

"*Okay*," said Dinah, exasperated. "I promise that I'll talk to you if I do anything *large*."

"*Before*," urged Connie.

"Before, before, okay? Can we get our massage now?"

Dinah was dreaming she was rolling around in bed with Rudy. They were in each other's arms, kissing, nuzzling playfully, laughing. Dinah noticed that there was something in the bed, little things underneath them. Rudy got up to go to the bathroom and Dinah looked down and noticed that the bed was covered with little wooden animals, toys from the ark. Dinah began sweeping them off the bed, onto the floor. "Rudy," she called laughing. "Whose toys are these?"

"What toys?" said a man's voice, a voice that was not quite Rudy's. A face peered out of the door of the bathroom, smiling. It was the face of Joshua Souther, the actor who portrayed Blaine MacDonald on *Heart's Desire*. The actor who portrayed Rudy.

Dinah awoke with a start. Connie lay on the next table, her face covered with honey and cucumbers, her body covered with oil. She looked to Dinah like someone being prepared for sacrifice. Sacrifice to the great Kong. Anointed in oil, lathered and buffed. Presentable for marriage, for sacrifice to the Great Monkey that is all men. Bride of Christ, the full moon's Mrs. Kong, shine your light of reflected glory on me.

There was an enormous fat woman making her way to the table next to her, a bigger bride for Kong. The woman was Korean. She lay on the table, closed her eyes and began humming a song while another woman slaved over her with oils, with honey, did to her what was also being done to Dinah and Connie. The song the fat woman sang sounded like "Que Sera Sera," so Dinah started singing along with her. Now Connie joined in and the fat woman and the masseuses in bras and panties who didn't speak English laughed and continued massaging in rhythm to the song.

> When I was just a little girl
> I asked my mother what will I be.
> Will I be pretty?
> Will I be rich?
> Here's what she said to me.
> Queeeeee sera, sera . . ."

Dinah knew as they began singing the last refrain that she just might possibly go east to the Hamptons.

"Whatever will be, will be" thoughts crossed Dinah's mind en route to God knows what shit hole. "What time is it?" she said suddenly. My God, what time was it? She had been daydreaming—what if she had missed his call? Rudy was supposed to call. Now, or soon. She had to call home. What time had he said? She knew perfectly what time he had said. Two o'clock. "What time is it?"

"A quarter to one," replied Connie. "Why, what is it? What do you have to do?"

"I'm expecting a call," Dinah answered as she dressed. "Rudy said he would call before he left."

Actually, he had said he would try to call. How do you *try* to call? She pictured him reaching for the phone without quite being able to reach it, pushing numbers on the push-button phone, but somehow they wouldn't quite push in.

She parted from Connie in the parking lot, feeling invigorated and alone.

"Don't do anything. . . ."

"Good-bye, Con. Thanks," Dinah interrupted.

As Dinah walked to her car, Connie called to her back. "Just remember, Dinah, people that make over four hundred thousand dollars a year don't change." Dinah turned. Connie continued, "And Rudy makes well over that."

"And I make well under, is that what you're trying to say?"

Connie opened her car door. "Not well under, but under."

Dinah shielded her eyes against the sun so she could see Connie better. "What are you saying, that I should change?"

Connie slid into her car and called, "I'm saying that he *won't*," and slammed her car door.

Dinah headed home, waited for Rudy to call, and when he didn't, she packed her suitcase, locked her house, got her dog, loaded her car and headed for the airport for a flight east. Began her driven drive, her frenetic flight to the older, longer-settled coast, the cradle of Rudy and his child bride, the garden where she puttered, the fights they never had, the nights they shared, the deep sleeps, deeper kisses, heaven. Dinah died (a little) and flew the Red Eye straight to heaven, the gray highway stretching out in front of her toward the airport, an asphalt river emptying into Rudy's ocean of love, a heart-shaped body of water where he floated with Lindsay . . . happy . . . happy . . . held aloft on a current of air, suspended weightless, the arrow of the airplane shot into the heart of the Hamptons, drawn helplessly toward Rudy's world, deeper and deeper behind the lines, between the lines . . . enemy lines . . . que sera . . . the ex–Mrs. Kong flew on.

The tiny male spider approaches his relatively huge mate and begins to couple. The female devours him in an act of copulatory cannibalism. She chews away the head, leaving the rest of the male's body sexually functional, so his sperm can pass into her body. The male tarantula has a pair of curved appendages on his front legs with which he holds open the female's jaws so that she cannot snap at him during mating.

8

She drove her nondescript rental car into Southampton one mid-morning. Past a deli, Elizabeth Arden, a library, cars, trees, people—turned left on Three Mile Highway, heading out to East Hampton. There weren't as many stations on the radio now. More static, fewer choices. No waiting. She found "Moondance" by Van Morrison. A song made up in a small room, she thought as the scenery lay smooth and summery around her. She turned up the music and slipped into its sound, allowing it to close tightly over her head, resting between a voice and a guitar. Shingled homes, water sparkling to her right, long grass, beaches, trees. She headed on farther into Long Island to East Hampton, to Amagansett— pulled by Rudy's happiness. Drawn by some invisible cord to the vicinity of his newly found domestic bliss. Rudy summering with Lindsay—writing a new play about her, dedicating it to her. Lindsay catering to him, nurturing, feeding, soothing, kissing—it was too much. Dinah searched for a loud, thought-dispersing song. She finally found "Sultans of Swing" and played it full throttle as she blasted up the highway, headlong into nowhere specific.

It seemed that everywhere she looked there were couples. Holding hands, laughing, engaged in something offhand and intimate. The pairing-off was ongoing. As the Ark was once again imminent, looming. Dinah turned the music up louder. Listening for two. She left her world and entered his.

A fly caught in his jar.

Rudy's enthusiasm for his fellows was limited, finite. And when it evaporated, Dinah registered what she came to call "The Stink Off the Swamp." And when the smell would come, when his ability to be with others almost happily would end, she would simply try to hightail it out of his sight. If you were caught in his sight once the stink came, you could see the critical light go on behind his eyes. He was a solitary man who came among us from time to time to favor us with his presence. But in the end he must wander back to his onesome, leaving us in his watchful wake, reeling.

Having, as he did, a solitary job, eventually his use for others would ebb, then run dry. And when the dryness set in, Dinah would have to get out, though she would frequently miscalculate and get contaminated in the chaff of his disfavor. She would sense that she had somehow done wrong. She had either spoken too loudly or too much, arrived late, overslept, watched too much TV, received or made too many phone calls, had too many friends, so-called friends who called too much. She used to say that when he answered the phone and it was for her, he looked at her as if she had just shot a cop in his living room.

She didn't know why people loved each other sometimes. Maybe it was simply that if you were ready, there was an opening and somebody walked through it, getting into your system, his pheromones mingling with yours, and suddenly you're undone and only that somebody can

131

put you together again. You grow toward his sunlight, live according to his law. You're strung to his tuning, come to his dog whistle that no one else can hear. And all because your ever-closed flower was open that day when his sunlight poured into you and you haven't been able to grow toward anyone else since. It's unfair, it's inconvenient, demeaning, dependent, inane. You were ever after obedient to the fact of him, a whim of his, a heat he had. Obedient and bowed.

She arrived in Amagansett about noon. "Village of Amagansett, settled 1790." She spotted several realty offices as she drove into town, and she drove to the back of the second one on the right, mainly because it had a parking lot. A sign in front said "Summer Rentals." But then all the realtors had signs in front that said "Summer Rentals."

Dinah parked her car, leaving a forlorn Tony in the front seat, and walked up a little ramp and into the office through a sliding glass door. A fat girl sat behind a desk.

"Hi," Dinah said. "Uh, I wanted to rent a house, I think."

The girl's smile was seriously sunk in flesh. "Surely, let me show you to one of the realtors." She took Dinah through a door that led to a large sunny room with many aluminum desks and filing cabinets. A man of about fifty sat in the corner talking on the phone. Two women sat on opposite ends of the room, also on the phone. The receptionist took Dinah over to the man in the corner. He wore glasses and had extremely large bunny teeth that his lips could not cover for too long. A plaque on his desk said his name was Barney Shout. Barney indicated to Dinah that she should sit in one of the two chairs in front of his desk. The fat girl mouthed the word "rental" to Barney and he nodded patiently. She waddled away and Dinah sat and listened to Barney finish his call.

"Well, think about how much you'd like to extend past the season, say until October. Because, as I say, they are interested . . . uh-huh . . . surely—take your time . . . fine, then I'll talk to you toward the end of the week . . . I will . . . Thanks so much, Mrs. Adelson. . . ." He smiled a great big bunny smile of an almost audible width for the benefit of Mrs. Adelson and returned the receiver to its cradle lovingly, gradually moving his enormous smile to Dinah. He rose slightly and put out his hand. "Barney Shout," he said amiably as Dinah took his hand. It was cool.

"Dinah Kaufman," she said earnestly.

Barney sat back down. "Well, what can I do for you?"

"Well," began Dinah doubtfully, "I wanted to rent a house."

"Certainly," said Barney easily. "It is very late in the season, you realize that. Most rentals have already started."

"Yes, I know," said Dinah. "It's kind of a last-minute thing. I thought maybe I could get kind of a last-minute discount or something."

Barney laughed. "Maybe so, maybe so." He opened a book of listings in front of him. "Let's see what we have here." He frowned happily. "What price range are you thinking of?"

Dinah pursed her lips. "I don't know. How much is the average cost . . . rent . . . whatever?"

Barney smiled and licked his low-impact lips. He wore a plaid shirt and a vest. "The price for the season can go anywhere from a couple of thousand dollars all the way up to seventy-five thousand. Depending on size, view, pool, you know."

"Seventy-five thousand!" exclaimed Dinah dramatically. "You could practically *buy* a house for seventy-five thousand."

133

"Not a very nice house," said Barney sadly. "A good down payment for a house, sure."

"Or several cars," said Dinah. "Or living expenses for a couple of years."

"I take it you want something on the less expensive end of the scale then?"

"You take it right," said Dinah. "I had no idea they were that much. I used to come out here with my . . . hus . . . boyfriend, but he always paid for it. I mean, I don't know, I never thought to ask him how much it cost. Wow."

Thinking now that she should have asked Rudy for alimony. What, asked . . . *sued.* Sued him for damages. But then he'd have that story: Dinah the dependent. Dinah the leech. Why should she sue for alimony? She made a decent living. Why? I'll tell you why. Because then she'd have money now. Enough money to rent a house near Rudy and his new girlfriend and have loud, fabulous parties. Alimony parties. With her as the pretty good Gatsby. Gatsby, the not-quite-great. Situated across the Sound. Audible, as opposed to liquid.

"So . . ." said Barney expectantly, folding his hands in front of him on the desk, his plaid shirt pulling unflatteringly around his shoulders, forcing Dinah from her reverie.

"So, more like the several-thousand range," said Dinah. "The less the better. Oh, and I also have my dog with me. A little dog."

"Well, that limits us a bit more then." He narrowed his eyes and scrutinized his book of listings. Dinah waited, feeling somehow as if she were in the principal's office. Barney flipped to the back of the book. "Let's take a look at the Springs."

"Where's the Springs?" asked Dinah.

"It's a Hampton," replied Barney. "It's more or less the economical Hampton."

134

"The cheap Hampton," murmured Dinah.

Barney pulled four or five listings out of his book and he and Dinah drove around the Springs in his beige Eldorado, looking at little tiny cottages, the last dregs of the rentals for the season. Places with depressing linoleum and leftover furniture. In between these elfish hideaways, Dinah sat slumped down in Barney's Eldorado gazing out the window at her dappled surroundings. Tony sat obediently in the backseat, his tongue out, panting.

"Maybe I should just try to sell my car and get something halfway decent," said Dinah gloomily. "Actually with my car, we might not even get a third of the way to decent. Besides, I don't even have a car—I have a *rental* car."

"Now, don't be that way," coaxed Barney as they arrived at their last option of the afternoon. A sign read "Salter's Cottages" as they drove up the graveled drive. It was at the far end of Fireplace Road in the Springs. "What is your profession, may I ask?"

"Writer," Dinah replied as he came to the end of the drive. "Television writer," she added guiltily in case she could be accused of fooling him into thinking that she was an artist of some kind making some valuable contribution to a Third World society somewhere.

"Really? Television? What shows? Do you mind my asking?" He turned off the car and looked at her inquisitively.

"Soap opera. A soap opera called *Heart's Desire.*"

Barney Shout beamed at Dinah. "Aw, that's terrific. I'll have to tell my wife. She watches those shows all the time. What's the name of it again?"

Dinah opened the car door. *"Heart's Desire,"* she said as she got out of the car.

"Heart's Desire," intoned Barney solemnly as he opened his door and got out. *"Heart's Desire."*

There were many tiny cabins on a patch of land leading up to the water. A larger house at the bottom of the land had a laundry line leading from it to a tree. Two white T-shirts waved gently in the breeze. "That's Mrs. Salter's place," said Barney almost confidentially. "I'll just go get the key."

The gravel crunched under his shoes as Barney marched gingerly up to the house, his head down, watching his feet as though to help them go.

Dinah stood forlornly in the drive looking past several cottages to the water sparkling beyond. I hope I like this place, she thought, as a dog barked in the distance and boats bobbed on the horizon.

Barney emerged from the house happily. The screen door slammed behind him. Sun flashed across his glasses. "Got it!" he announced, raising his clenched fist full of keys victoriously into the air. "It's the last house on the right, almost on the water." They crunch-crunch-crunched their way past two other little shingled cabins. "It was rented to a couple but apparently one of their relatives fell ill and they couldn't get away," explained Barney. "Otherwise, a place like this would be gone very early on in the season, let me tell you. These cottages are real bargains for what they rent. This close to the water and all that."

They came to the last cottage on the right, the one almost on the water. There was one other cabin between it and the water. "It's a hop, skip and a jump to the beach," said big old Barney, fitting the key into the door. He reminded Dinah of a puppy wagging his tail as he opened the door. "I told Mrs. Salter that you were a writer and she said that they get lots of writers here. She said there's a couple here right now. In fact, one of them is in one of these two cottages on the water." He gestured vaguely beyond them. Dinah squinted halfheartedly to the houses beyond as she followed puppy man into the cottage.

They walked into a tiny living room with a little black cloth sofa, two wooden chairs with beige cushions, a table in the corner with a huge red lamp. An old yellow rug with forlorn tassels covered part of the linoleum floor.

A TV stood facing the couch-and-chair area. Barstools stood under the counter. The sun shone optimistically through windows with curtains with brown and yellow flowers. There was a musty, forgotten odor. Dinah could see dust caught in the sunlight. The overall effect was that of a hideaway for a mildly wanted criminal.

"Cozy, isn't it?" remarked Barney impartially, as he strolled toward a door on the right and opened it.

"It's less depressing than the other places we've seen. Less modern. Not as much like a furnished closet," said Dinah.

Barney laughed from the other room. "Furnished closet—that's a good one. I'll have to remember to tell that to the wife. *Heart's Desire* and furnished closet. This in here's the bedroom."

Dinah padded across the small room and peered into it. There were a bed and a table next to it, with a small reading lamp and a rotary phone.

"This here is a new mattress," he said proudly. "There's your closet right here and that door there leads to the bathroom." Dinah nodded. "And through here is the kitchen. . . ." He led Dinah out of the bedroom through the living room and into the kitchen. Dinah noticed a little tear in his pants. "All new appliances," Barney said, gesturing around. "Through here," he continued, opening a door next to the yellow refrigerator, "is your porch area, where you can eat or write or whatever you want to do. It's nice and sunny all day. And private."

They stood on a deck where there was a little picnic table with two benches and a chair. It had a partial view of the water and the back of another cabin that was directly on the water.

"How much is this place?" Dinah asked, as cavalierly as possible.

Barney smiled wistfully and looked down at his hands. "I'm afraid this place is a little bit more than the others because of the view."

Dinah closed her eyes and hung her head. "How much?" she asked apprehensively in the direction of her shoes.

"Four thousand," said Barney sadly.

"Four *thousand*? But it's just a shack!"

Barney shrugged helplessly. "You said yourself that it was nicer than the others—that it wasn't a . . . furnished closet. When they're nicer, they're more." He sounded apologetic. "I mean, this isn't really a *view*, but it has tremendous view potential. . . ."

A man rounded the corner, walking past Dinah and Barney to the beach or the house beyond. Dinah stopped talking and stared at him. He had dark, curly hair and intense blue eyes, was medium height and slight. He wore light-tan loose-fitting slacks and a white shirt with the sleeves rolled up at the elbow. He carried a book: P. G. Wodehouse.

"Hello," he said in a friendly, nervous voice. "Are you moving in?" He smiled an uneasy, beautiful smile. Dinah was transfixed. He was attractive, uncomfortable and altogether new.

"Yes," she said automatically. He could just as easily have asked her for her firstborn son. No. Yes. She flushed and looked at Barney. "I mean, I think so."

"Great," said the new, nervous man. "I'm Roy. Roy Delaney. I'm staying in that cottage there. We'll be neighbors." Roy seemed to be alive with movement. His hand ran through his hair, over his mouth, in his pocket, and out again. He shifted his weight from one foot to the other. His large eyes flashed and smiled. He was like a

Richter scale for a country with constant tiny earthquakes.

"I have a mood named Roy," said Dinah, smiling shyly. "I'm Dinah Kaufman," she added quickly.

"And I'm Barney Shout." Barney put out his hand and Roy took it.

"Are you both moving in?" Roy asked as he reached for Barney's hand and dropped his book. He shook Barney's hand briefly and picked up his book. His hand reached behind his neck, his weight shifting. Controlled epilepsy.

"Me?" laughed Barney. "No, no, I'm just the realtor."

"Oh, oh, I see," said Roy, smiling and dropping his book again. "Ooops," he said as he picked up the book and wiped it on his pant leg. "Well . . ." he said, looking at Dinah and nodding slightly, "welcome." Their eyes met. Both smiling. Nervous. "Neighbor," he added, running a hand through his hair and shifting his weight from one foot to the other.

"Neighbor," she echoed, nodding with him. For a moment they were like those dolls with the bobbing heads in the backs of cars. Roy raised his free hand.

"See you," he said as he backed away for a few steps and then turned and walked toward his house that was essentially Dinah's view.

"See you," said Dinah as he disappeared into his house and the screen door slammed behind him. Dinah turned to Barney, who stood smiling with his hands in his pockets. She tried to look stern. "I still say it's too much money."

Barney just smiled apologetically and looked at his enormous hands.

Dinah thinks that if she can get someone to love her, then she doesn't have to love him anymore. Love for her is a one-sided thing—having to do with pursuit and entrapment—not a state of rest. Once someone loves her, her job is done, she must move on. It was as if she largely loved in order to be loved. The great thing, the essential thing about Rudy, was that she could never win him entirely. She once said to him, "I want to win you over." To which he replied, "Hon, you won me years ago."

"Yes," she said, "but now I want to bag your demeanor."

A thing she could never do. What she wanted from Rudy was his approval—a thing he was incapable of giving. Consistently. Enthusiastically. Genuinely. And confusing love with approval as she did, it became an endless arena for her to act out her dysfunctionality in. If Dinah would love Rudy until he visibly approved of her, she would love him forever.

"You seek too much approval," he informed her. "I'm not a person that overpraises. I don't bullshit. You can really believe it when I give a compliment."

"I've only known on some level that you care," Dinah said, "even if I don't actually *see* it."

"Of course I care. Besides, how can you trust what you see?" he asked. "Someone wearing their feelings all out in the open like that? You'd never trust that anyway."

"No," she agreed sadly.

Since she would probably never feel loved anyway, it was a lot easier to feel that that was a result of someone's behavior toward her, rather than some deficit in herself. That their problem was her problem. But finally, however indirectly she perceived it, it was her problem.

Dinah was driving aimlessly around Long Island, from Amagansett to East Hampton and on to Sag Harbor. She saw a handmade sign with a picture of a gypsy and an arrow on a tree. She followed the arrow to a building or, more precisely, to the side of a building. As Dinah drove up, there was writing on the wall. It said "Psychic

Parking." She imagined herself telepathically parking her car as she eased into a space underneath the prophetic writing on the wall. She walked around the building to the front, where a neon moon and star shone over the promise: "Sag Harbor Psychic Tarot Readings." Dinah entered a small room that was fairly bare with only a beige couch, a round mirror over it and a little table covered with magazines. Dinah appraised the room mildly. Three thousand a month, she concluded, continuing to look around. A beaded doorway was in the corner. Sounds of a television came from the room beyond. Dinah picked up a magazine as a young man's dark head appeared through the beads.

"Just a moment," he said with a startled look, his head disappearing back into the psychic's lair.

What am I doing here? Dinah wondered. Perhaps the psychic would know. Dinah opened the magazine, just as a small, heavyset Indian woman burst through the pink beads and then stood there with them swaying dramatically behind her.

The Indian woman motioned for Dinah to follow her. Dinah walked behind her, around a corner and through another bead-covered door. These beads, however, were gold, amber. They clicked and swayed as Dinah and the little woman walked through.

In the little room, there were two chairs facing each other. The women sat, their knees almost touching. It was more a cubicle than a room, the psychic's lair, the voting booth of the dead. On a low shelf was some sort of altar, a string of colored lights, tarot cards, candles. A picture of Jesus gazed mournfully from the wall above the psychic's head. Dinah got a good look at her now. She had metal-gray hair and dark-brown skin that hung on her as though it might have once belonged to a larger woman, second-hand skin, hand-me-down skin that clung to her like a shy child. She had tiny golden eyes surrounded by the heavy guard of wrinkles. Her face was quite flat, a manhole with furtive eyes. She had a slight mustache and white, white teeth. False teeth. Dinah was nervous and hoped this would prove to be somehow effective and not too expensive. The psychic smiled like a double agent. Someone trapped between this world and the world beyond. A Jungian world, the parallel universe.

"I am Mama," the woman said with a heavy accent as she picked up the deck of tarot cards. "Cut the deck, please." Mama watched as Dinah cut the deck, then she took one-half of the deck and spread the cards in a fan, picture cards facing Dinah. "Pick four cards," she said, her piercing eyes apparently studying Dinah.

"Can I look at them?"

"Of course," Mama replied.

Dinah chose her four cards carefully, as though everything were riding on this. One was a man and a woman holding a goblet, another was a man and a woman under a rainbow, dancing with two children, the next was the high priestess and the last was an imposing-looking page. Dinah handed her four cards to Mama and looked up inadvertently to Jesus. She looked away guiltily.

Mama studied the cards. "You will have a long life," she pronounced.

Well, thought Dinah, good. At least that's out of the way—or covered—or in the cards. She winced.

"You are healthy."

Dinah smiled a practically home-free smile. Can't be bad, she thought.

Mama gazed at her impassively. "You smile on the outside, but there is sadness within."

Oh, great, here we go, thought Dinah. I've got a long, healthy, sad life to look forward to. Perfect.

"Understand?" probed Mama intensely.

Dinah nodded with what she hoped would pass for solemnity.

"You are lonely," said Mama. "Understand?"

What could be clearer? Dinah nodded.

"There is darkness over you—a cloud—understand?"

Dinah nodded the tiniest of nods. Mama didn't notice. "What's your birth date?" she continued.

Dinah told her.

"You're born on the twenty-seventh degree of your sun sign," she explained. "Well, this degree is very interesting. The point right between the twenty-sixth and the twenty-seventh degree is called the Pleiadean Degree. People that are born on the twenty-seventh degree of their sun sign are really channeled from our star source, the Pleiades. My ancestral source is Pleiades. The Star People come from this source. It means that you are a very old soul for one thing, and it also means that you have been many other places very recently and that you are in tune with the Celestial Forces in a way that not everyone is. That isn't easy, because it makes you really alone and really different. And so you don't have brothers and sisters to talk to, who know who you are because you come from a very different place. You agreed to come here, you didn't have to come here this time. But, once we come, we get caught up. We want to taste the extremes, what the Celestial Beings told the Star People to do when they came to Atlantis."

Ooops, Dinah thought. There it goes, the duck just dropped. The Spiritual Duck. Atlantis. Right.

Mama continued, "They were supposed to teach and uplift the consciousness of those people. But they were not supposed to physically interact with them. But the gift of this planet is the flesh, and flesh is another form of experience. The experiential for you is just as profound —profound—you feel everything so much. You will do very extreme things just so you can feel them extremely. You are a teacher and you teach in the way bad parents teach. You teach what not to do. To yourself. It's the force you have chosen to represent. There's no wrongness in it, but it appears backward. Moon..." she mused. "But you are one of the Pleiadean Beings, the cusp people, they have to do twice as much as anybody else, because there's the force of two beings pulling at them. You're like Kali, the Destroyer Goddess; you do all these intense things; it takes long to understand that. You won't come into your power of discerning until you are forty, and you're not forty yet, are you?"

Dinah shook her head. "Twenty-eight."

"Ah," continued Mama, nodding slowly, as if this were the last piece of the puzzle that now made everything fall into place, "you are in your Saturn Return."

"What's my Saturn Return?"

"It's a period when your life is turned upside down, all around. Everything is in turmoil. Many changes."

"Ah." Dinah didn't really believe this stuff that much, but it was interesting, and, just in case it was true, she could at least say she'd been around it all. In case there were Star People, Atlantis and gods, she would flirt on with spiritual matters.

"When you get to be forty, you will be able to discern in a different way, and then you can find more humor in it. Your north node is in Scorpio, so power, power, lots of power."

Dinah interrupted. "My north node?" Mama nodded. "That's great, because I was wondering where my north node was. I hadn't seen it in ages."

Mama smiled. "You are so fun-loving. You came to earth because you wanted to have a good time. You're really high-minded and you like people that are high-minded. Artists. People with a philosophy of spirit. It's such a power dance, such a power dance. And because it's this tenth degree, you're really strong for a woman. Even though you are small and delicate and beautiful."

144

Here Dinah smiled and blushed. All this for, hopefully, a low, low price.

"You're so strong, a man would rather have this force than you. So it will take a strong man to be able to counter this force. At the same time, a lot of soft men will come to you."

"Soft men," mused Dinah. "A lot of soft men. Ugh."

"And you will not be feeling good about yourself as a woman, because it makes you feel like you're too hard. The right relationship is in your future. You're not supposed to spend your life alone. The dance by the hearth is not something that you're given easily. You demand a mate, a counterpart, but you end up being more like a king than a queen. Which makes you feel unsatisfied with yourself as a woman. You have a tremendously powerful chart. There's bright fire in you. You're just so extreme. I see you ripping your hair out, ripping your clothes off. And I see you standing in the middle of it saying, 'How did I do this? How did this happen? This is so wonderful. Where is my mate?' You've reawakened some powerful, ancient stuff. You need to study black-widow medicine."

Dinah nodded. "Okay. Is there some sort of black-widow medical school in the area?"

"All the women dreamers, they really honor the spider. The black widow is so significant. You know, the male black widow, if he is very clever and fast, he can impregnate the female without losing his life. It can happen. But . . . there is such a counterpart that understands what you're doing, what you weave. With your Uranus at eleven Leo, you ought to be able to do revolutionary things with the film industry. You're instinctively in the right place at the right time; you funded that force when you came into this body. You are not for yourself, you do not belong to yourself, you belong to the world, and that's another reason it's so hard. Down here it feels bet-

145

ter if you belong to somebody. But there's nobody down here that you could keep without killing. Sort of. You belong to your star source. Your lack of fulfillment will produce your fulfillment.

"Hold the money in your hand and think of two wishes. Thirty-five dollars, please."

Dinah picked up her purse and fished around for the money, thinking thirty-five dollars was not bad for a sad, lonely dark-cloud type reading, delicate and beautiful. Dinah put a twenty and three fives in her hand, bundled disrespectfully into a wad.

"Now, tell me one wish."

"I wish to have a child." Why had she said that? It had never occurred to her that she wanted a child. Well, not never. Just not lately.

Mama nodded. "Ah." She smiled gravely. "You have someone you wish to have this child with?"

Dinah nodded, hypnotized. Why stop here? Why not be completely insane? Let's go with full-out psycho Norman Rockwell. "My ex-husband."

"Ah," smiled Mama as though she'd known it all along. Knew Rudy, knew hundreds of women who wandered in off the street wanting children with ex-husbands who were currently in recent, successful relationships. Her head continued nodding, bobbed, almost bobbing on the water of the world. "But there is trouble."

She knows! thought Dinah. She can help me. This is real!

"Someone is trying to keep you apart. There is darkness around your head. A maldocchio."

So that was it! A darkness, a maldocchio. I knew it!

Mama pointed to the card of the man and the woman holding the cup. "See."

Dinah looked at the card closely, narrowing her eyes. It was true. There were tiny gray spreckles surrounding everything that she hadn't noticed before. But maybe

146

that was the pattern of the card. Maybe this was a hoax. A squeak of doubt leaked into Dinah's hope and head, a little feeling that told Dinah that she might be a fool.

"Understand?" asked Mama.

Dinah thought she might have seen the doubt, felt the foolishness. She nodded hard, hoping to hide it all.

"Something happened to you with your father that keeps you from being with this man."

Yes! That's true. She knows! But then something happens with everyone's parents that keeps them from being with anyone. Oh no.

"But, there is someone else—two people who do not wish you together. If you want, I will take their bad wishes away."

"No," said Dinah sarcastically, "I want to keep the bad wishes. They'll help me to build character. What two people?"

Mama crossed her arms and gazed at Dinah impassively. "I will take the darkness from around your head, but it will cost you more."

Here we go. A costly maldocchio clung to her cranium. Her cranial cathedral where she worshiped the god of inappropriate men. Dinah cleared her throat and said doubtfully, "More?"

Mama looked impatient. Her skin draped cavalierly over her muscles, her bones. "I will put colors around your head. Understand?"

Dinah didn't quite understand but it sounded nice in any event.

"Usually, for this special blessing, I charge . . ." Mama paused dramatically. "One thousand dollars."

Dinah's eyes widened in astonishment. The squeak of a doubt spread. She found herself looking at a con artist. The doubt doubled, tripled, till there was nothing but doubt. Fucking people from Atlantis, I should have known. Raving on about this berserk star-source shit and

147

the black-widow school. Black widows killing their mates and there's no one I could keep without killing. Well, that's probably true. Or not. I'll probably never know what's true. What if it is true and I don't believe it and this is my one chance at—what? Then an edge of this blooming doubt browned and curled in the light of some other thing. Didn't things cost a lot because they were worth more? Like when men became more desirable? How could you determine till you got them? They seemed so desirable till you got them. A thousand dollars to remove a bad aura, to put a rainbow of colors around a formerly cloudy head. "Gee"—she looked at Mama like a bewildered child—"I don't have that kind of money."

Mama's golden eyes gazed impassively at Dinah. "How much do you have?"

Dinah furrowed her brow and clutched her bag. "One hundred." Said almost like a question, a polite request.

"Have you a check?" asked Mama, folding her hands.

"No," said Dinah earnestly, opening her purse toward Mama as if to convince her by allowing her to search.

Mama was unmoved by the yawning bag. "How much have you at home?"

Now Dinah lied. "Two hundred," she replied in a small voice, the voice of a grown woman lying to a psychic with hanging skin.

"Do you live far away?" pressed Mama.

Dinah hesitated. "I'm staying in the Springs." The cheap Hamptons, she added to herself. The humiliating Hampton, the Hampton of the hexed.

"I will make a blessing for the colored lights—I will remove the obstacles to your husband. But it must cost more. You will thank me. You will love Mama and bring her gifts. I will light candles."

148

Dinah watched Mama as she said these things. She was afraid to look directly into her eyes, but when Mama stopped talking, she suddenly found herself staring into them, hypnotized.

"You must trust Mama, you must trust her completely." Mama's eyes narrowed. "There is another man also."

"Another man," said Dinah hopefully, deciding not to withhold her trust entirely until she heard about the other man. She watched Mama warily.

"But it is your husband you love."

"Sure," said Dinah curtly, "but what about the other man?"

"When can you come back with the two hundred?"

Dinah smiled the tiniest of smiles. "That partly depends on my star source . . . and the other man."

Mama regarded her sternly. Both women sat in the tiny cubicle, knee to knee, presided over solemnly by Jesus, gazing at one another, both greedy for something. Finally, Mama laughed a laugh that started slowly from deep within her. The skin around her neck seemed almost to vibrate. The laugh increased. Mama threw her head back and slapped her hands on her knees. Dinah watched her, smiling.

"What about the other man?" Mama repeated, mimicking Dinah. "What about the other man?"

Dinah flushed.

Mama finally settled, wiped her eyes and looked at her. "Give me your right hand." Dinah did. Mama held it with both hands. "The other man is your brother from another life, you were both boys, twins." She looked at the side of Dinah's hand. "There is another man here." Dinah leaned forward to see the man on the side of her hand. "This man is a younger man, a friend."

"You mean he's already a friend?"

Mama nodded. "Maybe he is a Japanese man. Maybe.

I say what I see. You have many men. Men are made for the world. Women are made for the men. When will you return with the money?"

Dinah considered briefly. "Tomorrow afternoon. Many men, you say?"

Mama folded Dinah's hand into a fist and gave it back to her. "I will put colored lights around your head —do not worry. You will have your husband."

Dinah nodded absently, thinking, What Japanese man?

She told Mama that she'd return, glanced at Jesus and left.

What Japanese man?

Those Japanese are getting into *everything*.

She left Sag Harbor and returned through Easthampton to Amagansett, driving half purposely, half aimlessly. Maybe she would get a pizza and go to a movie.

She drove down a street called Further Lane and, out of the corner of her eye, she saw a wooden fence. Rudy's house. She stopped the car. Behind the fence she saw a lawn dotted fairly densely with tall trees at the back of which, partially visible, was a gray-and-white two-story Cape Cod house . . . Rudy's house . . . Rudy and Lindsay . . . happy . . . happy . . . Dinah had come to a stop and was staring at the house, through the house to a time when she had been with Rudy in this same house in the late afternoon, watching TV. Rudy was watching a Yankees game. The Yankees weren't doing very well, so Rudy wasn't doing very well, a man and his team. . . . Dinah sat with her portable computer on her lap, working on next month's plot breakdown of *Heart's Desire*. She looked up occasionally at the game, at Rudy and the game. Lou Pinella hit a fly ball. He ran to first. The ball was caught somewhere outfield. Lou ran back to the dugout—what Dinah normally referred to as the cockpit—

and, as he ran down the steps into the dugout, another player hit him on the ass. Dinah had looked up and was watching all this with some interest. She shook her head and smiled, saying, "That's so great that guys have that whole male-bonding sports thing. Girls don't have anything like that."

Rudy looked at Dinah impatiently. "Oh, Christ, stop complaining."

Dinah was slightly taken aback.

A horn honked, startling her out of her reverie. She put her foot on the gas and moved on.

And just think. That was the good part, albeit the end of the good part. Things had actually deteriorated from that point. The Yankees lost and Rudy and Dinah deteriorated.

She looked in the rearview mirror as she drove away. In it, she vaguely saw a girl with blond hair, honey-colored hair. Dinah's heartbeat quickened. Was that Lindsay? She drove away and looked in the rearview mirror when she got to the stop sign. She didn't want to look before then and be caught and seem desperate. And sure enough, the car was gone. Dinah shut her eyes and put her head down. What was she doing here?

Oh, Christ, stop complaining.

Somewhere in the space between loving Rudy and not loving him, Dinah lurked. She found herself wedged between these two worlds. She loved the memory of him, the possibility of him. What the fact of him said about her.

Dinah respected what Rudy did. He was good at his job. And since she had been brought up to believe that a woman had to get behind what a man did, she wanted to get behind someone whom she truly believed in, someone to whom she could say, "Go on, honey, do that thing you did again. You do that good. Really you do." She could be more articulate, say it more sincerely and mean it. It didn't seem to Dinah that men had to get behind what women did as much. They didn't have to look up at their mates so much as over at them. Hopefully, they wouldn't be embarrassed by what their women did—but if a woman was beautiful, that was almost enough of a trophy. But to Dinah, the more valuable trophy in a man was for him to be rich, to be powerful, to be talented. And the men you looked up to, those men tended to need looking after. These were the men worth winning and getting behind. Dinah didn't believe that this was right so much as it was so. Men looked for a breeder, women looked for a provider. And she figured that you had to accept the way things were before you could change them. Could you change them? What Dinah's friend Connie said was largely so: that women get their identity from their men and men get their identity from their work. So get a man with a good job. Sure women could get a good sense of themselves from a good job, but really to feel a sense of accomplishment, she must get a great guy or a good guy—or, after a while, any guy at all. It was, after all, thought Dinah, still a man's world. Oh yeah, look at films. The plots centered around a man's drama and the woman was largely the love interest, a reference point, not the focal point. Maybe not so much in television, but . . .

So Dinah had at least partly been drawn to Rudy because she admired what he did. And Dinah had thought that Rudy was with her because she was pretty and he wasn't embarrassed by what she did. Dinah could get behind Rudy and say, "Good, honey, do that—do what you did again," and feel not like a hypocrite, but instead like a supportive companion.

She admired his discipline—the way he could decide to do or not do something and it would be done or not done. He had bold resolve. She had no resolve. Willpower was not her middle name. Rebecca was.

152

Rudy didn't think he was disciplined so much as organized. Dinah thought that she, at best, was right-brained. At times, though, she said she got left-brain results out of her right brain. She pulled a left-brained bunny out of a right-brained hat.

But Dinah's job had begun to grow like a distracting fungus, eating away her attention. Now, when she stood behind Rudy, she was on the phone or working on a script. Dinah's wish to support a supportable man became vague or obsolete. She no longer had the time or took the time with Rudy and resented the job. She'd say, "If you want nurturing, you should get an IV hook-up." Or, "If you want me to watch you all the time, act like TV."

Let's just say her day job began interfering with her night job.

What Dinah tended to need in men was very often something she felt she lacked in herself. The men she was drawn to were somewhat formidable, intellectual, artistic—even respectable, admittedly an abstract quality, but a quality all the same that Dinah required in a man. So Dinah basically did not think that she was intellectual, artistic, mature or respectable. She combed the earth in search of her better half. Once she found him, she thought, Who does he think he *is?*

In Rudy's presence, she tended to feel wrong, stupid and young. Which made Rudy, of course, right, smart and older.

Dinah looked in her rearview mirror where the honey-haired girl in the light-blue car had disappeared. Had she gone to Rudy's house? Was she standing behind him even now, whispering, "That was a great play you wrote, honey—write another one." Dinah knew as well as she knew anything that she was.

She drove on past the town of Amagansett, deep in the shadow of the spell of Rudy that was cast over her. A castaway adrift in a Rudyless sea. Maybe no man is an island, but some sure look like them.

Dinah's insides felt jumbled and dark. Over the years when she'd felt like this, she had written her way out of the darkness, untangled the jumble with her pen, scratching her itch out in ink. Then, with her job on *Heart's Desire*, her writing went from inclination to obligation, and now she rarely wrote unless it was for the show. But here in Amagansett, for the first time in a long time, she felt like writing. But she was without pad and pen. She drove back into East Hampton, parked and bought herself a legal pad and a Papermate pen. She got back into the car and eagerly wrote in her big, childish scrawl, as if ridding herself of these words once and for all.

I have something for you.
I don't know what it is, but it knows itself and it knows
you. It waits for you. It is yours, I think.
I noticed it soon after I noticed you.
It fought its way across my life and lay in waiting
        for some
way you are, some thing you say, a heat you have.
This thing knows you, it names you, it longs to be
        near you.
Oh, I tried to give it a piece of my mind, but it ate that
piece and smiled.
It has me and it wants you.
I drive it around, try to lull it to sleep, but it refuses
to listen to the strange music of reason.
Instead, it sings your praises, looks for you in other
people's faces. Recalls you, involves me.
It's all very distressing.
I have something for you.
A big corny thing with me inside it, stunned,
        waiting for

the shoe to drop.
A thing for you that has taken me hostage and
     asked for you
in ransom.
It made me write this note.

She finished and felt much relieved, having gotten this parcel of words off her chest, from out behind her breasts where it was lurking. In the garden of the horrible flower.

She drove back to Salter's Cottages, her new home, resolute about something, but she didn't know what. She no longer wondered why she had come here, she only knew that she had to come—that she had been right in coming. The day was dying a beautiful death, tender and glowing. The radio played "Stop Dragging My Heart Around" as she drove through the Springs, resolute with her tail between her ears.

Dinah waited for the truth of her predicament to be revealed to her. An insight to bubble from below into her brain. It was strange, very strange that she had come all the way across the country—the entire width of America —to place herself in precariously close proximity to her ex-spouse's newly discovered domestic heaven. It was strange indeed. Stranger still because it did not seem at all strange to her. It felt urgent, necessary, absolutely right. Like driving by the scene of an accident and slowing down to get a better view of the destruction—rubbernecking, they call it. Rudy's happiness was, for her, a little destruction, was the scene of a car wreck where someone had gone through the windshield and, when she slowed down to see the body, she noticed it was hers and was not surprised. She knew all along it would be.

So, here she was in the Hamptons, rubbernecking Rudy and Lindsay's love wreck. A collision they survived and she somehow perished in, a casualty of their happiness. She didn't want to be simply hurt by it; she wanted to be taken over by it, lose herself in their love in order that she might find herself again. Make a pilgrimage to the altar, the shrine of their happiness, happiness she was never able to share with him—that he shared with someone else. The idea of them sharing anything—their lives, happiness, room space, a bed—seemed almost unsanitary to Dinah. She felt closed off from their world, an exile from the land of perfect love. Rudy now had with Lindsay what he could never have with her. Didn't he? She suspected solemnly that this could only be so. She was the missing link, the defective partner. What he couldn't have, even with great effort, with her, he had now achieved simply, smoothly and easily with Lindsay. Dinah drove home from the Sag Harbor psychic tormented by such thoughts, past houses built for happiness, architecturally designed to enhance coupling with another soul. A sympathetic soul, while she had rented an overpriced shack outside of town, next door to a nervous writer. A cabin designed for one. A rabbit hutch, a dwelling for a lone creature with a dark cloud over her head and a long, sad life stretching out in front of her like train tracks to nowhere. Dinah drove in the late-afternoon light with everything looking as if it were lit from within. A tender light, trying to remember where she went wrong with Rudy, with men, in life. "You Really Got a Hold on Me." Dinah changed the station. The Stones sang "Miss You," a song that had played the night she met Rudy. Dinah's eyes filled with tears. One slid out of her eye, out from under her sunglasses and made its way toward her chin before it reached its southerly destination. Dinah brushed it away and drove on, peering through her sunglasses, her windshield, searching for the turnoff to the Springs.

· · ·

156

Dinah got back to her cabin, fed the dog and got ready for bed. Then she slipped herself between her envelope-like sheets and mailed herself off to sleep.

That night, she dreamed she was in a hotel lobby with Lindsay. And she loved her. She thought she was one of the most charming girls in the world and somehow she felt she had to protect her.

She woke up sweating. She was lying in bed in her bare bedroom in the Springs, bathed in mid-morning light. Her dog Tony sat beside her, a sentry into consciousness. But, as familiar as Tony looked to her, her surroundings appeared as strange. It took her several minutes to orient herself fully. The older coast, the interesting coast, Rudy's world. Stranger in a strange land. Honey-haired girls, light-blue cars, Cape Cod houses, dark cloud over her head, maldocchio, colored lights, Kong's bride, good Christ. Great Kong, redeem me.

"Anybody home?" a voice called, apparently from outside her head, the first in too long a while. Was it from outside her head, or had her head simply expanded outward, colonizing the space around her, growing and growing till her head had spilled into everything, till she couldn't tell the difference between her and everything else? Ubiquitous Dinah. Dinah without a difference, girl without end.

"Hello?" A male voice from high above her head. "Miss Kaufman?" the voice said, disembodied and warm, just as she liked it. "It's Roy Delaney from next door."

Dinah sat bolt upright in bed. Tony barked. "I'll be right out!" she called. Tony jumped off the bed, looked back up at Dinah and wagged his tail. Dinah swung her legs onto the floor and looked at her feet doubtfully. Her pinky toe was so small, a delicacy in Southeast Asia; it was so tiny, she couldn't move it. She concentrated very hard and tried to move her baby toe. Nothing. "Well, maybe not *right* out," she said to her lifeless toe.

"I hope I didn't wake you," Roy called apologetically.

"No, not at all," assured Dinah. "What time is it?"

"Almost eleven."

"Jesus!"

"If you wanna come by when you're . . ."

"*What?*" said Dinah. "What could I possibly be?"

"Up. More up," said Roy. "I've just come back from the farmer's market and I have some muffins."

"Great." Dinah listened to Roy's footfalls as they crunched a rhythmic path to his cabin. She stood warily in front of the mirror and looked at her face. It had the appearance of something that hadn't quite set. Unfinished, uncertain, in transition. Something that needed ten more minutes in the oven—or put over a low flame, in the freezer, on a sill. She put her head down and ran her hand awkwardly over her closely cropped hair, realizing that she should never have cut it so short, should never have left herself so exposed.

She had cut her hair when she first got to New York eight years ago. All off. It had fit into the starting of her life strategy. New job, new haircut, New York. But as soon as it was gone, it haunted her—phantom split ends, dry fly-by-night, never-to-be-seen-again hair. She looked to herself like a feminine boy, a sick pixie, someone bad at sports, introverted, androgynous, shy, a renegade choir boy. It seemed symbolic at the time, as she marched up the stairs to the hairdresser and bravely offered up her locks to be shorn. *Symbolic of what?* she thought now. She wanted her hair back. She looked like an elfin peach, a bewildered thud, an aging tomboy for peace. It looked to her like someone else's hair around her face. *There must be some mistake.* It was supposed to look better, make her new life start sooner, coax her toward some happy center, a core where life became easy, a corps where life became easy. Still, she had kept it short, if for no other reason than that she could imagine how much better she would look if she would only lose five pounds and grow her hair back. That was all that stood between her and true attractiveness. With this haircut, she felt like damaged goods—something marked down, this week only, don't miss this consumer opportunity, prices slashed, everything must go—so she mentally took herself off the romantic market. She closed her face, held her breath and listened for the sound of her hair growing.

She turned on the rickety shower, pulled off her nightgown, her underwear, and stepped into the warm spray. The ritual of preparing herself for the Great Monkey had once again begun.

A half hour later a new Dinah, scrubbed and painted, stood on Roy Delaney's next-door porch, with emancipated resignation—surrender without a smile. "Hello," she offered.

"Hey," came Roy's reply from well within his summer-hut home. Dinah saw him coming toward her through the screen door. "You came," he said, smiling, running his hand through his hair and opening the door.

A thug, thought Dinah, looking at him. A wonderful thug—Captain Dream Thug.

"I came," she said in reply. *Don't make any jokes,* she thought, then amended, *Don't make any bad jokes.*

"I heated up the muffins, but I'm afraid they're not as hot now," said Roy, shifting his weight.

"I prefer my muffins tepid," said Dinah politely, following Roy back into the house.

Roy laughed nervously. "You're just saying that."

Dinah smiled. "Yes, I am just saying it. I don't have a strong muffin ethic."

Roy laughed and almost tripped over a chair. "Oops. No muffin bias."

"Exactly," said Dinah. "No MB."

Dinah had followed Roy into his kitchen and stood

159

watching as he got two plates on which were two tepid muffins. "Someone's in the kitchen with Dinah," said Roy with a small smile. "I bet you get that a lot."

"Well," considered Dinah. "Not *a lot*. I've never had it said to me while actually *in* a kitchen."

Her emotional world could sometimes be described like this: She was in a house on a hill alone at night and . . . someone was in the house.

Looking at Roy, Dinah realized that if they had a baby it would have hardly any upper lip. Nice eyes, though, if it got his eyes. Her eyes were a dark hazel. His eyes were a light, faraway blue. Wouldn't her eyes be the dominant color then? She hoped it'd have his eyes and neither of their upper lips. Was this that biological clock? Ticking images whenever you looked at a new man's face, the possible man, the impossible man, a man?

Fantasy gripped her brain like a vise and wrestled it to the ground. She imagined herself married to Roy, happy with Roy, effortless with Roy; he was the one she had waited for. It hadn't been her at all. She just hadn't met the right person. There really *was* one person for everyone in the world, and just when you despaired of never finding him, there he was and so easy to be with. Just add water and live. Someone she was made for, who accepted her exactly for who she was, and she didn't find fault with that. She admired his taste, his gestalt. Oh, brother. She wanted to run barefoot through his gestalt, singing songs from *Brigadoon*.

She really had been right to be dissatisfied with the rest. It wasn't fear of intimacy; it was intimacy with the wrong person. Claustrophobia. If it's the real thing, they never annoy you, they never bore you, they stay with you. In the fantasy, she loved Roy and Roy loved her and everything was fine. Life had worked out—the last shoe

160

had dropped, doubt and death ceased plaguing her. Que
sera.

Roy and Dinah
Sitting in a tree
K-I-S-S-I-N-G
First comes love
Then comes marriage
Then comes . . .

Dinah tried to get her mind back into her own personal custody, free from the terrible jaws of this intoxicating fantasy. It was the female version of an erection
in an awkward place. Boy meets girl—boner. Girl meets
boy—marriage, perfect life. The first one fucks if he gets
lucky. The second one gets fucked unless she's lucky.
Fucked by a fantasy. Actually seduced by the fantasy and
fucked by the reality.

You meet a man and visions of husbands and potential breeders plod through your head. The morning erection of mental images: the part where one half of your
body wakes up before the other half. That was the only
thing Dinah missed about not having a penis—well, not
the only thing. That and jerking off to *Penthouse*. And
dressing to the left.

One reason that Dinah wanted to have a baby was
that she had read somewhere that women who have children run less of a risk of getting cancer. She was occasionally preoccupied with death and thought that having
a child would lessen the horror of dying. Leaving, as she
would, some part of herself behind. Someone to carry on
the tradition of her, whatever that was. Not that she even
really had a tradition, but in case one should crop up later
on, she could feel confident that her offspring would
carry it on into the New World and make jokes about it

at some high school cafeteria table. If Dinah couldn't live in fact, she wanted to live in part, a strain of her song playing through her offspring.

> K-I-S-S-I-N-G
> First comes love, then comes marriage
> Then comes baby in a baby carriage.

"You're so quiet. What are you thinking about?" Roy said to Dinah, his head tilted sweetly to one side.

Dinah looked at his upper lip and smiled. "Nothing," she replied, shaking her head. "I'm just not awake yet."

"You look like an eight-by-ten," he said as he went to his kitchen counter. "I'm just looking for the signature on your hand."

Dinah dismissed the compliment. "I have too much lipstick on for breakfast." She wiped her mouth with the back of her hand. "There," she said. "Now I look like an eight-by-nine." She sat at the little table in Roy's kitchen, watching him pour coffee.

He looked at her over his shoulder as he stirred. "And a little like Florence Henderson with a migraine. A good Florence Henderson."

Dinah considered responding to this and then decided to change the subject. "Your cabin is bigger than mine."

Roy brought a cup of coffee and placed it in front of Dinah. "Milk?"

"Yes, please," said Dinah. "Everything—car parts if you have them."

Roy walked over to the refrigerator and got a carton of milk. "If my place is any bigger, you can bet I'm paying for it. Out here, you pay by the square inch and square view."

He poured milk into Dinah's cup. "Say when." Roy poured milk into Dinah's cup for what seemed like a while.

Finally, she said, "When."

Roy looked at her strangely and sat down opposite her with his black coffee and cool muffin. "So . . ." he began, crossing his legs and leaning forward. Dinah watched him from over the rim of her cup. "What brings you to the Hamptons?"

She looked at him blankly; somehow, it hadn't occurred to her that she would be asked this. "What?" She was confused.

Roy was sympathetic. "What brings you here—vacation?"

Dinah's skin shone pale in the midday sun. She looked like someone everyone might have gone to school with. She nodded. "Vacation. Enforced vacation. There's a writers' strike in L.A., so . . ."

"You're a writer?"

Dinah nodded apologetically. "Soap-opera writer."

"Really," said Roy eagerly. "I'm a writer too. A screenwriter."

"I know. It was a selling point for this place," said Dinah sadly. "Or a rental point. The realtor said there were lots of writers here. You were the prime sample." She shrugged and took a bite of her muffin. "I wanted to be part of the community."

Roy laughed. "The writing community of the Springs. Tangleweird."

Dinah laughed. In her mind they were married, having breakfast, life had worked out. He was out there, finite, a concept. A net. Heaven. And if she was a good-enough girl, she'd get to go there. Her great reward. Mrs. Kong. She smiled.

Her mind described things back to her, like an echo, a translation—simultaneous, from the visual to the ver-

163

bal. Beating them into some sort of syncopated under-standing. Describing things back to her as she felt them, from the emotional to the mental, the wet to the dry, a translation, Cliff Notes to a complicated world. Bagging everything into her word bag, her brain barn, beaten into some controllable submissive understanding, where she was safe. Dinah, lurking eternally between a pronoun and an adverb, brain-dry, dreaming.

"Are you here to work?" she asked politely.

"Yes," he replied. "I'm working on a novel. It was going to be short stories, but now it's a novel. I'm hon-oring the strike, which is no big deal for me. I have a film coming out in the winter, so I want to wait till that comes out anyway, because I can probably make a better deal. Why am I telling you all this? You don't care about this."

"I don't care *passionately* about it, but it's interest-ing in the abstract. People tell each other things to elicit some sort of response. You know, to impress each other, or to show how funny or how smart or how interesting or how successful they are. To give us a kind of flattering context. I sometimes just want to cut to the short form. Just ask people straight out to like me or to think I'm interesting or funny. Maybe give them references from other people who've thought that I was interesting or funny in the past."

"So I guess the short form of what I'm telling you is that I'm someone and that I do something that has some value."

"I'll take your word for it. You seem like someone, at any rate."

"So what's your short form?" he asked.

"I'm interesting and funny . . ." She drifted off.

"Yeah?" said Roy.

"And I'm going through a kind of rough period right now. My ex-husband has a new girlfriend and is very happy. What's the short form of that?"

"You're human."

"I'm obsessive. And he's here."

"Ah. So that's why . . ."

"That's why. But who knows? Maybe I'll do something constructive too. Like get a tan. Or go home."

"Don't go home. Who will I share my tepid muffins with? Everyone else around here has a strong muffin bias. Besides, I need another female for my stories."

"Where is your usual female?"

"Well, I have a wife who's in a mental hospital and a girlfriend who's angry that I still have a wife and thinks I should leave my wife and marry her. But I can't leave my wife because she'll kill herself."

"The short form of this being that you're very popular."

"Too popular."

"So I guess you wouldn't want to have an affair with my ex-husband's girlfriend."

"I thought you said they were happy."

Dinah shrugged. "I thought it might be good material for your book."

"The short form of this being that you don't like the idea of . . ."

Dinah got up. "This is a lot for one day. I think we should continue this later. When we've known each other longer. Longer than ten minutes." She moved to the door.

Roy stood and followed. "So I'll see you longer, later. See you later."

Dinah smiled and pushed open the door. "So far so good, but so soon so what?" she recited, making a clean exit as she crossed his porch and disappeared around the corner.

The air around her was lighter than air, sweet as child's breath, weightless, buoyant, pastel. The mist of someone spread too thin, someone warm and willing.

Someone wonderful.

She went back to her cabin and let Tony out. She stared at the phone. She did all she could for as long as she could, which was for seconds, and then couldn't help herself. She lifted the receiver and dialed. Dialed Rudy's number, hoping just to hear the sound of his noncommittal voice. Instead, she heard a busy signal and ended up listening to it for a while, feeling connected to him somehow, the busy signal becoming the sound of her heartbeat, her broken heartbeat, beating for him, beating on her, country-westerning her; she ached inside with a feeling that painted the back of her ribs the cold color of vulnerability. She passed her hand over her hair, watched the dust dance in the sunlight, an orphan in this estrogen storm, this estro fest. After trying to read *Madame Bovary* for a while, she turned on the television. *Jane Eyre* was on. Edward said to Jane, "It's as if there is a string traveling from beneath my ribs and reaching out of me and into you. I fear if you traveled too far from me the string should snap and I would slowly bleed to death."

Dinah switched the channel. *Heart's Desire* was in the midst of a flashback.

———

Blaine sat watching television. A Yankees game was on. Rose had a portable computer on her lap that she was typing on. She looked up at the television just as a fly ball was hit somewhere outfield. The batter ran to first as the ball was caught. The batter ran back down the steps into a dugout and another player hit him on the ass. Rose shook her head and smiled, saying, "That's so great that guys have that whole male-bonding sports thing. Girls don't have anything like that."

Blaine looked at Rose impatiently. "Oh, Christ, stop complaining." And with that he stood and stormed out of the house. Rose put aside her computer roughly and bolted after him. She opened the door and called, "Go on, leave! Well, don't think I don't know where you're going. The whole town is talking. You're seeing—"

———

Dinah switched off the television, she decided that she needed food; she would take a drive.

She was in the Amagansett Market, staring vacantly at the fruits, the produce. Rudy liked fruit, didn't he? Yeah. Rudy ate fruit. Lush red apples . . . Snow White, Prince Charming. Maybe she should get some bananas . . . bananas are good for you. But aren't they the fattening fruit? Maybe, but then it's the good kind of fattening. Not empty calories, but the other kind. Besides, bananas are more fun to eat than apples. Like baby food, toy food. Apples can be upsetting on the gums, and they're so *loud*. Bananas are soft and tender. Dinah reached out for a bunch of bananas, having finalized her decision, and there, just behind the scale, was Rudy's brother-in-law, John Delman.

Dinah drew her hand back, as if something had bitten her—as if, in doing so, this apparition would disappear. John would vanish and the bananas would remain. Instead, John's startled face said, "Dinah, Dinah, I can't believe it! How are you?" He moved to embrace her. She was caught off-guard and held on to him for balance. John pulled back. "Let me look at you. Christ, I haven't seen you since—"

"How are you, John! You're looking well." She hated to be looked at, but more than that, she hated being told she was being looked at. At these moments, she tried but could not remember what she looked like. And it seemed so important.

"Can't complain, can't complain. Put on a couple pounds—but I needed it, I think." John was of medium height, about forty-five, and very, very thin. He had a small nose, someone else's nose, and a mustache. As long as Dinah had known him, John's face had always been gaunt. Like an aristocrat or an Indian. A loud Indian aristocrat. Somehow, he looked to Dinah like someone whose face you would see on a bottle of salad dressing.

"How's Laura?" Dinah asked politely. Laura was John's wife, Rudy's sister.

"Oh, fine, fine. Still trying to quit smoking."

Dinah smiled. Laura was the most high-strung person Dinah had ever known. As low-strung as Rudy was, Laura was that high. She was always laughing, crying or smoking. "Will you give her my love?" asked Dinah.

"Well, but you must come *by*," pleaded John. "Just because you split up with Rudy doesn't mean you've split up with us. We're still your in-laws." His hands were deep in his pockets. He drew them out now and smoothed his mustache, looking at her. Dinah took a banana off the counter and began to peel it.

"That's nice, John," she began slowly, chewing. "But it's still kind of awkward, I think."

"Nonsense," said John expansively. "That's all in your mind."

"*A lot* of it is in my mind," she said, her mouth full. "But there's a portion in my emotional world too."

"Well, the only way to deal with that is to confront it dead-on."

"How do I do that?" she asked timidly, thinking it would be much more pleasant to deal with something broadside.

"You can come home with me right now and have lunch with us."

Dinah squirmed and wriggled, but she was caught, ensnared in the web of Rudy's world and gradually being drawn to the center, where his reality would close over her head and she would sit stunned as trapped prey.

She bought a bunch of bananas and three corn muffins and a small pack of Band-Aids for her thumbs, putting them on as she walked. This was a potentially tense situation and her thumbs tended to bear the brunt of her nervousness. She walked out to her car and saw John waiting in his for her to follow him home to the dreaded lunch. Wasn't this what she had wanted? To gain access to Rudy's life through a variety of side doors. To discover the mystery of his newfound union, expose its flaws. When she hadn't been tormented by the loss initially, it was because she hadn't lost him really, just misplaced him. He existed in the world out there for her somewhere. A fact. Like Greenland. He wasn't hers, but he wasn't someone else's either. But now he was not only not hers, he was also someone else's. She had lost him and someone else had found him.

Greenland was truly gone.

She followed John's brown BMW dutifully. Obedient. She was now positioned to hear the inside story of Lindsay and Rudy. What if the news was good? She vowed to take it like a man. But how do men take it? she mused, turning left onto Egypt Lane. Stiff upper lip, good sport, that sort of thing. Like an Englishman. Like Oscar Wilde. Well, maybe not so much Wilde as—who?—J. B. Priestly? Kingsley Amis?

Dinah decided then to go headlong into this situation, whatever it was. Aside from everything else, she liked leading with her head. To be carried along, as it were, as it happened to be. She had come this far, now she must go the rest of the way, whatever way that was. She looked around her. It was a beautiful day, beaming proudly around her, shimmering with bold resolve. A perfect day for a decision—even if it was deciding to do what you were already doing. Choosing what you had chosen. The bell had rung, the Roy had sounded and Dinah sped along in her car, greeting her onslaught of facts, armed with her preferred fiction. John's car pulled into the drive of a gray-and-white-shingled house. Dinah pulled in behind him and parked. A dog barked hysterically from within and then came bounding out of an open screen door.

"Down, Mitch," warned John as the terrier ran to Dinah and peed happily on her shoes.

Dinah kneeled down, petting the dog, calming him. "That's okay," she said, as the dog licked her. "Aren't you good," she murmured to him. "Hmmmm? Aren't you?"

A squeal came from just inside the house, followed by a moaning sort of laughter. Dinah saw Laura coming toward her, her arms outstretched, her big blue eyes streaming.

"Look who I found at the market," boomed John. Laura made her way to Dinah with a speed and a purpose that Dinah found alarming. She backed up a step as Laura fell on her, holding on to her as though she had been looking for her all her life. Dinah returned the embrace tentatively, staring bewildered over Laura's shoulder, as John looked on approvingly.

"I can't believe it! I can't believe it!" cried Laura through Dinah's hair. "You're here! When did you come? Why didn't you call?"

Dinah's brain felt like a big baby that she was trying to birth through the small hole of her throat. "I just got here," said the baby, out now and breathing. "I would've called. Try to think of this as me calling."

Laura looked perplexed. Then the sentence took shape in her head; it fought its way over the back, dark curve of her brain and dawned there, her eyes widened and she laughed. "Think of this as you calling." The words laughed out of her in rhythm as she took Dinah's arm and led her into their home. "This is me answering then," Laura said, crossing the threshold, John smoothing his mustache, following behind.

Their home was cool inside. Cool and white. The front of it was all screened and glassed, leading out to a porch facing the sea. A bird cried from overhead and Dinah inhaled the mild salty air gratefully. As Laura went to fix them some iced tea, Dinah opened the screen, looking out at the water, the water of Rudy's world closing tightly over her head. Boats on the water, children playing somewhere down below, their squeals carried aloft by a breeze. Laura emerged from the house carrying the tea.

"Here we go," she announced cheerfully, her dark hair falling around her face. Her pale-blue eyes had a faraway quality, like someone in the process of remembering something curious or sad from long ago. "John's taking a shower," she continued apologetically, as though admitting some dark ritual he engaged in that she didn't understand. Dinah found Rudy's face in Laura's— his sharp nose stranded in Laura's soft face, his stern mouth now smoothed by his sister's wide range of emotion, till it was almost unrecognizable. Still Dinah, looking for it, found it. The mouth spoke. "Incredible about this whole Quayle thing," it said.

"What whole thing?" asked Dinah. "Who's Quayle?"

"Who's *Quayle?*" said Laura in disbelief. "He's Bush's running mate. Where've you been? It's all over the news."

Dinah blanched with embarrassment. "I've been . . ." She thought for a moment, then said, ". . . distracted. Traveling. I've been a bad American. Don't tell anyone. Is Quayle bad?"

Laura shrugged. "Dumb," she said. "But dumb is bad if Bush . . ." She sighed and changed the subject.

"Have you seen Rudy?" Laura asked innocently, as innocently as possible.

Dinah smiled, ducked her chin, shook her head.

"No," she said. "Not here. In L.A., I saw him—but not here."

Laura tilted her head, looking at Dinah. "*Will* you see him here?"

Dinah sighed a laugh. "I don't think so. He has a new girlfriend, so . . ."

Laura sat back, holding her tea as if for balance. "So, he told you?"

Dinah nodded, watching Laura. "Have you met her?" she asked nonchalantly, crossing her legs and affecting an expression of detached, benign interest, like someone long past the need for the petty attachments found in human relationships; an evolved benign creature, showing polite interest in social customs.

Laura seemed relieved to see Dinah's smooth, unflustered exterior. "Yes, well, we've met her several times since they've been together. She's very nice, I think, quiet."

"Who's quiet?" boomed John from the doorway, showered and changed and followed by the dog.

"Certainly not you, dear," said Laura impassively, turning to him. John sat down by her side, his hair still wet, shining in the sun. "We're talking about Lindsay, honey," explained Laura patiently. "Rudy's new girlfriend."

"Ah, yes," said John, sweetening his tea. "Sweet girl," he continued. "On the whole, very good for him. Wouldn't you say, hon?"

"Of course, no comparison to you," offered Laura quickly, turning from John to Dinah, mild alarm in her pale-blue eyes. "But since you two couldn't seem to . . . work yourselves out—someone like Lindsay is the next-best thing," she finished brightly, hopefully, to Dinah.

Someone like Lindsay, thought Dinah. That's probably what she's like, someone like someone, someone like herself instead of actually herself. Instead she said,

172

"Absolutely. That's great for him." As though she were now completely past it all, free at last.

"Why don't you bring out some of that tuna salad, Laura?" John said energetically to his bride. Dinah noticed that his collar was up in that silly way that men's collars sometimes are, as though they had been in a strong, fashionable wind. Laura left for the kitchen, leaving Dinah alone with John and his renegade collar.

"I'm happy for Rudy, actually," continued John expansively, theoretically. "I really think he's on to something with this girl. This could be the one. Has he told you of his new theory of relationships?"

Dinah paused before saying, "I don't think so."

"Well, it's very interesting, if I can get it right. Let's see . . ." He put his hands behind his head and squinted his eyes against the sun. Dinah waited. "I think it's basically that you should pick someone and make it work."

Dinah digested this pronouncement. Finally, she repeated tonelessly, "Pick someone and make it work."

John nodded. "Yeah, something along those lines. He said that it's going to be difficult with anyone—no, wait, did he say that? Maybe not. At any rate, something like pick someone who can spend some time with . . . not all this big love stuff . . . and just make it work with them. That's it, someone you like and that like will eventually grow into a kind of love."

"I see," said Dinah. She didn't see; she barely wanted to hear. John folded his arms and continued, looking out at the sun on the water.

"I actually think he'll marry this girl," he said.

This knocked the wind out of Dinah. Something at her center dropped away, leaving an ache howling through her, a moaning somewhere inside her. It all sat at the back as she said flatly, "How great."

"It's great for him. After the whole thing with you guys, I didn't think that he had it in him to try again.

You know, you have plenty of time, but he's a lot older than you. So, if he wants to have kids, he can't wait too long."

"You think they'll have kids?" asked Dinah, her voice hollow-sounding. Hypnotized, rooted to the subject, rooted to her spot as the Chinese Water Torture dripped on.

"I hope they have kids. I know she wants them. She's that age. Well, she's *your* age." Dinah nodded mutely. John rambled on. "I know they've been looking at new apartments in the city. She'd like a fresh start, I think."

Dinah went deaf at this point. A new apartment in the city. She could never get him to get a new apartment in the city. And children. Jesus. Jesus. The tuna salad arrived. Dinah moved it around; Laura looked at her with concern. John now talked of other things. New films, the weather, Barbara Bush, Marilyn Quayle. She watched his mouth, sipped her tea and finally got up to leave. She was sick and silent inside. She embraced Laura and promised she'd call.

"You're sure you're okay?"

Dinah couldn't remember saying she was okay to begin with. Anything was possible. Rudy was engaged and anything was possible. "I'm fine," she said, getting into her car, finally away. "Thanks for the tuna." She started the engine and drove. Straight to Rudy's house. Like an arrow singing toward her target, straight down center, over the plate, home.

When Dinah drove, she felt incredibly directed, in control, a force to be reckoned with. Even though her present circumstances were less than structured, far less, she could entertain the delusion of rational purpose when she was at the wheel.

She pulled up to a streetlight in Amagansett behind another car with a couple in it. The man and the woman put their heads together like two dark peaches and bit into one another's sweet fruit. Dinah imagined the juice running down their necks. She wondered, Where is my dark peach?

She found Rudy's street and parked her car down the block from his house at a discreet distance, got out of her car and locked it. She crossed the street with her head down and slipped into the yard of the house next door. Walking up their driveway, assuming the air of someone who belonged, she looked at Rudy's house through the trees that divided the two drives. Everything seemed still in the summer heat. Dinah wiped her brow and kept walking.

Rudy's car wasn't in the drive. The pale-blue car was also absent. Don't they drive together? Dinah wondered as she stole through the bushes and into Rudy's back-yard, looking down and behind her as she went, her heart in her throat. She walked quickly across the yard and up the stairs onto Rudy's porch. What if someone's here, oh, God, what am I doing? I'll be caught, remember to breathe, what do I say if I'm caught? Hi, I was just in the neighborhood? Did I leave my red bathing suit here three summers ago? I should go, start a new life; I did start a new life and look where it got me, smack dab in my old life like a prowler. She was at the back door now, looking at two pairs of sandy shoes next to the door. His and Hers. Theirs. She tried the door and, sure enough, it was open. Now she was in. She crossed the threshold into truly inappropriate behavior.

She stopped. No. There are limits. Even she knew that. What was she hoping to find? Evidence of a lie? Lindsay's clothes? Yes, that was it, perhaps most of all. She wanted to see how Rudy's new woman dressed. She wanted to be reassured or enlightened about who Lindsay was or wasn't. And how that related to who she was or wasn't. This was suddenly wrong and small and sad, fool-

175

ish. She turned around and started to leave. That was when she saw Rudy's car driving up the drive.

Dinah froze, saw everything stock-still around her. The furniture, the house, the carpet, the walls, the doors, the trees, the sunlight held her momentarily suspended as she watched Rudy's steel-gray Mercedes come to a stop through the side window of the house. Then the engine stopped, which served to start Dinah, who, in the wake of its silence, bolted farther into the house. Standing in the living room . . . where should she hide? The hall closet? Come on, now . . . they're coming . . . make a decision . . . uh, uh, which way . . . go . . . go . . . up the stairs. No. Not there. Where then? . . . The hall closet. Go . . . the door . . . open the door. Dinah ran toward the closet as she heard Rudy's voice and steps, footsteps, footfalls, falling up the porch steps. She climbed in, jumped in—did she make too much noise? Had they heard her? She pushed herself in among the coats and shut the door as gently as possible behind her and found herself in complete darkness. The hall closet was halfway between the living room and the bedroom. Life was passing her by in a slow car, jeering.

Sometimes Dinah felt almost as though she knew exactly what she was doing. It seemed a very delicate feeling, though. As if, if she sneezed too hard or bent down too fast, it would go away. Just now crouched down in the closet, between the coats and the shoes, she realized that it was gone. Totally gone. This, then, was the absolute limit of polite masochism. Anything after this would be hard core. Dinah had been seemingly striving toward closeness—but she always did it with people who kept her somehow at arm's length. That was what she relied on. She felt that she desperately longed for connection with this man, these men, but if it was connection —really connection that she wanted—she would never have chosen this man. She chose him for the bad and the good reasons. Maybe bad and good is too strong, more like neurotic and valid. And all these reasons were hopelessly intertwined. You love the very thing that hurts you. You think that you love it in spite of the suffering, but you somehow love that semi-stoic suffering. It is fraught with a meaning that makes sense to you. The not-good-enough message from your childhood.

The air in the closet was stagnant—it clung to Dinah, a woeful thing. Trapped by old air. Senile, palsied, attic air. Dinah wondered if it had been there when she and Rudy were still together. She picked one of the protective Band-Aids off her thumb and began to tear the skin there. Well, this is another fine mess you've gotten us into, Roy old mood, Dinah thought. She held her breath in the hush of the closet. Her shoe squeaked. She shut her eyes tight, her face tight. If she couldn't see anything, she couldn't be seen. What you can't see, can't hurt you, unless it's a germ or a gas. The screen door slammed.

"I mean, we should pull our troops out of Japan and Germany and then see if their economies thrive so much," said Lindsay from beyond the door, from in the kitchen. "Here, give them to me." Dinah opened her eyes as if revived by the sound of Rudy's new relationship, whole through proximity to his new better half. Lindsay.

"Lindsay, we can't just pull our troops out of Germany and Japan. We have agreements with those countries. Anyway, I'm gonna go take a shower." A crash of silverware.

"Oh, God," said Lindsay. "Leave it. I'll get it."

Rudy cleared his throat. "Are you sure?"

"Yes," she said.

Rudy's footfalls approached, the floorboards squeaked, he slowed in front of the closet. Dinah's heart pounded, the telltale heart, tattletale tell-all heart. "Did you move my sneakers?" he called, right there now, just at the other side of the door, so close she could hear him breathing. Could he hear her? She clenched her face tight into a fist and put her head down onto her knees, making herself as small as possible. Small and silent. Please, God. She can have Rudy. They can have each other. Just don't let them find me. I couldn't survive that humiliation.

"Where were they?" called Lindsay.

"Here," he replied, "on the landing."

"I probably put them in the closet," she said.

Oh, God. It's over. They'll commit me. I'll just stay small. I'll die.

"Which closet?" The handle turned. This isn't happening.

"Upstairs," she answered.

"I love this girl," Dinah said inwardly. The handle was released.

"Hon, don't move my stuff, okay? I leave them on the landing so they'll be right there when I run in the morning." His footfalls went up the stairs.

"Sorry," she called.

"It's okay," he consoled, upstairs now, in their bedroom.

Lindsay turned on the water in the sink, opened the refrigerator. Dinah listened to her with affectionate relief. Her neck ached and her toes were asleep. Just let me get through this, God. I'll go home, I swear. I'll be good. I'll have a normal relationship. I'll suffer that, whatever it takes. I'll write a script, I'll go to church, to temple, somewhere, anywhere; just don't let them find me here. Even if he did call her hon. I'm hon. I was hon. We're all hon. She moves slightly to take the pressure off her knees.

I'm a psychopath, she thought. A hedonist and a psychopath. She straightened slightly, her face in the coats, in the dark, then sat down hard on some boots, making a small, muffled thump. She grimaced and waited in the resuming hush, listened for approaching danger. Instead, she heard Lindsay singing softly as she rustled around in the kitchen.

"Flintstones, meet the Flintstones, they're a modern stone age family. From the town of Bedrock, they're a page right out of history." In a sweet high voice.

Dinah smiled to herself in the dark closet.

Maybe this is what they meant by mood-affected behavior. Things like this probably didn't happen to just anyone. Where impulses become edicts, laws that you must obey. Things that begin ordinarily enough, but which, as they continue, grow from a leak to a flood, from being on the edge of things to straight in the middle and out over the other side. It was something Dinah refused to look at; if you didn't look, it wasn't there, advice she gave herself that didn't always make her the best driver, among other things. Serotonin, that's what they called it. The fluid in your brain that flowed between your electrotransmitters, making them connect. And she had too much serotonin. Nor epinephrine. Neither a lender nor epinephrine be. Or too little. Depending. Roy and Pam. The tide is in, the tide is out. Which was it now? What wave had washed her up and into the closet? Serotonin. Where her mood wrote the music and her head wrote the words. The Serotonin Operetta. "Let's drive with the family down the street, through the courtesy of Fred's two feet."

Really? Dinah had never known that lyric. Well, there you go. Dinah remembered commercials, sound bites from commercials that had lodged in her brain, media mantras, a thought-dispersal technique that she had developed over the years when there wasn't any TV or radio to lull her out of the moment and into her mind.

"How's it going?" came Rudy's voice over her head, coming down the stairs.

"Fine," mouthed Dinah in the dark.

"Fine," called Lindsay from the kitchen. "Do you want brown or white rice?"

"White," called Rudy from just overhead. "I'm watching my cholesterol, remember?"

"Maybe we shouldn't have gotten Chinese then— we should've gone to the Japanese place."

Beautiful, thought Dinah, nodding. There it goes. The duck dropped. The relationship duck. The Peking duck. All the Chinese take-out he had grown sick of sharing with her, he now grew fat on with Lindsay. She picked the protective bandage off her other thumb and began to pull away the skin under what was left of the nail there.

"That's okay," Rudy's voice assured her, coming down the stairs just over Dinah's head. "The chicken cashew isn't bad."

"And the pea pods," chimed in Lindsay. "Pea pods are okay."

Dinah mouthed, "Pea pods are okay," to herself in the dark as she listened to Rudy's footsteps walking by her closet hideaway and into the kitchen.

"Pea pods are fine," he now agreed with her. Dinah listened as the two of them puttered around the kitchen in food preparation. The refrigerator opening and closing. The crack of the ice tray and then the dropping of one, two, three, four in a glass. Liquid poured over the ice into the glass. The squeak and pop of a wine bottle. Plates set down on the table, chairs moved back and presumably sat in.

Dinah listened hard, her ear pressed against the door. What did this girl have that she didn't have? Or did she have less of something Dinah had too much of? Probably. Not so many opinions, probably she was more agreeable, pliable, a loving frame for his overall picture; less demanding, more thoughtful; less ambitious for her, more ambitious for him. More reliable, more interested, less interesting, less complicated. A wife, for God's sakes, a wife. Well, fuck, I want a wife too. No, no, that's not true really. I want a partner, a companion, an ally, someone who shares with me the secret handshake of shared sensibility. Someone whom I find endlessly interesting. Well, maybe not endlessly interesting, but mostly. Mostly. What does he think, even if I don't agree? What did he dream, what will he say?

The only light shone through a thin uninterrupted line around the door. The dense musty smell of the small closet tickled her nose. Dinah scratched it hard with the back of her hand. She carefully moved a rainboot that was uncomfortably wedged into her leg. She felt as though she had been kept after life, punished by an angry religious parent. Banished to a closet to contemplate God and all of her trespasses. Locked in this crypt for coats, the guilty secret Rudy barely knew he kept.

"I bought some new cookbooks today," said Lindsay, apparently after some eating. Dinah shifted herself quietly to get closer to the door, since they spoke more softly now and were farther away.

"Really," replied Rudy slightly muffled, his mouth full. "What kind?"

"One is New England—for that clam chowder I told you about," said Lindsay, "and the other is a surprise. For tomorrow."

Dinah shook her head mournfully in the dark. A domestic surprise. Oy. How could she compete with a domestic surprise? She peeled a long piece of skin off the corner of her thumb. It stopped abruptly and Dinah had to bite the skin off with her teeth, drawing blood. She sucked the wound thoughtfully as their conversation continued.

"So you have to stay out of the kitchen all day," Lindsay continued earnestly.

Dinah heard a chair push back and the refrigerator open and close. "Why all day?"

"Well, the chowder takes about four or five hours to really make perfectly," said Lindsay thoughtfully. "I mean, chopping all the ingredients and simmering. And then organizing that along with—the surprise . . . well, it'll take most of the day. Of course, I'll make your breakfast first. Some melon and muesli. And then just something light for lunch. Maybe a tuna salad."

Dinah's head fell forward in dismay. She sighed a quiet sigh. Muesli and tuna . . . Fuck it, I can't compete with this. I don't even know what muesli is. The only thing I can make is banana bread and bad veal piccata. She rearranged herself so she could lie down. She didn't know how much more of this she could take seated.

"Tuna sounds good. Or maybe just some turkey slices," said Rudy.

Christ, thought Dinah, arranging a small pile of boots to lay her head on. She had never known Rudy to take such an interest in food. Maybe if she'd had someone ready and willing to fulfill all of her culinary fantasies, she'd eat too. An attentive mother for a girlfriend and no siblings to fight with for her attention, someone to dedicate her deeds to, like the governess in *The Omen*, hanging from a noose. It's all for you, Damien. Dinah yawned, breathing in sharply, inhaling some of the stale, scarce air as she did. In doing, she sneezed a sudden little squeaky sneeze. Jesus! She clapped her hand over her mouth and waited in terror, her eyes staring out into the dark surrounding her, surrounding the thin white line around the door.

"Did you hear something?" asked Lindsay quietly.

There was a pause while Rudy wondered. A chair was pushed back and footsteps took him past Dinah to the front door, which he opened, checking. "I don't see anything," he said finally, returning. "It's probably nothing. Maybe a bat."

182

Dinah closed her eyes in relief, relaxing once again into the boots. A lonely forgotten taste in her mouth, an undomestic taste. The taste of someone who eats in restaurants, who orders in. She ran her dry tongue over her lips and closed her eyes. Maybe she wouldn't think about this now. She would think about it tomorrow. As God is my witness . . . can God see this?

Lindsay was saying something. "When is that fireworks thing? Saturday, right?" A chair was pulled back again, dishes were collected.

"Yeah, Saturday," answered Rudy faintly; the water was running now. "Saturday at dusk. And we have to leave early or we'll never get a place to park."

Dinah shifted in the dark, putting her arm under her head, settling in.

"Don't worry, I'll wash up," offered Lindsay. "You go write."

Dinah smiled, almost sleeping. This is so heavy, she thought. This girl is perfect.

"You sure?" said Rudy politely from nearer now, just outside the closet.

"Sure," said Lindsay gently. Dinah could feel her smile; it soothed her. Rudy's steps walked up the stairs and over Dinah's head, a loud preamble to dreaming. He hovered over her head like a cartoon.

"Rudy?" called Lindsay from the foot of the stairs.

Rudy stood suspended there, hanging by the thread of Lindsay's voice. "Yes?" he said, stopped now, waiting.

Dinah was lying precariously between them. Almost asleep, dreaming of them, dreaming his reply, dreaming her voice as it said, "You don't really think there are bats, do you?"

The steady monotonous jingle of crickets, their cry spread out on high. A long line of music, a carbonated hum, a one-noted plea. A thin strand of singing strung just above Dinah's head, strung cavalierly through her ears, through the dark needle of the night. A round thin sound, farther away and all around, a percussive cricket undercurrent, a current that carried Dinah along and down into the place of dreaming.

───────

Rudy is going to two parties without Dinah. She is very upset and looking for pills at Chuck and Connie's house. They have a new funny-looking baby. She goes away sulking and pill-less. She is followed by a rat, a doting rat, that she can't seem to get rid of, which is more annoying than anything else. Finally, she loses it somewhere and is suddenly in a TV show in the street. There are roses somewhere. Dinah feels relieved, as it is something good for her. Some attention. She goes to find Rudy, feeling invigorated from the recent attention. It is a long, complicated way. Finally she finds her father in a neck brace with several other people. It seems that there has been some trouble with the baby.

───────

Dinah woke with a start, cramped and disoriented, her face stinging from the imprint of some shoelaces, her thumbs hurting, her heart beating its rapid, interrupted-sleep beat. The crickets cried faintly now from the other side of the door, from outside the house. Dinah raised herself on her elbow, her eyes adjusting to more darkness, to a now fainter line around the door. She sat up and into the coats, pushing them back with her arm, listening for signs of life, married life. Soon-to-be-married life. The house was silent. The crickets cheered their rhythmic, pulsing cheer from the sidelines surrounding her. Egging her on, coaxing her out. She rose slowly, carefully, and put her hand on the door. Her heart beat a middle-of-the-night beat, a recently awakened clump. She turned the knob and opened the door cautiously. The house was silent. She rearranged the telltale jumble of boots and shoes to their former pre-Dinah order and closed the door on the crypt of her recent past. She stole through the house, out the back door and onto the porch, where she paused. Maybe she should steal upstairs for a quick peek at Rudy and Lindsay sleeping. She imagined them nestled like slumbering spoons, dreaming the same dream, digesting the same food. Synchronized heartbeats, sympathetic hearts thumping as one, keeping her at bay, at arm's length, out. She crept back through the house and gingerly up the stairs, stopping stock-still halfway, stunned by the lightning crack of the floorboards' creak. She slipped up the remaining stairs without a sound, down the hallway to her old room and stood in the doorway teetering on the precipice of Rudy's new improved life. Dinah registered their two forms, lying there in the darkness. Stood there dry-eyed, blinking, then escaped back into her own life, where she hoped someday to belong.

The crickets cheered their lazy 2 A.M. cheer and dew glistened on the grass as Dinah, taking her heartbeat and her ravaged thumbs, moved down quietly back to her car and drove off into the night.

The female bat, after copulation, emits a loud squeal which, it has been suggested, acts as a signal to other females to choose the same male for a mate.

9

Dinah ripped a strip of flesh carefully out of her thumb and a thin line of blood appeared. She squeezed it, so that the line became a round, quivering dot and threatened to drip, whereupon she sucked the blood away thoughtfully. She hadn't meant to go that far. To draw blood. But these were the hazards of peeling your thumbs. She didn't bite her nails. She actually had rather nice nails. But finally they only served as a kind of arsenal to tear the skin off her thumbs till they were angry, creased-looking nubs sporadically dotted with tiny scabs.

It was a gray, overcast day, as Dinah drove toward East Hampton in search of a bookshop and a drugstore. Trees lined the highway, a yawning green entreaty of trees grouped under the mottled sky. The road rumbled beneath her as she pushed her sunglasses farther up on her nose and sped along.

This, then, was unhingement. After all the other things about her she was afraid. Afraid of being left alone just outside life's door and listening to all the laughter coming from inside. The inside joke being so far inside that by the time you got there, it would stop being funny.

There was something in her that no one could get at,

not even she. It lay just outside the grasp of language, inhabiting that wild world. Translating loosely from the Sanskrit of feeling, of no talk, of how can I put this? A thing that would hold her finally apart.

She was a lighthouse in the raging sea of the world, shining a light out of her eyes, searching, scorching— determining the danger, keeping everyone at bay, crashed up against the rocks of her personality. Not who she was, but what she did about who she was. The rocks of what she did about who she was.

A world at arm's length. See it out there at the end of her hand. Crashed up against her rocks, built up out of it. She proceeded as though the answer would be no and she was the question. Looking for humans to hold on to so she might not blow away when the strong wind of "Where is everybody" and "Whoopee, we're all gonna die" came swooping down on her.

She felt, at times, that her mind were a longish message in a bottle, a brain bottle, left afloat in her skull by some wiser, playful being. Just as a joke. An impractical joke. Very much made for the world and not made at all for it. Made with something else in mind. Some dark whimsy. *Serious* whimsy. The Full Wallop.

Most of the time, she tried to situate herself evenly between the deadly seriousness and the big-joke aspect to the whole thing. Inhaling deeply and imagining herself there, physically holding them apart, herself together.

She parked behind the drugstore and got out of the car, brushing the tiny pieces of torn skin from her lap to the pavement below. She went inside, combing the aisles for treasure, for booty, for more Band-Aids for her mangy thumbs.

She bought two different kinds. The fabric kind, because you couldn't rip them off, and the plastic kind, because you could. She bought some Tums, because it was a fun way to take calcium and she didn't want to end up all hunched over like her great-grandmother. Hunched over and blind. Of course, there wasn't much that she could do about the blindness; she would cross that bridge when she came to it. Cross it with a cane.

She bought some Jolen Cream bleach as an after-thought, in case the hair on her arms grew dark over-night, and took her items to the cashier. Satisfied now that she was prepared to meet life headlong, unhunched, light-haired and smooth-thumbed.

Dinah paid for her items and darted across the street to the bookstore, putting her Band-Aids on as she went. The cookbook section was just inside, against the wall on her right. She stood awkwardly in front of it. So many varieties. The *Joy of Cooking. The Cholesterol-Free Cookbook.* Chinese, Japanese, Vegetarian, Breads, Soups, Desserts. *New England Cookbook.* Mexican, Gourmet, Middle Eastern, Salads, Soufflés. Maybe that. Maybe soufflés. If she could make soufflés, she could make any-thing. Did Rudy like soufflés? Didn't everybody? Besides, that really showed culinary artistry. That would over-shadow Lindsay's clam chowder. But, just to make sure, she bought a soup book too. Soup, soufflés and the *Joy of Cooking.* If there was a joy to it, she certainly didn't want to miss out on that.

Dinah wandered farther into the store, clutching her three cookbooks, and found herself in the self-help sec-tion. She chose *Give Him What He Wants Without Feel-ing Like a Fool; Smart Couples, Dumb Relationships; So You Want Him Back;* and, just as a joke, *Your Genital Is Your Friend.* Between these books and the cookbooks, it promised to be an interesting weekend.

She was slightly embarrassed when she handed her purchases to the cashier, but the woman never batted an eyelash. So, for good measure, Dinah added *Thin Thighs in Thirty Days* from the counter display. With all this cooking, it couldn't hurt. She reached for the bag with

190

her bandaged thumbs, and as she left the store thought, Who have I become?

As she crossed the street, she thought, Whoever it is, I hope she can cook.

The soufflé she chose to make was a dessert soufflé. Primarily because it was easier and that made buying the ingredients more straightforward. She dog-eared the page of the yogurt soufflé with bananas and rum. Just for starters. She stopped by the Amagansett Market, this time without incident. Without running into anyone she or Rudy knew. At one point, she had considered making a carrot-and-squash soufflé, so as not to be making just a dessert soufflé, but it required shallots, and as she didn't know what they were, she decided against it.

She gathered the ingredients for the least odd-looking soup her cookbook offered. But even the least-odd seemed quite odd to her. It was called American Vegetable Soup, which seemed straightforward enough until you got into ingredients—like yucca and red peppers and hominy. What the hell is yucca? she wondered and was about to abandon it like the shallots when she stumbled upon it. It turned out that it was a white, lumpish thing that came frozen. She rounded up the rest of her items and approached the checkout stand, hoping to be mistaken for a housewife. Someone with a husband and children. Someone with a life.

Dinah emerged triumphant in the hazy late-afternoon sunshine, laden with goods. A mole in the house of domesticity. Lost in the dark woods of *chickdom*.

It turned out that the American Vegetable Soup was South American Vegetable Soup. The yucca was like rubber and tasted to Dinah vaguely of wood. The recipe called for a lot of dicing and, not being exactly certain what dicing was, she improvised, cutting everything up

191

into tiny, hopeful cubes. As the cutting progressed, however, she grew more and more impatient with the tininess and the cubes grew larger and less cubelike. She lost the tops of two nails in the process and her Band-Aids grew wet with onion juice, causing the raw flesh to sting.

She realized halfway in that she should've cut everything up first and not started heating the onion and garlic, but it was too late. Besides, how did you mince something? The recipe called for minced garlic, which sounded awfully small indeed, so Dinah grated it, which proved fairly unsuccessful, since it was extremely difficult to get the garlic off the grater afterward. The onions didn't make her cry, which she took as a good sign: it made her feel stoic and capable. She concentrated very hard, playing beat the clock with the browning of the onion and the dicing of the carrots, green beans, celery, peppers, and the dreaded yucca. But finally it was all in a big pot over a low flame, looking multicolored and exotic, and Dinah started working on her dessert soufflé.

The egg whites were the bitch. For the life of her, she could not make those damn things stiff. She considered going out and buying an egg beater or a Cuisinart or something to expedite the matter a little and then thought, No, other women make egg whites stiff all by themselves, so there's no reason why I shouldn't be able to.

But, after fifteen minutes of wrestling with the bowl and the whisk, after trying a fork, switching from one arm to the other and back again, she had to admit that there was little more than foam to show for her efforts. Jesus, this cooking thing might be a kind of nightmare. But she refused to be daunted by this setback, this minor failure, the egg-white impotence. Instead, she decided that perhaps "foamy" was a sort of stiffness in miniature. Maybe it was enough after all. It was inconceivable to her that all women everywhere had the strength and perseverance to turn out stiff, snowy mountain peaks of egg whites. So her soufflé wouldn't be a gourmet soufflé. It would still be a soufflé. Rudy would see. She'd show them all. She'd feed them all. Well, maybe not all.

She preheated her oven and went back to her egg-white Waterloo, adding the sugar and continuing to beat the eggs as the recipe suggested. But it said that the whites were going to get "firm but still glossy." They were glossy all right, because they were little more than liquid, but they sure weren't firm. Fine. She'd go to the other end of the recipe.

It was the yogurt soufflé, which she'd chosen because it sounded exotic in a low-cholesterol kind of way. And because the ingredients weren't complicated. She combined the yogurt and cottage cheese and beat the mixture until smooth. No problem there. Then she beat in the remaining ingredients: bananas, rum, maple syrup and lemon juice. These seemed to proceed without a hitch. Now it was time to add the egg whites. The decidedly unfirm egg whites. Well, Jesus, it was only her, trying out the whole cooking thing. Feeling discouraged but resolute, she added her watery egg whites to the rest of the concoction and hopefully stirred it all together, till there it was: a kind of beige creamy something. Having no idea what it was supposed to look like, she supposed it looked all right. Dinah put the bowl of beige surprise aside and buttered the only thing she had that might serve as a soufflé dish, which was a ceramic bowl of sorts. Despite the fact that the recipe called for "three individually buttered and sugared soufflé molds, refrigerated and ready to fill." But what if you didn't have three soufflé molds? What if you just had a ceramic bowl? Oh, please, she was just trying this thing out anyway.

Dinah poured her carefully and tragically prepared beige slop into the bowl and set it on the counter. Now the dessert would be ready. Ready to put in the oven. And her soup was simmering. Now she would . . . what? Now she would . . . what time was it? Just after six. Now she would . . . dye the hair on her arms. Yeah. Now she would go into deep Great Monkey Prep. Mrs. Kong had made her absent monkey man a light supper and now she would cleanse herself, dye her arms, smooth her skin in preparation for her imminent sacrifice.

She mixed the dye in a bowl over the sink and then removed her clothes, all except her underwear and a towel that she wrapped around herself. She then smoothed the preparation over the hair on her forearms and looked at her watch. Six-thirty. She had fifteen minutes till she could wash it off. She decided also to apply a face mask, getting both beautifiers over at once. Looking like a participant in some strange suburban ritual, Dinah decided to fill the fifteen minutes by calling someone. She combed her phone book for a friendly name, someone who might not ask her what she was doing, why she was in the Hamptons, who she thought she was. But it was difficult to imagine her friends not asking her where she was and why. She certainly couldn't call Connie. And then she saw the perfect name to call. In the middle of the phone book under *K*—Herb Kaufman, her father. She dialed his number in Bolivia slowly and carefully. What time would it be there? Not more than a couple of hours, right? It was below, not away. She heard the hiss of a faraway connection and then his number began to ring. And ring and ring. Dinah listened to her father's number ring for exactly twelve minutes, or 537 rings before she replaced the receiver and went into the bathroom to wash the bleach off her forearms.

Dinah stirred the soup thoughtfully, hypnotically, staring into it as if waiting for a vision, a message, as though it were vegetable TV. Vegetable cable TV. The sad soufflé concoction sat waiting patiently in the refrigerator for its impending trip to the oven. Dinah sighed as she stirred, wondering when she had gotten to be an observer rather than a participant. When had she stopped being excited about what was going to happen next? Had she ever been excited about what was going to happen next? Now the outcome of things seemed so clear, things once shrouded in mystery and excitement seemed almost dreary and not worth the effort. Rudy had been her companion and she had run away thinking life might offer her up more—something better, different—and it had, it had; but there was a sameness, she had seen it before, variations on a theme: who could people turn out to be, who could she turn out to be? She watched, waited, lived through a variety of similar outcomes, walked down streets teeming with young adults all juiced up with possibility, their arms slung around one another, smiling, talking, cigarettes dangling from the corners of their mouths, wondering what was going to happen tonight, who would be around the next corner, what party, what girl, what fun.

Dinah stirred her soup in the cool shadow of the outcome, a reluctant, inept domestic. No, no, no . . . wait. This was Pam stuff. Sure, she was in there, but Pam was clearly back. Standing at her back pushing her a little too far back, a little too far down. Dinah felt relieved. If she could name it, it wasn't as dangerous to her. It was still unpleasant, but it would end, it wasn't because she was a bad girl. Dinah smiled into her pot of South American Soup. Soup from the adopted land of her father. Chez Pam.

"Do I smell food?" a voice called. As if the message the soup contained finally had caught up to her, called out to her.

"Yes, sir," Dinah replied, looking in the direction of the sound of the voice. A face appeared at her window. Roy's face, sheepish, smiling in the dusk. Dinah removed her spoon and placed it on the counter. She wiped her hands like a true professional and went to open the door.

"You wouldn't happen to have a small dish of something or other for a struggling writer, would you?" he was saying. "Not that I'm necessarily struggling as a writer at the moment," he concluded brightly. "It's just stylistically how I generally function."

Dinah was about to open the door when she remembered that she still had the face mask on. She grimaced. "Can you wait out there for just a minute—in keeping with your struggling motif?" asked Dinah plaintively.

Roy hesitated a moment before answering. "Sure," he said finally. "It'll probably build character," he reasoned.

"Most things come to those who wait," she promised as she darted to her bathroom, washed the mask off of her face, and applied the smallest, quickest amount of makeup. Satisfied with her appearance, given her time allotment, she returned to the front door, fluffing her hair up as she did, wishing she had a little more makeup on, making that her next priority.

"A dish of something or other is exactly what you'll get if I cooked it," she said, waving him in. "If the quickest way to a man's heart is through his stomach," she intoned, "show me another road."

"Low or high?" asked Roy.

"High, how are you?" she replied, smiling.

"Fine," said Roy, standing awkwardly just inside the doorway.

Dinah indicated the kitchen table. "Take a seat," she said. "How do you want your eggs?" she asked, moving back into the kitchen and getting some bowls out of the cabinet, getting some forks and spoons, some glasses. Setting the table for Roy.

"We're having eggs?" he asked thoughtfully, removing his jacket and considering his egg options.

196

"It's just an expression," she explained patiently. "We're having soup."

Roy looked relieved, then confused. "Only soup?"

Dinah explained that it was a light meal, a trial meal of soup and soufflé, of things starting with *S*. They continued talking as she dished them both out some soup and put the soufflé in the oven. She opened a bottle of wine and turned the radio on low. She was really nesting now. Here was a man to try out her domestic-woman routine on. And the bitch of it was, she liked it. Liked the way the soup had turned out, that she had made it and that Roy enjoyed it. Liked it as much as almost anything else she had accomplished, with the exception of the first few shows she had written for *Heart's Desire;* she felt that she had done a good, big thing. She sat back and watched Roy finish his second bowl of soup, feeling quite pleased with herself. At one with the suburban universe. The conversation had drifted swiftly to relationships. Roy was talking about both of his, his girlfriend and his wife.

"I'm not actually seeing Karen for the moment," Roy said, pushing back his empty bowl. His eyes looking vaguely at something in the distance, to the left and down low.

Dinah pursed her lips, then said, "And Karen is . . . ?"

"My girlfriend," he said, then continued. "She's upset about my wife. That's still a potentially viable situation. Which also makes her suspect me of other liaisons." He now looked at Dinah directly, vaguely mistaking her for Karen. "But that is simply not true," he stated vehemently. "It never happened." Dinah watched him; his blue eyes flashed beneath his dark curly hair. "She thought I saw an ex of mine, when I didn't. But she refuses to believe me. Besides, the whole thing with my wife—Karen doesn't understand why I don't divorce her. I told her that it's very complicated. Cindy is very fragile and—" He sighed and looked at his hands in front of him. "There's still a lot of feeling there. But Karen can't understand that. She's very possessive and wants to have a baby." He paused now, looking at Dinah again, pointedly. "Come to think of it, Cindy wants to have a baby too. To them I'm just a breeder. I have to service their biological clocks."

"We ought to put you out to stud," she said, grinning.

"Do you ever feel that urge, the biological—whatever—to have a child?"

She shrugged, sitting back down. "I guess, sure. I want to experience everything that there is to being human. It's part of my gender package. It's horrible to be a woman sometimes, believe me. We have to try to get men to marry us or go in the other direction and pretend we don't care. Or other stuff. Last week I was in a store, in the lingerie section, very earnestly engaged in hunting for panties and nightgowns and I'm looking at this stuff, circling my prey, and all of the sudden I look up and I see all these other women similarly engaged, and I think, Look at us, we're chicks lost in the netherworld of our gender, absorbed in the world of potential purchase, why do we do this? Why is it so endlessly interesting? I mean, who gives a shit if Ultima comes up with a new shade of lipstick? I do. Very, very much. Just like you. Like guys. You have to watch the basketball playoffs. Do you know why? No. I comb stores for the right underwear and lipstick to wear while you watch the playoffs."

"I'm actually not that interested in basketball," admitted Roy almost coyly.

"Whatever. So you're like one of the seven guys that don't like sports."

"I like hockey." He leaned toward her, his elbows on his knees.

"There you go," she said victoriously. "Nice and violent." Dinah got up, clearing the soup bowls in her wake. Roy started up as though to help her. Dinah pushed him back down. "No, no," she said, stacking the two bowls and holding the two glasses between her index finger and thumb. "This is an experiment in domesticity for me," she said, taking the bowls into the kitchen and placing them carefully into the sink. "How far can I go without chaos? I'd ask you if you want coffee, but . . . I only know how to make instant. Do you want instant? Or wine? What?"

Roy considered for a moment. "Wine would be good. Let's just keep going with the wine. Do you have enough, or do you want me to go to my cabin and get some more?"

Dinah ran the water over the plates as she checked the refrigerator. "One more bottle," she replied, holding it aloft as evidence. "But you have to open it. Opening bottles is a guy thing. I only opened the first bottle because we hadn't had a major gender discussion yet."

Roy got up and took the bottle from her. She handed him the opener. "You're the only sexist female I've ever met," he said.

Dinah opened the oven carefully and studied the soufflé within. She took two oven mitts from the counter and placed one on each hand. Her face looked earnest. "I don't think of myself as sexist so much as practical. Things have progressed to the point that now women can work—even if it's for less pay—we can work, but the home thing is still really our domain. So now we have to do both. The work thing and the whole home nightmare." She carefully removed a sad-looking object in a pan from the oven. "I don't think this is right," she said, worried and serious. Roy came behind her and peered over her shoulder.

"What's it supposed to look like?" he asked generously, looking at the contents of the ceramic bowl Dinah held between her mitted hands.

"Not this," said Dinah, shaking her head slightly. "I'm pretty sure it was supposed to rise up higher in the pan. And be a . . . better color."

Roy went back to the table and continued opening the bottle of wine. "Let's give it a shot," he said, struggling with the cork. "How bad could it be?" Dinah looked at him with a mixture of gratitude and doubt.

"We're talking about loyalty here," she said, going over to the cabinet and getting some fresh bowls. "I'm going to call this Loyalty Soufflé. How-Bad-Could-It-Be Soufflé," she continued, spooning up a small amount for each of them. The cork came out of the wine with a pop. Roy went over and got two new glasses and poured them each a glass of wine.

"Look at it this way," he said, "the wine can always kill the taste."

"Great," said Dinah, placing a bowl of gray mystery dessert in front of him. "A sort of vintage Roach Motel."

A dog barked in the distance as they tasted Dinah's unrisen, bland wonder. Roy rolled the dessert around his mouth with a look of concentrated introspection. "Well, it's certainly not *awful*," he began. "It has a sort of . . ." Here he trailed off, apparently looking for a metaphor for this food. But, before it could be found, Dinah interrupted him.

"It tastes like chalk," she announced grimly, taking a mouthful of wine.

"But *fun* chalk," he offered brightly. "Sweet mortar."

Dinah tilted her head and regarded him with affection. "You see?" she said sadly. "This truly is the Loyalty Soufflé." Looking at Roy over the rim of her glass, Dinah hoped that he liked her. Not so much because she liked him, but because she needed him to like her. She didn't really know if she liked him so much as she knew he *must* like her, and she would like him until he did just that. And she would be kind of hurt if he didn't. Not that she knew who he was or what she would really do with him, she just knew that she wouldn't be able to live with herself until Roy wanted to live with her.

Roy and Dinah looked into each other's eyes for a beat too long, betraying a certain biology. A physiological tie-in, connection, the inadvertent mating of mammals. Both looked away quickly. Dinah closed her eyes tightly, pushing the estrogen storm back. The estro fest that was feeding on her. Change the subject. Find a subject. Anything. They both began talking at once.

"So you—"

"Why did—"

"Go ahead," he said expansively.

She shook her head, smiling. Flushing. "No," she said. "You."

"So you think you're going to get back with this guy?" asked Roy, leaning back in his chair and looking at her expectantly.

"Who?" asked Dinah absentmindedly, then, instantly, everything was crashing back in on her. "Oh, my ex-husband!" she exclaimed, suddenly remembering him and feeling foolish for having forgotten. "You mean live with him again?" Dinah looked sternly at the soufflé in front of her, looked within herself, and answered her own question. "No, no, we didn't live together well. I basically don't know what I'm doing. I'm in process. The thing before the question."

"Ah," said Roy ironically, thoroughly baffled. "Well, that was my other question. Were you the thing before the question?"

Dinah laughed and sipped her wine. "Or are you just glad to see me?" she countered softly.

Roy continued. "No, but like . . . so . . . what's the

deal? You couldn't stand the idea of him having another relationship, or what?" Roy crossed his legs, put down his glass and wiped his brow.

Dinah shrugged, looked embarrassed. "I guess," she replied. "Maybe. I have to admit, it does bother me." Suddenly she looked at Roy. "What would you do? I mean if Karen—or—"

"Cindy," Roy offered helpfully.

"Cindy," Dinah nodded, continuing. "What would you do if Karen or Cindy got another boyfriend?"

Roy smiled and looked down at his folded hands. "It already happened," he said. "Karen went out with this actor. It was horrible. I'm pretty sure she did it to torture me. I was in marriage counseling with Cindy at the time and Karen wanted me to stop. So she went out with this actor."

"And what happened?"

"I stopped," he said simply. "The bad thing about that is, that if she's fucking someone else, I will artificially get hotter for her and I don't want to force her into a lifelong relationship where she has to keep having sex with other people to keep me interested in her."

Dinah nodded hesitantly, attempting to pick up on the loose thread from his thoughts. "You want her interest to go to someone else so that you can have something to pull it back with?"

Roy nodded evenly. "Right. And you know something? I think maybe I'll have to have a lifelong relationship like that. Be one of those guys that has relationships with women I have to lure back from other men."

Dinah leaned forward, her hands around the bottom of her glass. "Well, that's what I like about Rudy. He was always interested in me in this not-interested-in-me way. And the tragedy is that would almost be enough. I could maybe be sort of happy."

"Almost enough. But it won't be," Roy stated matter-of-factly. Dinah was slightly affronted.

"But I don't want enough. Because then what would I have to do?"

Roy looked confused. "Huh?"

"What do I have to do if I have enough? There is no challenge. How do I get my workout?"

"Ha," noted Roy, looking relieved. "I know what you're saying and I agree, but I don't think *that* has to be the challenge to get your workout. I mean, you're going to find dark holes in everything. And so there'll always be challenges. I don't think it has to be that. You know what I mean?" Roy looked at Dinah expectantly, warmed to his subject. Hot. "You wanna hear a challenge?" he continued intensely. "God forbid? You have a deformed child. There you go—"

Dinah looked doubtful. "Well . . ."

"I'm saying, life—you know, throws you things."

Dinah sprang to life with a new thought. "So what does a wife have to do for you? I mean, does Cindy cook? Pack for you? Give you back rubs?"

"Well, I mean, she's in a depression clinic now," he said diffidently.

"I know that," said Dinah, waving away the fact with her hand. "I'm talking about before. *Ideally.*"

"Oh, well, *ideally*," conceded Roy. "I can do without any service that I'm willing to purchase. So, you can't purchase . . ."

Dinah interrupted eagerly, "Back rubs?"

"No, you *can* purchase back rubs."

Dinah nodded idiotically. "Right, yeah, I know you can."

"You can't purchase point of view and sensibility," Roy reminded her gently. She smiled gratefully, apologetically.

"And sex," added Dinah. "I mean, you *can* . . ."

"No, but you can't purchase that kind of sex. I mean, sex that's meaningful."

They both sat back thoughtfully, exhausted. A fly

circled the dishes in the sink, finally landing on a dirty fork. Tony groaned from the couch in his sleep. Roy stared at the empty space before him and sighed almost wistfully.

"The one thing I've never done is be so much in love and so close and have that become this . . . immense soul connection and not . . . not . . . just . . . someone who's dating someone else." He fished a bit of cork out of his wine with his thumb and forefinger. Dinah watched, absorbed.

Roy continued. "Either I'm too damaged to see that this is the one or it's not the one. These are not the ones. Either way, the results are the same and she has to deal with the results. They. They have to deal with the results."

"Yeah," said Dinah, slightly deflated. "Because it's the perfect excuse and it's not the perfect excuse for nothing." She paused for a brief moment, collecting her thoughts, then pushed on, her hazel eyes sparkling with amusement. "Here's how men think," she began, looking once more intently at Roy, about to try out some of her best material on him. "Ready?" she asked playfully.

"Ready," he replied, leaning forward, his arms on the table.

"Okay," she said, starting, counting on her fingers as she enumerated. "Sex, work—and those are reversible, depending on age—sex, work, food, sports, and lastly, begrudgingly, relationships." Roy started to say something, but she cut him off, continuing. "And here's how women think." Her hands were back in fists, poised for the female count. "Relationships, relationships, relationships, work, sex, shopping, weight, food." Roy shook his head in wonder. Dinah felt slightly foolish. "It's not really a foolproof theory, but you get the overall gist of the drift."

Roy wiped his brow with the heel of his hand.

"Yeah, I think I get the gist of the drift. Women think a lot about relationships."

They were both silent for a moment. A breeze blew through the window screen. A train whistle sounded in the distance, a lonely sound. The fly found itself in oily waters and flapped its wings frantically, trying to get out.

"It's hard for me to be alone," Roy continued finally.

"You're alone now," she pointed out.

"No," said Roy, part hurt, part joking, "I'm with you."

"You know what I mean," she said in a slightly admonishing tone.

Roy shifted in his seat, didn't meet Dinah's eye. "Yeah, well . . ." he improvised. "I'm on the phone a lot and when I'm not . . ." He shrugged. "It's hard. I have trouble falling asleep."

"Me too."

"I sleep better when someone else is there."

"I don't mind being alone," she said. "Actually, I like it. I learned to like it in the last couple of years. But I still have trouble falling asleep. Always have."

"I dread it. I dread finding myself alone with my head, my thoughts. I've always had trouble falling asleep. That's why I drink."

"I only ever drink when I'm shy or want to do something I wouldn't ordinarily do. Usually sexual." Why had she said that? She was drinking now. She took her hands off her glass and sat back guiltily, hoping Roy wouldn't notice the wine there. He didn't seem to. His head leaned to one side and he regarded her curiously.

"You aren't usually sexual?" he said.

"I don't think so. I try not to be." Dinah began to peel the Band-Aid off one of her thumbs. Subtly. Under the table.

"Why is that?"

"I don't know. I was brought up pretty strictly and

. . . it's a hard area to control. I mean, once you have total sex . . ."

Roy interrupted, leaned forward, his eyes twinkling in amusement. "Total sex?" he said in mild disbelief.

"You know, the procreative act," she explained hesitantly, her eyes down, looking in her lap. How had they arrived at this subject? thought Dinah dismally. It has to be my fault. At least half my fault.

Roy made a wild guess. "Making love?"

Dinah grimaced. "Making love always sounds like something you need a recipe for. You know, with cinnamon or vanilla or baking soda."

"Intercourse, then," Roy amended politely.

Dinah tucked in her chin. "You could say that, yes," she said, still not looking at him. "Once you have that—and I speak now as a woman—then all these expectations start crashing in. With sex comes the assuming. Making it something else in your head. Does he love me? Will he call me? What does this mean? Will it work out? It's just voodoo time and you stop owning yourself. Everything is thought of in terms of him."

She looked out the window, imagining one of the people who lived out there, a Long Islander, hacking through the landscape toward her. The melting, shifting, yawning landscape. As if offering up its only son. The only human thing that it could produce. She waited to see what the landscape would bring her and then realized that it had probably brought her Roy.

"Sounds pretty grim," he said. What were they talking about? Oh, yes, what boys and girls were always talking about.

"That's why I mostly just made out with people and hoped they wouldn't get mad instead of just hoping it wouldn't get crazy." The Band-Aid came off. Dinah smoothed it in half and dropped it discreetly under her chair.

Roy looked confused. "I don't think I quite follow you."

"It doesn't matter," said Dinah. "It's just my looniness. I like kissing. I mean, making out is like babysitting for my whole head . . . but I don't want to be a tease." Was this an advertisement? They both wondered. She started on the other Band-Aid.

"Uh huh," agreed Roy. "Well, kissing is nice."

"It is, isn't it?" What kind of conversation were they having?

"Of course, I'm also a fan of sex. Of—what did you call it—procreative sex?"

Dinah laughed. "Procreative voodoo. It's . . . I'm not really fluent in sex—I speak it—but it's more a second language."

He laughed and shook his head. Their eyes met again and the other Band-Aid came off.

"Procreative voodoo," Roy repeated, murmuring. A warmth invaded Dinah's face. Her hands felt weak and Band-Aid-less. She stood up.

"I should go to bed," she said, looking in the direction she would be going, then back at him.

He stood. "Yeah, me too." She followed him to the door. They faced each other.

"Well . . . ," she began, holding a hand out, a raw thumb partly exposed. "Good night," she finished generically.

"Good night," he said. "Thanks for the . . . friendly chalk."

"*Fun* chalk," she said, correcting him.

"*Fun* chalk," he echoed obediently. They had exhausted all probability of conversation. Neither moved. Rooted. Held by some invisible force field of pheromones. Roy bent down suddenly and kissed Dinah. Dinah kissed Roy back. Desire mingled with relief.

The fly in the sink suddenly broke free of the water and flew toward the light.

"What are we doing?" moaned Roy breathlessly.

"As little as possible," mumbled Dinah faintly into his mouth, arms encircling him, smoothing over his soft shirt. Henry Stark. Thursday nights. No, this wasn't Henry. Who was this one? Not Rudy, she was sure of that. Who were these people? Feeding on her, feeding her. Tangled fingers through his hair. Inhaling him, inhaling her, touching the back of her neck. Pressing his hardening body into her softening one. They maneuvered over to the couch, falling back on it, Roy on top. Disturbing the sleeping dog, who jumped off the couch disgruntled and settled nearby on the floor. Dinah and Roy talked through the kissing, a closer conversation.

"Unexpected," he said.

"What?" she said.

"This," he said.

"High school," she said.

"High school?"

"This is like high school. You're my high school sweetheart. Andy Hardy." Actually, it was *Love Finds Andy Hardy*, she thought. But this wasn't love, was it? No, it was probably just Andy Hardy. One more Andy Hardy. What was her name? Judy Garland. No, the character. Couldn't remember. Can't. Just, "We can use my barn."

"You'll have to wear my new ID bracelet," he was saying now, smiling into her smile, hands in her hair. She pushed him onto his back, lay on his chest, resumed kissing him, on top now, on top at last. No one she could keep without killing. Killing them softly. Her new Andy Hardy. The next not-Rudy, him.

"I'll give you a hickey," she said, elbows on either side of his head, hands folded on top of it. He bit her chin playfully.

"We'll go to the prom," he vowed.

They pressed together tighter as she said, "Can we?

Oh, can we?" She raised her head from next to his as he turned his face to her.

"Absolutely." Her face fitted into his. Her hands moved back through his thick dark hair. They bit into one another's heads, peach eating peach. Tasting the sweet dark head meat. Her hands ached. He pushed her smoothly onto her side, her back against the back of the couch, his back to the room. A car rumbled slowly down the road beyond.

"What are we doing?" he asked her again intently.

"This," she replied, kissing him, as much to close her eyes as to kiss him. She continued breathlessly, her forehead touching his. "We were so nervous. This helps us to calm down."

He laughed, a drop of sweat trickled down his brow and into his hair. "We were nervous, weren't we?" he admitted. "Maybe that soufflé was an aphrodisiac."

"*Anglodisiac*," she joked, shifting her weight slightly, moving her top leg over his.

"What?"

"Anglodisiac, if anything," she said. "First of all it's us, and second, I would've had to add a lot more melanine."

He laughed. "I see."

"I feel better now," she said. "Don't you?"

He kissed her. "Much better."

Infatuation fizzled through them, their kiss burned on, glowed inside them, her head, his loins. A temporary eternal flame. That heavy beat, beat, beat. A gentle hammering. A surging, then quiet. A sensual riot. The shoe that falls into this world, lands with a mighty thud. The shoe that hovered precariously at the back of all this pounding. Dinah didn't wait for the shoes to drop anymore; she just looked for them on the ground.

"Roy," Dinah said, just to say his name.

"Dinah," Roy whispered, moving her onto her back.

209

She pulled him to her. "If I said nice things, I'd be saying them now," she said softly, sweetly.

His hand moved gently over her breast, a cloud over her sun. Hearts thumping, the loud music of lust, of proximity, of new, unvanquished blood. He reached back and turned out the light next to the sofa. On the way back, his arm struck the side of her face. She inhaled sharply in the darker room. Not Rudy. Who?

"Oh God, sorry," he exclaimed, pulling back to see her. Her head was on his chest, her teeth clenched.

"It's okay," she laughed, embarrassed. "It goes with the territory."

His hand found her face, pulled her gently back, holding her chin. Placing his nose next to her nose, his mouth onto her mouth. "I don't want to hurt you," he murmured into her mouth gently, sucking her bottom lip. Dinah shifted uneasily, reminded of something. She'd heard this before, done this before, remembered the ending, shot to the exit. "I would never want to hurt you," he repeated, his hands exploring, finding her ass. Dinah tensed slightly, passed through the door. Rudy's face appeared and disappeared on the back of her closed eyelid. Didn't it?

"Physically or emotionally?" she said lightly, pushing her hair back from her forehead, opening her eyes so that Rudy was gone and Roy, once again, appeared.

He pulled her to him once again, kissing her deeply, briefly. "Neither," he said, the kiss now complete.

"So, don't," she said in the same tone, now struggling to sit up.

Roy held her back. "Where are you going?" he chided, pulling her playfully.

Dinah resisted. "Don't," she pouted, struggling. He realized she was in earnest and let her go. She sat up. He lay back, looking at her silhouetted in the half-darkness. Dinah readjusted her clothes, herself. The mute thud of the shoe, invisible to the untrained human ear, fell somewhere in the room. Tony, the dog, heard it and awoke from a wonderful dream. He sat up suddenly, alarmed.

"What's the matter?" Roy asked, his hand on her leg, stroking her, coaxing her, back, back. Come crash against my rocks. A siren. The song of persuasion.

But Dinah heard only her smoke alarm. "You don't want to hurt me," she said, still smoothing. "Well, I suddenly remembered that I don't want you to hurt me either."

"Jesus!" he exclaimed to a ceiling he couldn't see. "I'm not going to hurt you! How am I going to hurt you?" He sat now, a condemned man. Condemned to this world partly populated by women. He stood, wanting a cigarette, removing a crushed pack from his back pocket.

"I don't know," she replied wearily. "I'm sure it's a mystery to you too. But you'll find a way." She put her hand out. "Give me one." He handed her a cigarette, felt his shirt pockets for a match. He lit her cigarette, the match illuminating their faces briefly in the dark. Two prisoners in a cell, a holding tank. How many times can I do this, thought Dinah. This thing with guys. Who are they? She sighed, exhaling. The smoke hovered in front of her face, then was reabsorbed into the evening.

The dog got up and wandered over to the couch and jumped up beside Dinah. She petted him absently, regretting the turn of events, making up for them by being nice to her dog.

"Jesus," Roy said in a boyish, baffled voice. "We're already talking about me hurting you and I haven't even known you a day."

Dinah inhaled the smoke deeply. Her eyes stung. She sat back. "Well, we'd get to it eventually, so why wait?"

Roy sat back down next to her. "Why wait?" he said incredulously. "I'll tell you why wait. Because it's fun.

The time between meeting someone and 'I don't want you to hurt me' can be really fun."

She looked at him, her eyes adjusted to the darkness. "I told you I wasn't fluent in sex," she said finally in a low voice.

She got up and went into the kitchen wearily, rummaging through the cabinet for a saucer to use as an ashtray. She turned off the radio, returned, placing the saucer in front of the two of them, flicking an ash before she placed it on the ground, sitting back down beside him, wondering how she looked, glad it was dark. Oh, fuck it. Roy sighed, crossed his legs pensively.

"I'm a romantic lost cause," he said finally. "Like the Spanish Civil War."

Dinah looked at him. "Was the Spanish Civil War romantic?" she asked.

"Sure," answered Roy. "Haven't you read *For Whom the Bell Tolls*?"

There was a pause. It beat down on them, held them in the hollow of its warm darkness, feeling them trapped and struggling there.

"It's so quiet," she remarked sadly, running her free hand through her hair. There was a pause as proof. "Oh, God," she exclaimed apologetically. "I'm sorry. But men are always saying that they don't want to hurt you, you know?" she said, then continued. "Well, you wouldn't know, would you? Not from my side. What do you all think? That we're deeply in love with you? Held captive by the hope of some life with you? That I'm just another chick hurling myself onto the roaring pyre of your availability? I mean, I do have a tendency to fantasize, but I have a strong practical counterside." She abruptly stopped speaking and took another drag on her cigarette. "Never mind," she added quietly, smoke coming out of her nose and mouth. They both sat quietly in the darkness, smoking.

Finally Roy said, "I'm so afraid to say the wrong thing to you now." He shook his baffled head. "I just wanted us to enjoy each other."

Dinah sighed, smiling slightly. "We're very alike in a way, I think."

Roy relaxed at her approving tone. "Alike, how?"

Dinah put out her cigarette. She sat back. "Well, we both do this charming thing," she began thoughtfully. "We're winning. We perform the same function. We render each other obsolete. Village idiots. And you know what they say. Too many village idiots spoil the village."

Roy leaned forward, putting his cigarette out, and half-laughed, half-sighed. "I see," he said, not really seeing.

"See, I figure there are two types of guys. Daddy men and sibling men. And you are a sibling guy." Daintily, she removed a sliver of tobacco from her tongue.

"Jeez, you've really thought about this," Roy said appreciatively, lighting a second cigarette. "Want another one?" he asked politely. She shook her head. "What is a sibling guy?" he asked, a cigarette dangling gangster-style out of the side of his mouth.

"A sibling guy is a more easygoing guy—approval-seeking—and a daddy guy is someone whose approval you're after—approval-withholding," she replied simply. "See, the thing about us—you and me—ultimately, aside from the fact that you have two other relationships, is that we can't win each other, 'cause we're each so busy trying to win each other. You know, checking for a reaction instead of having one? Creating a response, instead of feeling one? We are charming rather than charmed, winning as opposed to won over. Always needing something to achieve, persuade, or coax. Coax in from the ledge of indifference." She said the latter in a singsong, taunting voice.

213

Roy shook his head. "You really *have* thought about this."

Dinah leaned back, her hands spread on her knees. "I always think about all this stuff," she said. "It's my job. Mostly I'm just voice-activated, though. I'm a mind reader. Engaged in reading my own mind."

"You know, if you want to destroy the possibility of us becoming anything, fine," said Roy, slightly irritated now. Dinah raised her eyebrows in surprise. "But you know what I think? I think you're just doing it before I do. I think the medical term for this is 'The Rush for the Exit.' You may end up alone but you'll have gotten there first, so—"

"Anyway," Dinah interrupted, flushed and stifling a manufactured yawn. "You don't need any more complications in your life. We'll just be friends." She turned to face him engagingly. "So, will you do me a favor, now that you're not going to be my second husband?"

Roy put his hands over his face, moaning, "What did I ever do to deserve this?"

"Probably something," Dinah replied sweetly. "Will you?"

Roy removed his hands. "What?"

Now that they had gotten through the negotiation of what it was, they could relax. Bask in an absence of agenda, as it were, as it happened to be. Now they could just be friends, just enjoy each other without making it count toward some greater, future good. Now that they both knew they were going nowhere, they could simply enjoy the ride.

Dinah wouldn't let herself want anything from them —men. Then, when she didn't get it, she didn't want it anyway. She befriended them quickly, defensively. A friendliness that concealed a deeper, more hopeful seduction. She demanded to be accepted as an equal. Not really as a female—as a pal. A consort. A consortionist. She'd get a little from him and him and whomever else, and finally, it would be enough. A feast of fast friends, making her immune to a full meal of a man.

"Where do you think this is going?" A thing she'd never say. She picked them to be protected. Conspiring to get them to want her, nest with her, *breed.* Feeling ashamed. Afraid.

Along for the ride, she'd bask in the warm short blasts of reflected glory. A shared identity, a double identity. Someday surrounded on all sides by folks with claims on her affection. Daughter, wife, mommy, grandma, great-grandma, pretty-good person, parading to the grave. The cloying fantasy of double identity, intoxicating her with its evil spell.

No.

She would live in her mind. High up in her head, where they couldn't get at her. Up high in her mental lighthouse, high above the seas that raged around it, she'd watch the mayhem and haw.

She was sometimes comfortable in crisis and confusion . . . needing an occasion to rise to. At certain points, she didn't know who she was anymore. She became the same with everyone. But then again, maybe there was something nice about that. Constancy. She wondered when things would cease to be something she was able to describe and become something she experienced. Something she more than understood. She wanted to feel what she described, experience what she explained.

Dinah wanted to get it right, get it understood by whomever she was putting it out to. She was proud that she could name things. She was proud that she could, at times, be clever about things that a lot of people were afraid of in themselves and couldn't name. She could name it. She could choreograph it and get it to do laundry. It was hers. Her information was hers. Wasn't it?

215

She rhapsodized. It gave her pleasure. Her effect on people gave her pleasure. Dinah felt as connected up with herself as she ever did when she was with people. She needed the restriction of making herself understood. Clear.

It took them forever to park. They had taken Roy's car, since Dinah thought it was more appropriate for the guy to drive. He had a small dark-green MG and, aside from its being a much nicer car than Dinah's rental, and the whole gender aspect of the whole thing, it was a compact car and would be easier to park.

Traffic gathered at the intersection from both directions, waiting to make the turn out of the main road. As they drove down the road leading to the shore, cars were parked for almost a mile leading into or up to Boy's Bay Park.

"We should have left earlier," said Dinah as she watched families pile out of their cars carrying hampers of food or big coolers hoisted up on a shoulder, marching slowly toward the impending festivities, teenagers and tots in tow.

"Don't worry, this baby is great for getting at those hard-to-get-at parking spaces." Hunched over the steering wheel, Roy peered out of the windshield for a challenging slot for his vehicle. Tiny herds of humans trudged toward the choice spot on the bay from where the fireworks could be seen best. There were boats on the water at the end of the road, floating in the dusky light.

"Maybe we shouldn't be doing this anyway," Dinah said, sitting back and crossing her arms. "Maybe our not getting a parking space easily or near is a sign."

"It's a *challenge*," growled Roy with mock intensity, looking at Dinah briefly, then back at the line of cars on either side of them. He was happier now that Dinah was over the little hump of their brief encounter, now that the radio was playing, now that they were closing in on someone else's little drama, not his. He had spoken to both Cindy and Karen that day, and both conversations had been largely pleasant and relatively without incident. He had managed to charm both women, without either of them guessing that it was partly due to the fact that he felt a little guilty about his aborted encounter with Dinah the night before. It was true that he had not really cheated on the two women in his life and so he was relieved that his status as faithful had not really changed.

Dinah pulled the visor down and looked in the mirror, smoothing her hair. She appraised her face haughtily, hopefully, then replaced the visor and sat back, disappointed. It was still her face. It was always still her face. "I don't know why you're so anxious to go," she remarked gloomily. "If this shit ends up in your book, I'll kill you."

Roy laughed a short, sinister laugh. "Hey," he said, "this is the shit I do *instead* of writing, not *in order* to." He saw a tiny little slot on top of a sandy slope. "Oooh," he exhaled as he pointed his car toward the little hill.

"Oooh what?" asked Dinah, looking at where Roy's car was headed, seeing his ambitious idea of a parking space. "Oooh, *that!*" she said, pointing needlessly, as they were now navigating the slope, tires spinning in the sand. "Oooh, *this*," she modified. "This is not a parking space; this is a . . ." But she was at a loss as to what it was, because whatever it was, Roy was making a Herculean effort to guide the MG into it.

"Look," he began, looking over his shoulder, turning the steering wheel hard, his tiny car making all sorts of whining noises. "Do you or do you not want to torture your ex-husband somehow?" he asked with some effort as he maneuvered the MG dramatically into this almost unmaneuverable space.

"Yes, but . . ." began Dinah.

Roy interrupted, speaking with some effort as he steered the back tires away from an inconveniently placed tree. Sand flew everywhere. Dinah hid her face in her hands. "And do you or do you not agree that, by your definition, driving is a 'guy thing,' and I am, for the moment, the guy?"

"Yes," Dinah acquiesced, her face still hidden, her legs now curled up beneath her. Hunched over, protecting herself from this preposterous parking stunt. The car roared and lurched forward slightly. Roy turned off the engine and sat back victoriously.

"Then, as the official guy, I say"—he grinned impishly—"it's torment time."

As far as the eye could see and beyond, where it couldn't see, but could only guess at, a blanket of people was covering every available space on the ground. People stepped over people, on people, lay side by side, sat grouped on blankets, towels, waited in lines to buy drinks or food. An ambulance stood by valiantly, ominously. The event hovered precariously on the brink of itself, teetering, about to fall in. It was a clear, warm night. A sickly breeze blew briefly over the mob, soothing them.

Roy and Dinah followed a path through tall dark trees that lined the road leading to the sea of people anxiously awaiting the festivities. As they approached, walking by the ambulance, Dinah's heart quickened. Somewhere in this peopled place, Rudy wandered benignly with Lindsay. Dinah took Roy's hand. "Nothing personal," she assured him as they made their way through the milling throng. Babies wailed amid the laughter, the talking, the general hubbub of the hubbing and bubbing. Plastic glasses lay strewn along the path, abandoned. The smell of—what was it?—corn on the cob and barbecued chicken perfumed the evening breeze.

218

Boats lay on the water beyond, their dark silhouettes standing in the bay.

A house up on the embankment glowed with light, a buffet on a table was spread out before it, next to a small uninhabited pool. Candles glowed from amid some groups as Dinah looked everywhere for Rudy and Lindsay, clutching Roy, her neighbor and accomplice. Small radios blared here and there, dogs barked in the twilight.

"Let's get a drink," suggested Roy, pulling her toward a table, getting into the little line that led to it.

"You're so practical," crooned Dinah, leaning against him, holding his hand with one hand and his arm with her other. Her short black dress was swaying gently in the breeze. "It's times like these that I'm almost sorry that you aren't my second husband," she said, smiling up at him.

" 'Almost' isn't good enough," Roy whispered, chiding. Dinah squeezed his arm, watched the crowd for Rudy's forbidding, lovable demeanor.

Having gotten their drinks, they moved gingerly through the people, searching for a space to sit in. They passed a small old woman hunched over with age.

"Me in four years," declared Dinah. As the woman passed, Dinah realized with a start that it was the psychic to whom she had promised to return with several hundred dollars. She averted her head unnecessarily as she watched Mama move through the crowd toward the food.

"What's wrong?" asked Roy.

"Nothing," said Dinah innocently. A tall man came toward them now with large sticking-out ears. "You in a dream sequence, dancing with devils," she informed him happily. As she said this, the spray of a squirt gun hit Roy in the leg. He took it heroically.

"It's nothing," he assured Dinah. "Just a flesh wound."

A microphone crackled, an announcement was made. "Good evening, ladies and gentlemen. And welcome to the twelfth annual Boy's Bay firework display," said a clipped New England male voice. A Bostonian voice. There was a smattering of applause and some children cheered. Dinah and Roy made their way to a tiny, moist patch of land near a short hedge, surrounded by families, and sat on their haunches, so as not to wet their clothes. They clutched their paper cups and looked at the sky, waited for it to do something. The music from *Rocky* blared from large speakers somewhere on either side of them.

"Your theme," whispered Dinah.

"Shhhhh," one of the children near them admonished. Roy gave Dinah a mock stern look as a small, glowing light, the introductory rocket, climbed the night sky. The crowd murmured as it hit the dead center of their vision and exploded, popped into a cluster of stars, an electric chrysanthemum that hovered briefly in the dark sky, the aurora borealis gone berserk, illuminating the crowd beneath on the shore, who cheered and applauded as the bright flower dripped out of being, into memory. The festivities had officially begun.

Roy and Dinah smiled at one another. He gallantly removed his sweater and smoothed it on the ground beneath them so they could sit.

"I don't deserve you," she whispered.

"Exactly my point," he whispered back.

The sky exploded in three colors, from high and low, then whistled and twisted into darkness. Everyone's heads were thrown back, throats exposed. Americans agape in a group, eyes fixed on the heavens in wonder. The sky glittered and sparkled, exploding in colors and light, as it ought to do more often, in Dinah's opinion. A wondrous short circuit in heaven's TV. Lovely lightning,

220

choreographed, carbonated, glorious. Hundreds of happy lanterns hanging, thrown and splashed against the dark-blue sky. Melting stars—melting into blackness, a fiery, flaming weeping willow, crying out of the sky, briefly illuminating the water—silver, green, gold, red, blue, magenta. Holier than wow, than now, an electric trick Jesus that snap-crackle-popped, baptizing the onlookers beneath in the name of fun, the heavens' after-dinner mint. A swarm of fireflies, inverted shooting stars, dragging their smoky tails coquettishly behind them, the smoldering electric Alka Seltzer of the sky, phosphorous and refreshing.

The sky dripped in riches, exploded with treasure, shimmered. After several minutes, Dinah couldn't remember it being any other way. Wouldn't want to remember it as having been any other way. She hugged her knees closer and watched the sky do one of its neatest tricks. Roll over, sit, do-si-do, splits, stand up, sit down, fight, fight, fight.

For the grand finale, they played Neil Diamond's "America." The sky blazed in red, white and blue. The spectators oohed and aahed. A river of light poured, emptied out of the sky. The spectacle climbed to its patriotic pitch, hovered there, teetered, then went back to black. To blue. Pale stars twinkled in low-cal comparison as the display came to an end.

Dinah and Roy blinked expectantly at the recomposed sky, then shook themselves out of the glittering dream.

"Well . . ." exhaled Roy.

"Boy," breathed Dinah. They stood unsteadily and brushed themselves off. Roy folded his damp sweater. And there, just over the hedge, staring at Dinah, then at Roy, was Rudy, with Lindsay just behind him.

Dinah's center dropped out of her and fell away, her composure evaporated into the night air. Roy looked at

Dinah and then at Lindsay and Rudy, blinking in attempted recognition.

"Dinah," Rudy said in a sort of subdued amazement. Lindsay brushed her blond hair back from her luminous, open face. She wore a long white cotton caftan with gold embroidery at the neck and the edge of the sleeves.

"Hello, Rudy," Dinah said with a half-smile. The first half, the half that eats. *Les jeux sont faits.* Well, she was in it now. People mulled about them, oblivious, as the smoke from the fireworks cleared. A boat's horn sounded in the distance. A child cried from somewhere just beyond them. The four of them stood awkwardly, wordlessly, as Roy shifted from one foot to another. The pause circled them and closed in around them. Finally Roy gave Dinah a questioning look and then put his hand out to Rudy in greeting.

"Roy Delaney," he offered pleasantly to Rudy. "Nice to meet you."

Rudy took Roy's hand, but looked instead at Dinah. "Rudy Gendler," he said dolefully to her, clasping Roy's moist hand briefly. He then dropped Roy's hand and looked uneasily at Lindsay. "Lindsay," he said, looking at her with a flicker of compassion, "this is . . ." Rudy hesitated—who was she again? Dinah cavalierly took up the slack.

"Dinah," said the same, extending her hand with the bandaged thumb. "Dinah Kaufman—nice to meet you."

Lindsay pressed Dinah's hand politely, stealing a look at Rudy, sensing his tension, trying to ascertain its source. Dinah noticed Lindsay wore no makeup, her hair framing a pale face with heavy-lashed green eyes and a pert turned-up nose. She self-consciously touched her own face, covered with base, her eyes made up and her lips lined and painted. She felt like a fake. A painted sham. She rubbed off her lipstick with the back of her hand.

Roy's hands were plunged deep in the pockets of his cream-colored pants as he rocked back and forth on his heels, a gleam of mischief in his eyes. After all, it wasn't his drama. For once. Rudy started to say something when Roy cut him off.

"Say," he began almost joyously, "weren't you two married or something?" He looked from Dinah to Rudy happily. The color drained from Lindsay's already pale face. She looked in polite horror at Rudy. Dinah dug her nails sharply into Roy's arm.

" 'Or something' is more like it," murmured Rudy uneasily. He gave Lindsay an almost beseeching look. Lindsay put one hand to her throat as though for reassurance, for luck, and then looked from Dinah to Rudy, perhaps connecting them in her mind. Finally she looked at Dinah again, disconnecting them.

"I see," she said evenly. "You're *that* Dinah." She appraised Dinah with what was left of her cool. Roy laughed a snorting sort of laugh.

"How many Dinahs are there?" he mused ironically, trying to infuse some sort of false cheer into the little group. "I mean other than Shore and the cat in *Alice in Wonderland* . . ."

Dinah shot him her version of a withering look, cutting him off. An announcement was made over the loudspeaker regarding a lost child. It occurred to Dinah that it was a sign. A sign or a metaphor. Something.

Lindsay now looked at Rudy for some sort of cue as to how to behave. "Well . . ." began Rudy, running a hand absently over the front of his shirt, "it's been good to—"

"Say," said Roy brightly, sweeping the three of them with an optimistic, merry look. "Whattya say we all get a drink of something and let you two catch up? My treat."

. . .

223

Rudy and Lindsay and Dinah and Roy sat around a tiny table at a makeshift café around a pool in Boy's Bay. Sharp figures cut in the blur of hot, stock-still, no breeze. They sat in silence, the air infused with everything they didn't say, speech having run aground in contemplation. Chinese lanterns were strung merrily behind them, held aloft by the almost-said, the about-to-be-said. Sweat glistened on Roy's forehead, shone dimly in the pale light of the colored lanterns, his light-blue shirt stuck fast to his moist back. Dinah crossed and uncrossed her legs, looking at Lindsay, noticing her honey-colored hair glowing faintly, her sad pale-green eyes fastened on something soothing in the distance, her slender face alert to her insides, to Rudy, her full lips parted. Dinah looked away. It was the face of a guileless, beguiling child. Slender as a smoothly drawn line, draped over her chair, rather than seated. Dinah shifted uncomfortably, feeling her weight all around her, an earthbound thing surrounded by so much more of herself on all sides, trapped, while Lindsay seemed to end almost as soon as she began, an economic, lightweight waif. A sheaf of wheat, a shaft of light, a moonbeam to Rudy's moon. While Dinah sat there; another planet, dangerously close, a collision in space, when worlds collide. Not enough orbit to go around. Seeing Lindsay's delicate, hopeful face, a face turned bravely toward the future, catching its light, she realized that she should never have done this. What had she been thinking? She wanted to go home. Whatever home she had that wasn't Rudy. Whatever little lean-to of a life she had without him.

Rudy cleared his throat. Dinah ran her hand over her hair in response. Her body was pressing in on her. People were milling about them, navigating their way through the unfriendly current of the air. Suddenly Roy slapped both his hands on both knees, startling everyone back into this reverie, this now, this unfortunate now.

"Weren't those fireworks *something!*" Roy said in a

forced, cheerful way, looking expectantly at the little assembled group.

"Beautiful," said Dinah, startled by the sound of her voice. She beamed artificially at Roy and nodded. A cloud of cigarette smoke floated by. Lindsay coughed absently.

"When did you get here?" Rudy said, looking pointedly at Dinah, guiding himself by her once-familiar star. Dinah wrinkled her nose slightly, considering.

"Let's see, when did we get out here, honey?" she said, looking at Roy. Two young boys ran through the tables by the pool, screaming. One of them held a sparkler above his head.

"We *just* arrived," replied Roy, happily looking from Rudy to Lindsay. "When did *you* get here?" he continued, with his head tilted to one side, focusing on Lindsay now. She squeezed her clasped hands tightly, glanced quickly at Rudy, then back at Roy.

"We've been out here most of the summer," she said nervously. Roy nodded at her in comprehension. The conversation had, once more, run aground, its motor dead. Roy continued to nod throughout, stopping only to wipe his brow. Rudy watched him through narrowed eyes.

"What do you do?" asked Rudy finally, crossing his arms across his chest. Both his legs and arms were crossed now; he sat wound around himself waiting for Roy's reply.

"Me?" Roy said, pointing to his chest as though isolating himself and an activity lodged there.

"Do," said Rudy. "What do you—"

"I'm a writer," answered Roy, remembering. "A screenwriter. Silk screen. No, I'm kidding—not about the screenwriting, about the silk-screen writing. I know what you do, though. Playwrighter. One of the all-time great contemporary playwrights." Rudy's eyes narrowed as he attempted to detect irony in the compliment.

"Mr. Right, I used to call him," chirped in Dinah

quickly. "Mr. Play Right." She smiled a painful smile, pushing her suddenly heavy cheeks off to each side to allow it. She turned to Lindsay. "Rudy tells me you're an interior decorator."

Lindsay's eyes widened slightly in astonishment. "When did he tell you that?" she said, looking from one to the other, from Rudy to Dinah and back again.

Rudy uncrossed his arms and legs, and unguarding himself briefly, cleared his throat. "In L.A.," he informed her casually. "I saw her when I was out in L.A. I thought I told you that. Didn't I tell you that?" Lindsay looked at Rudy speechlessly.

Roy leaned in, a mock, innocent expression on his handsome face. "Who's thirsty?" he asked, looking from one face to the other with his eyebrows raised expectantly, a social bee pollinating his favorite flowers with the sweet nectar of his mood. "I don't know about you, but those fireworks took every ounce of liquid out of me. Rudy? Beverage?"

Rudy looked almost relieved. "Sure," he said, his hands folded in front of him, his blue eyes glittering, hard to read. "I think we have to get them ourselves. Over there." He pointed vaguely over Dinah's head toward the house. Roy rose abruptly, looking at Rudy.

"Well, why don't we boys go get them, while the girls hold down the fort."

Rudy looked doubtful, but stood. "Fine," he said, pushing back his chair.

An announcement was made over the loudspeaker that the raffle was imminent, with the grand prize being a motorcycle and one week at Gurney's Inn.

"I'll have a rum and Coke," said Dinah to Roy with as much cheer as she could muster.

"Wine, please," Lindsay said to Rudy, the tiniest tweak of panic in her eyes as she pushed some blond hair off her face, revealing the strong, gleaming forehead beneath. Roy and Rudy headed off through the throng in the direction of the house. Dinah looked briefly at Lindsay, lips stretched in the direction of a smile. Suddenly, she turned her head and called after the disappearing Rudy and Roy.

"And maybe some cigarettes!"

Lindsay looked at her sadly, a doleful-eyed stalk of wheat waving in the musty air. "I don't think they heard you," she said to Dinah hesitantly.

Dinah straightened her rounded, aching back. "I don't really smoke anyway," she said. "At least not intentionally. I just thought . . ." Dinah trailed off, shrugging. "It seemed like a good idea at the time," she concluded halfheartedly, sitting back in her chair and looking at the starlit sky.

"You write soap operas," said Lindsay almost brightly. The two women regarded one another cautiously, mosquitoes buzzing around their heads. The smell of hot dogs wafted delicately through the night air.

"Well, one," said Dinah. "I write one soap opera. *Heart's Desire.*"

Lindsay nodded in comprehension. She sat straight in the middle of her chair, her white cotton dress open at the throat, revealing a tiny round diamond that glittered when she moved ever so slightly. "I think I've heard of that," she said. "I don't really watch much TV, though. I'm usually working during the day. And when I'm not, I'm . . . outside if I can be. I like to garden."

Dinah slapped a mosquito off the back of her arm. "Rudy mentioned that," she said, wiping the bug's corpse off her hand.

"What?" said Lindsay. A line trembled between her bright-green eyes. The raffle began.

"That you like to garden."

"I see," Lindsay said, the line neither smoothing nor

increasing. Dinah felt as though she was going to sneeze. She put her hand to her nose, stopping it. Lindsay watched her. "Do you have any hobbies?" said Lindsay finally, generously.

"Hobbies?" echoed Dinah hollowly. "Gosh, I don't know. Hobbies always sounded so, you know, like stamp collecting and kayaking and—"

"And gardening," interrupted Lindsay sharply, her mouth pursed, the line deeper now, keeping her eyes apart, her wits together.

Dinah's stomach made a hillbilly noise; she put her hand on her stomach to quiet it. "No," she said emphatically, stressing this point with her other hand. "*Not* gardening. That's somehow less . . . Republican." She looked over her shoulder at the house for assistance. None was forthcoming. She put her hand to her cheek, her forehead. Checking for fever. That's it; she was unwell. Nervous and unwell from all this talk about hobbies. From all these fireworks and men. "Gardening seems like a very . . . Zen thing to do. Calming. Simple."

"Well, it *is* calming. But I don't know how simple it is."

"No, I don't mean simple, like easy—I mean simple, like basic. Pure," assured Dinah. Lindsay's diamond sparkled, catching Dinah's eye. "Hey, I *wish* I had a hobby! Writing used to be a sort of hobby, but now that it's gone from inclination to obligation . . ." She shrugged helplessly.

Lindsay looked at her, an open, barely offended look, then ran her tongue over her lips. "You should try gardening," she offered quietly.

"I *will*," Dinah said gratefully, leaning forward to emphasize her intention. A trickle of sweat ran from under her left breast and made its way to her waist. She crossed and uncrossed her legs. Lindsay waved a mosquito away from the side of her head. The two women had come to their first standstill, the end of the hall of their initial exchange.

Rudy should be with this girl, thought Dinah. *And I should be with a less-male guy. I'm not female enough for a really male male. Then there's too much competitive energy. Two yangs don't make a right. The psychic said many soft men will come to me. A soft Japanese man . . . like a pet.*

"What brings you to Long Island?" said Lindsay, startling Dinah out of her reverie.

She frowned slightly and sighed. Why did everyone ask her this? Did she look so out of place? Probably, she concluded. "Not much," she admitted sheepishly. "There's a writers' strike in L.A., so . . . I thought I'd come here."

"Do you know many people here?"

"Many?" she frowned. "No, not many. No. Do you?"

"Some," she said. "Not many. But I'm here with Rudy."

Dinah nodded rhythmically. "I know," she continued, nodding idiotically. "That must be nice."

"It is," Lindsay said pointedly. "It is nice." The two women looked at each other, poised, ready for almost anything.

Why did I come here? thought Dinah. *What was my plan?* "That's nice," she said again, sadly, waving away a nonexistent insect. The announcer read the winning number in the raffle. The motorcycle had a home. Someone near the water screamed and jumped up and down. Dinah squinted through the crowd to see.

Lindsay smoothed her skirt and sat back. "Roy seems nice," she said.

Dinah nodded vaguely. "He does, doesn't he? I'm not with Roy, you know, we just met, really. He's my neighbor out here at Salter's Cottages."

"Ah," said Lindsay. "That's too bad."

"Well, maybe, maybe," said Dinah. "I don't really know him well enough to feel the full import of what a shame it is not to be with him, though."

"I see."

"Roy has a very complicated personal life. He doesn't need anybody to further complicate it."

"I thought you didn't know him well."

"Well, you don't really have to know some people well to know them well."

Lindsay's eyes narrowed. "What do you mean by that?"

Dinah was startled, realizing how the remark might have sounded. "Nothing, I . . ."

"Here we are!" Roy swooped down on them, bearing the drinks, shattering the tension into a thousand invisible tiny particles that then infused the air around them as their evening bore down on them as though they were pack mules. Roy placed a rum and Coke gingerly in front of Dinah. Rudy put a white wine in front of Lindsay. They both carried beers.

"Sorry we were so long," remarked Rudy, peering first into Lindsay's face and then suspiciously into Dinah's. "There was a *line*," he explained, sitting. Roy sat down too, taking a long pull on his beer. The chair squeaked.

"Did you two have a nice visit?" he asked Dinah happily.

Dinah gave him one of her darkest looks, as if this were all somehow his fault. Lindsay. Rudy. Men. Women. Everything. "Yes," she answered curtly. "We talked about hobbies."

"*Hobbies.*" Roy nodded with mock earnestness. "*Really?* We talked about writing a little," he said, looking from Dinah's face to Lindsay's and back again. Dinah successfully suppressed a smile.

230

"Writing and sports," added Rudy, taking Lindsay's lily hand in his.

Dinah felt sick and alone. Like an alien; a cyborg; a visiting, barely welcome thing. With everyone all around her in twos—or, in Roy's case, threes—ready to board the looming ark. Ready for the couple spot check she knew would inevitably come.

"What would guys do without sports, eh? That's what I want to know," Roy said, slapping a mosquito on his hand, then wiping it on his pant leg.

Dinah shifted uneasily, looking briefly at Lindsay and Rudy and their clasped hands, then away again. "That's so great, that guys have that whole male-bonding sports thing," she said miserably. "Women don't have anything like that."

Rudy looked at Dinah impatiently and sipped his beer. "What about girls' basketball?" he said.

"And volleyball?" Roy chimed in merrily.

Lindsay looked uncomfortable, clouds threatening at the back of her luminous face. Dinah was dumbfounded —looking first at Rudy, then at Roy in order of the remarks. "Have you ever watched women's sports?" she asked in her most generous voice, the chairwoman of the Benefit for the Doubtful.

Lindsay nodded appreciatively. "They're awful," she said in a low, conspiratorial voice, smiling slightly.

"Teams of women that look like those ladies at the airport who frisk you," Dinah said.

"*Exactly*," said Lindsay to Dinah, smiling, the hobbies' slight almost behind them. "You can't be serious," Dinah said, "that women have something comparable to men's sports."

"What about sewing bees?" said Roy, winking at Rudy. "What about the NOW organization? The ERA?"

"Be serious," said Dinah. "What do we have bonding-wise?"

"I don't know," said Rudy, ready to move on; this was threatening to become one of Dinah's troublesome subjects. "Women don't seem to have too much trouble bonding. And men do. So we talk about sports—but not just sports."

"Sports and work," said Roy wistfully.

"Right. And women talk about men," said Lindsay.

"Right," smiled Dinah.

Roy and Rudy gave each other a long, bored look. Roy tilted his head to one side, peering at Dinah. "I thought you said you talked about hobbies," he said archly.

"Hobbies as a means to the men end," rejoined Dinah.

Rudy sighed. "You can't imagine how sick I am of this whole man-woman conversation from women," he said.

"What man-woman conversation?" asked Dinah, uncrossing her legs and leaning forward almost conspiratorially. Lindsay also watched him carefully from her closer quarters.

"I don't know," he said in slight exasperation. "This whole thing about how it's a man's world." He looked at Roy and shrugged helplessly.

"But maybe if you hear it from so many women, there might be some truth to it . . ." said Dinah.

Roy shook his head and laughed. "What kind of truth? Objective truth?"

Dinah leaned farther in, scooting her chair forward, now addressing Roy. "Well, probably not," she began excitedly. "It's a pretty emotional subject. You might have to be a woman to appreciate what we're saying."

Lindsay leaned forward now, bringing Rudy's hand with her. "Women are second-class citizens," she said, then amended, looking at Rudy, "well, maybe first-and-a-half."

"It's a man's world," summarized Dinah, slapping

the flat of her right hand on the table for emphasis. Rudy looked at Dinah for a moment and began to say something, but he changed his mind and turned to face Lindsay. "In what way?"

Lindsay turned to him, fingering her necklace with her free hand. "Well, God, in most ways," she said, blotches beginning to appear on her cream-colored throat. "Economically, politically—men rule the world." She stopped abruptly on this particular dime and turned her face back to the table, her eyes resting on the wineglass before her.

"Hey, look," Dinah said, "it's just easier to be a man on this planet than a woman. In every way. Biologically you can procreate almost indefinitely. We can't. But you can start families even after you cease to have vision or teeth. You can delay the decisions of marriage and children while our limit looms ever larger. Please. Men make more money than women on jobs."

Rudy frowned slightly. "Well, that shouldn't be."

Dinah sat back. "Great. Well, maybe you can talk to some people and fix that. ERA my ass."

Roy leaned in eyeing Dinah ruefully. "Women porno stars get paid more than men porno stars," he said.

Dinah grimaced, but Rudy looked alert. "Is that true?" he asked.

Roy nodded happily. Dinah sighed. "Perfect. Demeaning for dollars."

Rudy shrugged. "Hey, you can't lay the blame on men for their biological advantage—"

"It's not your fault, it's your world," said Dinah. "But it does continue, so—"

"Well, that's *everybody's* fault," Roy said.

"Men occupy most positions of government," remarked Lindsay, her pale face less pink now, her free hand touching Rudy's arm in entreaty.

Roy finished off his beer and set the bottle down

on the table in front of him with a flourish. A check-mate.

"What about England?" he snarled brightly at Lind-say. "What about Pakistan?" he continued to Dinah, looking from one woman to the other. Dinah's heart was pounding.

"Exactly," said Rudy.

Dinah looked at him. What had she ever seen in him? Then she looked at Roy. What had she ever seen in any man?

"What about fucking Iceland?" laughed Dinah sar-castically. "And certain Amazonian tribes in the north-ern part of South America! But we're talking everywhere else! Every goddamn where else," she concluded breath-lessly. Lindsay's diamond sparkled at her throat. She touched it nervously. A cloud of cigar smoke blew by her face and she coughed daintily, four fingers covering her mouth.

Rudy shifted, his chair squeaked. "Maybe some of that has to do with a lot of women not trusting each other," he said. "Do you think that if a woman ran for office, other women would vote for her?"

Lindsay turned toward Rudy and regarded him curi-ously. "Maybe not," she said. "Because, as you say, women don't always trust each other."

"Yeah," said Dinah. "Because we've been brought up in a culture where you're taught that men are superior. Where men can trade in their older wife for a new younger one and no one frowns."

"And we're not blaming you for that," Lindsay added gently to Rudy, putting her hand on his arm. Then she looked shyly at Roy. "We're not saying that it's right or wrong. We're simply stating the way it is."

"The way it seems to be," agreed Dinah with a sharp nod.

Roy leaned in, his arms providing a safe circular harbor for his empty beer bottle. "Didn't that woman who ran for Vice-President—old Geraldine Ferraro—didn't she cry when they didn't win?"

"Please, this is just that shit that's out there," said Dinah. "It's just the type of thing that men would focus on about women politicians. I'm not sure if it's true that she cried. Hey, Nixon cried, too, asshole. Nobody talks about—"

"What do you mean, nobody talks about that? Jesus, look at him," Roy said ruefully.

"*You* look at him," said Dinah.

Rudy interrupted. "Look," he said, "men have to succeed in the world. That's the main thing they have to do. Women have to succeed, but the pressure isn't as extreme. It's not as disastrous if a woman isn't a success, let's face it."

"Yeah," said Dinah. "Men are the providers, women are the breeders. Rich men and beautiful women. Crinkly old geezers with young, luscious—"

Rudy interrupted, his face hard, set. "Incredibly beautiful people make me uncomfortable. It's like someone having this big powerful thing that they had nothing to do with acquiring."

Lindsay sat at his side and sipped her wine nervously while Dinah gave him a brief impassioned look, then said, "If a rich older man marries a poor young, beautiful woman, it's the Cinderella story. I do the same thing and I'm fucking the cabana boy. Look at that rumor about Cher, when she went with that young guy—"

"Rob Camilletti," Lindsay interjected.

"*Whatever*," said Dinah, acknowledging her briefly, then looking back at Rudy, then at Roy. "They said when she saw him that she told someone to have him washed and brought to her tent. Well, Cher said she never said that. So that's just that shit that's *out there*. That's the swap. Men are valued for something they achieve—

power and money, or success—and women are valued for beauty—a birth accident."

"Or effective plastic surgery," said Lindsay. "If a woman doesn't get married, it's a disaster. She's an old maid. If a man doesn't, he's an eligible bachelor."

"If he's rich," said Roy sadly. "And people can inherit money just as easily as they can inherit good looks."

Dinah smirked. Lindsay looked at her, then back at her lap. Rudy smiled. "And don't forget," he said, "women get those seven extra years."

"What seven extra years?" asked Lindsay.

Both women looked at both men blankly. A boat's horn sounded in the distance.

"Women live seven extra years longer than men on an average," Rudy said. "I'll swap you those seven years for this supposed power in the world."

Dinah's lips tightened and paled. "Fine," she said.

Rudy laughed scornfully. "Oh, sure, you say fine, but I've seen people at the end of their lives, and those seven years are pretty important then," proclaimed Rudy.

Dinah leaned in, her hands clasped in front of her, her knuckles white. "I was at this doctor's recently and I was talking about this guy at work and he said how old is he and I said 42 and he said, 'Well, that's young—for a man.' And do you know why it's young for a man and not for a woman? Procreation. It's the end of the line for starting over—that second family option. Eggs die at forty while sperm wriggles on till the end. So fuck your seven extra years. You can delay making any kind of commitment indefinitely—stall maturation in terms of settling down—just keep going out with younger and younger women whose biological clocks aren't—"

Roy interrupted, patting Dinah lightly on the shoulder in what she perceived as a patronizing attempt to calm her down.

236

"What about hair loss?" he asked her gently. "Women can't lose their hair, while men—"

Lindsay leaned forward now and interrupted Roy. "All men don't lose their hair," she said with some heat. "Twenty percent lose it at twenty, thirty percent at thirty, forty percent at forty, and on and on." She looked at Dinah. "My brother is a dermatologist. A bald dermatologist."

"So what you're saying is that if we live till a hundred we'll all definitely be bald," Rudy deadpanned.

"What we're saying is that half of you go bald in middle age while *all* of our tits get fallen and forlorn," said Dinah.

Roy nodded absently, leaning back again. "Anyway," he said, "all this is pretty transitional at this point. Most women work now, the balance of power is shifting. Women are coming into their own."

"Right," said Dinah ironically, running her hand through her hair. "Now women just have to work *and* mind the relationship."

"Oh, Dinah, please," said Rudy impatiently, "how did you ever mind the relationship?" He glanced at Lindsay briefly, then sipped his beer.

"How did I mind the relationship?! How did *you* ever mind it? I suppose it ground to a halt because I didn't fulfill my end of the bargain—which was no *end;* it was the whole thing—and it was no bargain, believe me." The color had drained from her face and seemed to have gathered in her throat, her neck. She touched her neck with one hand. It was hot. She felt light-headed and looked fiercely at her glass on the table in front of her.

Lindsay regarded her compassionately. "We've fallen between the cracks," she said almost timidly. "We're the generation that was brought up believing in making a good match—marrying well and having kids—then, when we were teenagers, we realized that we had to get a job, too. Or instead. I never figured out which, the message was so mixed up."

"Hey, you girls should just buck up and stop your whining," cheered Roy. "Be a man."

Rudy fought a smile and lost.

"You should start some heterosexual women's pride week," laughed Roy, continuing. "Your anthem could be 'I Enjoy Being a Girl.'" Rudy now joined in, laughing, "Or Helen Reddy's 'I Am Woman, Hear Me Roar.'"

Roy laughed harder now—both men were laughing helplessly, Rudy with one hand over his mouth, his eyes tearing. Lindsay and Dinah looked at one another pointedly as Lindsay slipped her hand out of Rudy's and finished off her wine.

"Oh, c'mon, ladies, c'mon," said Roy in an effort to be serious. "Don't forget—women can have multiple orgasms."

"And periods and twenty-three percent more body fat," said Dinah.

"And the thrill of childbirth," added Rudy. "And a longer, later sexual peak."

"Sure, to make up for menopause," said Lindsay, pushing one side of her smooth curtain of hair behind one ear.

"And how many women do you know who have had multiple orgasms?" Dinah added to Roy.

"Without a machine?" said Lindsay, laughing.

"Yeah," laughed Dinah, looking affectionately at Lindsay, her eyes shining. "'Cause God forbids you to get any oral assistance. Head being the thing you get in the first couple of weeks—or when they think you're leaving."

Rudy colored and looked at Dinah with disapproval. Lindsay laughed, a silent, hard laugh, her eyes bright with tears. Rudy moved his look of disapproval to her as she put her head down and continued to laugh mutely

238

into her lap, her shoulders shaking. Roy leaned toward Dinah intently.

"Yeah, well at least you don't have to have erections," he said. "What if you can't? Of course, you always can when you don't care. But eventually we can't—and sometimes before *eventually*—and that's humiliating."

Dinah stared at the glass in her hand, unseeing. "Twenty-three percent extra body fat," she intoned, shaking her head with dismay. "All to keep fetuses warm —what about a blanket—that's what I say."

"Or a fire," added Lindsay. Both women smiled an open smile at one another for one long, beaming moment, then looked away shyly.

"What about we can have heart attacks at thirty-nine?" said Roy. "While you while away the hours into your fifties—protected by estrogen."

"*Haunted* by estrogen," retorted Dinah, finished with the subject now, looking at her hands in her lap. Particularly the one without a wedding ring. There was a lull. A charged lull. Rudy looked at the empty space before him; Lindsay at her hands clasped in front of her; Roy at his empty beer bottle; Dinah at a mosquito crawling on her ringless hand.

Roy sighed and stretched. "Basically, it comes down to what my father used to say: 'Men think women are crazy and women think men are children.'"

"Yeah," said Dinah, "there are a bunch of sayings like that. What about, 'Men hate women for what they do and women hate men for what they are.'"

Lindsay leaned in to Dinah. "Or, 'Women don't feel what they know and men don't know what they feel—'"

Roy leaned in to Lindsay, interrupting. "Can I go back to something you said earlier?"

"Sure," she said doubtfully.

"I was just wondering what kind of machines give multiple orgasms. Vibrators, right?"

They stood at the crossroads—each of them heading their separate ways to their cars. Dinah clasped Lindsay's pale, cool hand, somehow hoping to pass the torch that she had been carrying for years. "It was nice meeting you," she said, trying to communicate something to her beyond the words—goodwill, good luck, peace—something. "Really," she added, squeezing Lindsay's hand for emphasis.

"Me too," said Lindsay, nodding her blond head rhythmically. "Me too."

Dinah took Roy's arm with one hand and raised the other in farewell.

"Good night," said Roy gaily.

"Good night," said Rudy to Dinah.

She smiled. "Don't do anything we used to do," she said.

"I'm going to cry," said Roy melodramatically. "I'm going to cry like Nixon."

And while Lindsay and Rudy looked on, Roy and Dinah disappeared over the hill and through the trees toward their car.

She said good night to Roy, good-bye to all that, and went home to her hideout. Tony was thrilled as ever to see her. Dinah let him out and got ready for bed, dismantling the personality she had painstakingly assembled all the livelong day. Before turning off the light and turning herself in to the sleep police, Dinah dialed her father's number once again and listened to it ring its rhythmic ring out into nowhere, to nothing. She hung up and went to sleep.

Hippopotamuses can behave very strangely toward each other. A father may bite off the head of his son and a captive adolescent may suddenly gore his mother to death with his huge canine tusks. That is why the females seek to simplify their domestic lives by staying together, consorting with males only to copulate.

10

She dreamed that she had a baby and didn't know who the father was. Maybe it was one of two people. But the thing that was remarkable about the birth was that it was so easy. She remembered wondering why everyone had always made such a fuss. And the baby. The baby was incredible. Very happy and very alert. Dinah thought how lucky she was to have gotten such a remarkable baby. A great baby, one she didn't even have to work at to make great. Looking closer at it, she noticed that it was partly black. It had close-cropped, black fuzzy hair on its tiny head. She couldn't recall how it had gotten partly black, but it wasn't a problem for her. She then breast-fed the baby and that was quite different from what she had expected. The baby wasn't very hungry. It seemed too busy looking at things to eat. She remembered hoping that Rudy wouldn't be too angry that it wasn't his. That this one wasn't and that he'd still want to have one with her. Actually, she hoped that the subject wouldn't come up at all. The subject of the great baby.

Then she dreamed she was in the courtroom of the Federal Aviation Administration, where the jury was about to hand down a decision in the recent crash of Dinah and Rudy's relationship. The black box sat on the table before the judge. The jury looked on as he reached down to open the box to play back the tape of the conversation that went on between them before they crashed and burned. Dinah strained to see, to hear, to try to stop them. The judge pushed "play" and Dinah awoke, sweating in bright sunlight.

She heaved herself out of bed with a sigh. What doesn't kill you makes you stronger. Wasn't it Nietzsche who had said that? Nietzsche who hated women and died of syphilis? What didn't kill men made them stronger. What didn't kill women . . . made men breakfast. She went to the kitchen and opened the refrigerator, removing three eggs. She broke one, then another, then all three, then scrambled them in a bowl and poured them into a buttered frying pan. She peeled off three pieces of bacon and put them into a pan over a low flame, then got a can of Diet Coke from the refrigerator and opened it. She called Tony, who wandered lazily out of the bedroom and toward the front door, which Dinah was holding open. Suddenly, Tony began to run; wagging his tail, he ran through the door and up to Rudy Gendler, who stood on the path just outside the door looking like someone who was listening to music in the next room. Faint, beautiful music.

"Can I come in?" he asked.

Dinah passed her hand through her matted morning hair and halfheartedly smoothed her wrinkled nightgown. "Sure," she said softly. "I was just getting over you . . . but . . . sure." She held the door for him and Rudy brushed by her and into the cabin. Tony followed him in excitement. "I was making breakfast," she said. "Want some?"

"Yeah," he said. "Sure. *You're* cooking?"

"It's just a phase," said Dinah, scraping her eggs onto a plate and setting them before Rudy, who sat at the table. She turned the bacon and went to the refrigerator to prepare another breakfast for herself, and pour Rudy a glass of juice. She removed three new eggs and scrambled them. She drained the bacon and placed the strips gingerly on Rudy's plate, the glass of juice next to it, while Rudy looked on benignly. He began eating slowly, continuing to watch Dinah putter uncharacteristically around the kitchen. She moved the eggs around the pan slowly, almost hypnotically. "How did you find me?" she asked.

"My sister," he replied, chewing.

"Ah," she said. "Yes."

It was as if there were no blood in what they said. As though it were embalmed. "Maybe if I'd cooked before, we'd be together," she continued, as she scraped her eggs from the pan and onto a plate. As though she were talking about another couple she only peripherally knew, in whom she was only interested mathematically.

Rudy swallowed his food and sighed. "It isn't the cooking, Di . . ." he began. "It is her . . . her absolute, simple conviction that she wants me. She's sure. You were never sure. Oh, you loved me, all right, but you were never certain that you wanted to be with me. She wants to be with me, more than . . . anything else—not to the exclusion of everything else, but more than anything else. And that's really nice. You were my companion, but you wouldn't stay."

Dinah was looking down at her right hand. "My nail is breaking," she said softly, raising her first finger for him to see. "See? Right at the quick . . ."

Rudy held up his hand to silence her. "Let me finish. She may not be the companion you were, but she *is here.* I didn't have the energy to wait for you anymore. I want

244

a home life. And she wants me enough to give me what I want. You just love me and it gives me no peace—it gives you no peace. I have to have peace. My work was so screwed up by the last time with you. So much tumult and activity. I couldn't do my work and that was the thing that drove me crazy and would always drive me crazy, and in my world, that can't happen." He stopped talking abruptly and breathed.

Dinah placed her plate of bacon and eggs across from Rudy and sat, looking at him briefly as she did so. She sipped her Diet Coke thoughtfully. Rudy moved his eyes slowly along the smooth curve of his plate. Somewhere in the distance a car horn sounded. Tony stared at Rudy woefully, hoping for some small handout in return for his patient, pathetic demeanor. Rudy ignored him, wishing to be clear. Clear of any obligation in a correct, compassionate way, functioning crisply, as though he were clairvoyant and all right. He looked at Dinah, took a lot of himself out of the look, kept it in reserve, cleared his throat.

"I have to make my mark," he said thoughtfully, now noticing the dog. "Maybe this next play will really be a big success and then I'll have made my mark and the pressure will be off." He tore off a small strip of bacon and passed it to the attentive dog, who snapped it up hungrily, gratefully. Rudy pulled his hand back protectively. Dinah watched as though recording it for later. Dispassionate, alone.

"How much more of a mark can you make?"

Rudy sighed and brushed the fly away. "I don't know. Maybe it's just a game I play with myself to stay productive or whatever—but there you go. I have a lot of drive, so I have to make up a destination." He looked at her almost imploringly. "I have to do something, or what am I going to do?"

Dinah smiled sadly, looked out the window. Wished

she were indifferent to this inevitable outcome. This particular outcome.

"We had so much evidence that we shouldn't be together." She shrugged. "I was sort of . . . trying to amass some that we should. What is it they say, 'Better the devil you know . . .' You know, if you can't live with him and you can't live without him, live near him."

"Dinah, I'm not going to invest myself that much in someone again. I'm not going to be a gambler. I beat myself up about how stupid I was with you. Look . . . each case is persuasive—the case of being together and not being together—till you get to the conclusion, and then the other case begins. Hey, you never really liked being with me—you said you felt I was so . . . what was it? Critical." Dinah shifted and crossed her legs.

"With you, I never felt good enough. Like I was always . . . fucking up. You were either mad at me or . . . not. Never really happy. I mean, it was either punishment or non-punishment. Reward was non-punishment. You know, dogs are trained better. If you weren't getting exactly what you wanted, you weren't getting anything at all."

Rudy pushed his remaining eggs around his plate and cleared his throat. "So, Dinah . . . why are you coming around again? If I'm so bad, why aren't you somewhere else—relieved?"

Dinah laughed. "I'm not the relieved type. And I guess"—she shrugged again—"I love you."

"Yeah, well," he sighed. "I love you too, but . . ."

Dinah interrupted, "So, I'm *who* you want, but I don't give you *what* you want, so . . ."

Rudy interrupted. "We can't be together. We don't make each other—"

"I know," Dinah interrupted, her mouth full of eggs. "It's not a rational thing, you know—my being here. And my loving you isn't—"

Rudy interrupted, "Your paradox is that you're a center of attention who's drawn to centers of attention."

Dinah laughed. "It's like mixing oil . . . and oil."

"Hon, you don't really have any big domestic interests. So there's no home thing to share."

She swallowed some soda. "Hey, it's easier to domesticate an intellectual than it is to intellectualize a domestic."

Rudy nodded vaguely. "Yeah, but that can be interesting, though, you know—helping to educate someone, guiding them, watching them learn or take more shape."

"Sort of put them through Girlfriend University?" she said. "But anyway, if you do it that way, then they're learning just to please you. Not necessarily out of some . . . instinct or passion of their own. It's not a natural impulse. And this is not about Lindsay. I liked her. She seemed smart."

"She *is* smart. She's reserved and . . . a good person. But look, I can't help wanting what I want. Other people have it. And I don't want to be made to feel needy for wanting it. I don't want to be critical. I want someone on the team—and I realize it's a tough membership. And I can't stand the *sound* of me a lot of the time. I say to myself, 'Stand it! Stand it! Say what you think!' 'Cause most of the time, I don't say what I think."

Dinah regarded him steadily, holding her tepid can of soda in her right hand, as her left-handed fingernails picked at the skin on her raw thumb. She smiled. "It's funny," she said softly. "You're afraid to seem stupid. I'm afraid to feel stupid."

Rudy frowned, then relaxed, drawing the corners of his mouth down lightly in reluctant agreement. "I think that's so."

"I thought you'd think so," she said, laughing slightly. "You're so cynical."

He tilted his head to one side, smiling. "I'm not *so*

cynical. I'm appropriately cynical for my age and experi-ence." He leaned forward now, his arms down on the table, his face open. "Dinah, your life is bigger than mine is, and I was always afraid of being taken over by you. And I sort of want to be taken over, but . . . in a good way. Look, every situation has its compromises—don't you think I know that? I'm starting to see what they will be with Lindsay and I don't know if I'll be able . . ." he sighed. "God, *marriage*. All these people's illusions that they're putting out on a tray at a wedding. It's so compli-cated and twisting that it's impossible to say ' . . . and I will to you . . . and you and I will both . . . and we . . . and our lives will . . .' I want to just scream out, 'How the fuck do you *know*? . . . who knows what will happen?' It's like the nice ones are boring and the smart ones are difficult; so in the end, you're all difficult."

Dinah chewed, her mouth full of eggs and bacon now, and swallowed the whole thing down. The food stuck, the bacon perhaps lodged in sideways, the eggs compounding the problem. Her face turned red and she began to choke. She put her hand to her mouth and stood. Rudy was looking at his plate at first.

"Well, it's not funny," he said. He looked at her now and saw that she wasn't laughing. "What's the matter?" said Rudy in muted alarm. "Are you all right?"

Dinah walked to the sink and tried to breathe. Couldn't. Her eyes filled with tears. She panicked. Turned to Rudy. Couldn't speak. Couldn't breathe.

"Oh, God," said Rudy. "Oh, God, come here." Dinah was bright red now and doubled over trying to remember how the choking sign from the coffee shop read. Rudy stood behind her and hit her on the back. Nothing. Dinah gasped for breath. None came. Rudy now put his arms around her from behind and hit her hard with both hands between her ribs. Once. Twice. Three times and a chewed-up mass of breakfast flew out of Dinah's mouth.

She stood gasping, with Rudy's arms around her, holding her from behind.

"Breathe," he told her gently. "Breathe." Dinah slowly sat on the floor and put her head down. Her heart was beating hard and her head ached. Rudy knelt down beside her, she put her arms around his waist and put her head on his shoulder. They were sitting on the cabin kitchen floor, holding each other quietly.

"Your black swan from hell lives on," she said finally.

"There's more than one person for everyone—you'll see," he whispered to her after a while.

Dinah's eyes stung, her throat now dry and sore. "I don't believe that. I wish I did, but I don't." She sighed. "I believe . . . I believe that love is . . . rare and . . . when you find it—"

"You wouldn't be happy in New York. And you would always end up leaving and going back to L.A."

"What are you, clairvoyant? You should play the stock market. How do you know?"

"It's what I observe."

"What you observe or what you fear?"

"Both, probably. Relationships should be about pleasure."

"Sure, *yours*."

"Di—okay, not *about* pleasure. That's more of a by-product, but . . ." He cleared his throat, began again, "Look, it didn't work before. And my therapist says that people don't change—not fundamentally."

"Then why go to a shrink?"

Rudy shook his head. "Well . . . you can change a little." He cleared his throat again and continued. "I think that you say everything to me that you couldn't say to your parents as a child. The objections that you could never raise or articulate." Rudy stopped and sighed. "You know, Dinah, sometimes I don't want to be understood. I just want to be . . . someone. Being under-stood can get so . . . intrusive."

"So, what do you want to be? Admired, serviced, to make yourself over into some new person?"

Rudy just looked at her and brushed some hair off of her forehead. Traced her cheek with his hand. Dinah watched him quietly. He leaned toward her now. His lips moved to hers. She shoved him. They sat looking at one another, post-shove, surprised and glaring. Rudy shoved her back.

"Why do you keep coming around me if you don't want me?" Dinah's face was hot now. Red. Her wrinkled nightgown stuck to a circle of perspiration on her back. She shoved Rudy harder this time, feeling as though she were fighting for her life.

"Me?!" she said. "Me coming around *you!"*

Both were breathing harder now as Rudy shoved her once again in a rough, albeit restrained, way. After all, she was a girl. Dinah fairly leapt on him now, her hands around his neck.

"You started it!" she continued. "You came to L.A. and slept with—"

Rudy's hands grabbed Dinah's around his neck, his suntanned face livid, his eyes like boiled fruit. He easily pulled her hands away, pushing her off him. Dinah sat back on the floor, her nightgown bunched around her knees.

"You just want me to sort of—"

Rudy interrupted, smoothing his shirt. "I don't want—"

Dinah yanked her nightgown down back over her knees. "Wait for you," she interjected. "My whole life waiting for you, sleeping with you, while you—"

Rudy waved her away and started to rise. "Do what you want! Jesus, you're not really worth the—"

But his thought remained unfinished as Dinah leapt

250

on him again, sending him over onto his back, attempting awkwardly to straddle his chest, her nightgown ripping straight up the back in the process. Rudy pushed Dinah off him, using a fair portion of his strength. She fell onto her side, weak and winded. Tony ran over, wagging his tail, trying to join in the game. Rudy held Dinah down, red-faced and white-knuckled, keeping her at arm's length, at bay, at least. When convinced she would do him no further immediate harm, he released his grip and attempted to rise.

"You selfish—" she said.

Rudy got to his feet, his hands on his knees halfway up, composing himself. "I can't do this anymore," he said, half to himself, a realization, a relief.

"Inflexible—" she muttered now, sitting up herself and pulling her knees to her chest and her nightgown over her knees. She pushed herself back along the floor till she was against the wall, watching him through narrowed eyes, breathing hard.

"Let's just stop," he said.

"Fine," she said with some effort, swallowing.

"So Dinah, what if I changed and I was no longer inflexible or dissatisfied—arrogant—whatever negatives you perceive me to possess—who's to say that you would still want me? Let's say I had a car wreck and sustained a blow that made you experience me as the person you want me to be?"

"Yeah. So? What are you saying?"

"I'm saying that . . . I'm saying that maybe you're just getting off on bitching and moaning."

Dinah gazed at Rudy for a long moment, absorbing his remark, placing his face, putting it in perspective. She felt as though she was haunting the same house—only it had been redecorated. She looked down at her right hand. "My nail is broken off," she remarked. "It's gone."

Rudy stood poised at the door. Dinah looked from her hand back in his direction. Starting at his feet and working back up to his dearly departing face. "This is it then. No more contact," she said.

Rudy slowly moved farther through the door and hesitated there.

"I don't see why we can't talk . . . sometime," he said in a low voice, not facing her. Dinah just looked at him with all the impassivity she could muster, her chin on her knees. Tony sat between the two of them, looking forlornly from one to the other. Rudy scratched his chin and sighed. "But then I guess that's like having my cake and eating it too."

"Having your cake and *talking* to it too," Dinah said, closing her eyes now and putting her forehead on her knees so that she couldn't see Rudy holding the screen door open and looking back down on her.

He cleared his throat one last time saying, "You know, if you'd have come to New York that time like I told you not to, we'd probably still be together."

With that, the door slammed behind him, knocking the broom into the radio, turning it on.

> You made me leave my happy home,
> You took my love and now you're gone
>> since I fell for you.
> Love brings such misery and pain;
>> I know I'll never be the same since I fell
>> for you.
> Well it's too bad and it's too sad but I'm
>> in love with you.
> Oh, you love me then you snub me, oh,
>> what can I do?
> I'm still in love with you.
> I, I guess I'll never see the light,

I get the blues most ev'ry night since I fell
    for you,
  since I fell for you.

Dinah sighed. "Bye," she whispered. "Thanks for saving my life."

Tony went to Dinah, his tail wagging, and attempted to crawl through her arms and legs onto her lap, to lick her face. Dinah petted him absently, feeling as though her hands were filled with cool, narrow air. Anxiety. She clasped her hands together and, in effect, wrung them. Like someone in a French novel, she wrung her hands, but like someone in an American one, she sat with a dog in her lap, doing so, listening to this mocking, sad song. "Bye," she repeated, her eyes on Tony's brown-and-white fur, feeling frightened and jammed. She pulled the dog to her and wept into his musty fur. Tony licked her face. Dinah wept harder, feeling somehow as though Tony recognized her pain and was sympathetic. The dog pulled back in an effort to lie on his back and have his stomach scratched. Dinah cried harder, pushing him away. "Everything has its price," she said. She stood heavily and crossed to the radio, turning it off, then shuffled back to her bedroom, got into bed and pulled the covers over her head.

She was frightened and perfectly calm. Long-winded on shortcomings. She couldn't get at the thing in herself that was vulnerable and safe and her. She was frightened and cozy. Nestled in her fear. Hidden behind talk. Lurking somewhere between a pronoun and a preposition.

She was the type of person who liked to iron things out, so she usually looked for wrinkled situations. So, here she was in the type of hell that was heaven for her. Full-throttle struggle. World of shit. Her weakness, in effect, was part of her strength. Her strength was a sort of result of her weakness. Whatever. Her loving led her to where she was not wanted. So she refused to tag along.

She bore down and tried to birth that bright penny of pain that she carried, but no, but no. How could she be this girl? Not this girl, no, not this girl. No. She never wanted to be this self-pitying, lost. . . . No. A carefree girl. Yes. Oh, yeah.

So she put down her head, her cowardly, unwieldy dread. She lay down in that dark sea that tossed and turned her, scorched the white angelic sheets that now burned her. Dinah lay down in an attempt to put this thing to rest. Tumbling over and over it all in her mind. What could I have done, what good can I do? A man like an umbrella, sheltering me from harm . . . that's not the way, that's not right. And now here she lay back in the dark woods, the dark words, far from home, lost in the place of how to let go. To find the thing in herself that she had looked for in him. That's no way, that's not right. Clutching a pole in the raging sea. The pole, she thought, was Rudy, she was the raging sea. Wishing some warm voice would rise like a sun in her cold world.

Her mind churning, burning . . . oh, for a little perspective to throw on the fire that was burning in her head. Dinah could feel herself staring out of her head. She rolled over and picked up the phone and, once again, dialed her father's number. She listened to it hypnotically ringing its rhythmic ring.

As she was about to hang up, a voice answered. Her father's plaintive voice. "Daddy?" said Dinah, a mantra from deep within her mind popped out of her mouth mid-prayer. "Daddy—it's me."

"Hi, baby, long time no hear," he said, sounding a bit sleepy.

"Did I wake you?" she said, folding herself up—putting her head on her knees, holding the phone like a security blanket. "No, no—I was just lying here—what's up?"

"Daddy—do you think a wife should know how to cook?"

He laughed. "Well, gee, I don't know, honey—I guess it's sort of nice, but it's not necessarily essential. I mean, your mother sure can't cook. None of my wives could cook, for that matter."

"Yeah, but you're not married to any of them anymore."

"You can say that again," he said, laughing. "But not because they couldn't cook."

"Why then?"

He sighed. "I'm a romantic, I guess. It's childish, I know. I'm one of the fools. But . . . if you love and are loved in return, well, that's it. And I guess I'm still seeking what I've always sought—passion. And I know it fails, but I have known great passion and I guess I'll always seek it. But passion is a, you know, short-lived thing. Three years seems to be my limit. One of the problems today is that people live together longer 'cause people live longer." There was a brief silence while Dinah sat in the quiet overhang of her considering, of her crazy, drinking in her father's rare voice. Finally, he spoke. "Why, baby—has somebody tried to make you cook?"

Dinah laughed and she closed her eyes. "No, Dad, not really. I just . . ." She trailed off.

"Dinah," said her father, "some people are for marrying and some people are for loving."

Dinah straightened. "What do you mean?"

Her father laughed a long, bewildered laugh. "Well, that maybe you're like me. I was always drawn to women who didn't want me. I found their . . . indifference attractive. I don't know, it just seems like my wiring in this area was crossed. I wasn't interested in women that were interested in me. I found that boring. Well, now, in my old age, I realize that it would've been a lot better to be bored than killed." Dinah tilted her head in attempted comprehension. She petted Tony, who slept at her side, with her free hand, absently. Her father continued. "So, it seems to me, four marriages later when it's probably too late, that maybe some of us have to pick mates out of our heads, rather than out of our . . . feelings . . . our hearts. That that . . . thrill we feel when we meet certain people isn't love at all, but some . . . neurotic flash, and a reason to stay away rather than pursue. I always pursued it, but don't do what I did, do what I'm saying. Go where you're wanted. Relationships should maybe be about safe . . . about . . . about yes . . . instead of all that other stuff. 'Cause that stuff dies down anyway, and then who are you with? Look at me. I'm all alone. Oh, I wouldn't trade a lot of it. That passion. Those. But you're still young, you're still young. You've got a good mind. Choose some-one with that. I'd like to see you with a man you look happy with."

"Me, too, Daddy," she said softly. "Pop?"

"Yes, daughter."

"Would you want to be a woman?"

He stifled a yawn, saying through it, "Would I want to be a woman? No, I think it's more difficult to be a woman. I'm complicated enough. What is it they say? 'Men are victimized by their sexuality and women are victimized by men.' "

"Who says that?"

"I don't remember, my friend Sydney in Palm Springs, I think." He sighed. "Four marriages. Can you believe it? You know sometimes I think it was a way of staying youthful. You look into an old face—a face your age—and you think, 'I'm old.' You look into a young new face and you think, 'I'm young!' Maybe it's borrowing on their youth. Sometimes I felt like a sort of vampire. I loved the beginnings of relationships. I would just feast on all the white lean meat of a new situation. A situation filled with possibilities and . . . and then you hit the gris-tle and bone of who you both really are." He laughed.

"I'm talking to you with my bridges out in my lower mouth."

Dinah smiled, hugged her knees harder, loved her father more, loved in an effort to feel love, to be loved, to close the distance between her and—what? Everything. Everything out there at arm's length. The laughter through the door.

"Are you all right, sweetheart?" her father continued.

Dinah said, "Yes, Pop—I'm fine. I'm just . . . I'm just waiting to play the major chord after the minor one. You know, unless I'm struggling, I don't think there's anything going on."

Her father laughed. "Well, baby, all I can tell you is don't try to look for a bottom line in all this. As far as I can see, the fucker keeps shifting. But, I promise you this —if I get to it, you can have some of mine. Snort a little of my bottom line. Hey, that rhymes! How 'bout that!" Dinah laughed. She turned off the light and got under the covers.

"That's great, Daddy."

"Okay, sweetheart—I'm going back to sleep now."

"Me too, Dad. Good night."

"I love you, baby."

"You too, Pop."

She did what any sane, heartbroken person in her prone position might do. She turned on the TV. There was a show on about people with hideous facial deformities. The host said, "If everyone put their problems into the middle of the table—I bet that they'd want theirs back."

Yes, thought Dinah. Yes. Heartbreak over deformity. Yes. What were they saying now? Children with these kinds of impediments were often sensitive, talented people. Yes? "I want people to get beyond what I look like and see that I'm a good person." Okay. Yes. Life some-

257

times gives to people by taking away. The walking wounded can possess a remarkable gait. She turned the channel. The news was on. AIDS patients were storming the Federal Building to protest the difficulty—the impossibility of getting AZT or DDI unless one was rich or dying. Put all of your problems in the middle of the table. She considered marshaling herself, deputizing herself. Hey, she had her health. She had a job, a car, a dog, a house, no facial deformities. What would she do with a Real Problem? Somehow she thought that she would do better with another kind of problem. She could rise to a higher occasion. High Expectation, Low Outcome. No waiting.

"Race you to the end of my grief," she said to Tony. He wagged his tail in excitement. Dinah scratched his woolly head. "You won."

She felt like an unmatable thing whose counterpart was some rare, fragile creature who was only to be found in China or Outer Mongolia and who would surely die in the crossing.

She switched the channel. Laurence Olivier stood over Merle Oberon's dying body in a bedroom in Yorkshire.

"Cathy you loved me! What right had you to throw love away for the poor fancy you felt for Linton? Because misery and degradation and death, and nothing that God or Satan could inflict would have parted us. You, of your own will, did it."

Dinah groaned and changed the channel. "I *am* Heathcliff," she insisted to Tony, who crawled to her wagging his tail and licked her face.

Now, on the TV Rose sits in the front seat of a car looking through the open window at Blaine standing dramatically in the snow. They gaze at each other hypnotically through the large white flakes of the soap-opera snow that gathers on Blaine's jacket without melting. Rose writes her number on a slip of paper and passes it through the window to the blond man in the snow. He slips the number into his pocket. "You're such a girl," he says, leaning through the window and kissing her briefly on the mouth, his pale hair covered in shards of paper snow. "In what way?" Rose asks almost demurely, lowering her heavily lashed eyelids. "In the best way." Blaine smiles his startled, recently-thrust-in-sunlight smile, then strolls off through the swirling snow, his hands thrust deep in his pockets. Rose watches him go, a dreamy smile playing on her lovely, sad face as the camera zooms in to close up and they cut to an Oil of Olay commercial.

━━━

Dinah reached into her bag, rummaged around and found a pen, then searched the house for some paper, couldn't find any and finally wrote on the back of a manila envelope.

My brain like a car drives through what you are saying. I can hear it all around me, among it, nodding. The hum of the motor, of my mind revving. I am driving, driving into the next moment, hop on, feel the breeze. The roof of the car, the skull, windshield eyes, steer with my mouth. Veering all over the highway. Skidding. Boon companion. He is my boon companion. I brought myself up, all the while hoping, like a relay, someone would relieve me of my task filled with nuance, with oh so quiet desperation. My mind the car purrs, warms its motor and drives right over my hand. I soft into you, creeping into your corners for a look-see, a be-here anon.

My crazy, a cream, it melts into my mouth with a sweet taste. I have it here in the palm of my head where he loves me, bump, there's the ceiling, bump smack up against my limits they press me. Someone outbid me in my bid for immortality. He's there out there somewhere in the not-dead, the newly not-dead, the lively not-dead. Help me see it as all just one thing bump *the ceiling. The motor idles. I wait in the darkness trying to shape it into words or is it all one thing? Or is it all one thing? Or is it all one thing? Surf the brain waves, feel the curl.*

The whole love thing doesn't sit right with me. A bad fit, more epileptic than tailored. I love you, it's a round thing, round and running, bump *tick-tock. Some smart thing out there somewhere cracks the whip of his crazy, raises the welts on my haunches, rides me till dawn, rides me like a beast.*

House sprained but not broken. She waits for her beatings.

I'm who you want but my what is faulty which then chews into my who-ness. My, I thought I loved you-ness. My eeny meeny miney mo.

It can be so relaxing to unravel the world ball. Let the yarn bounce, bounce, bouncing down the stairs of the page.

"Hello?"

A voice outside her window. Roy's voice. A warm sun rose in her cold world. Dinah straightened and put down her pen. "Roy?" she called hesitantly.

"Yo," he replied. "Any loyalty soufflé left?"

Dinah smiled, swung her legs off the bed, stood and padded to the door. She opened it. Roy stood in the doorway, framed in sunlight, carrying the paper, smiling. Dinah regarded him happily. "You look like a hero," she said.

"What kind of hero?" he asked suspiciously.

"*My* hero."

Roy looked at her more closely now. "Are you all

right?" Dinah shrugged and wandered back into the kitchen, Roy in tow. "Mr. Fun was here, wasn't he?" he said. "I thought I saw him on the path."

Dinah poured them both a glass of juice. "I'm going to end up alone." She sighed.

"You can't use the words 'end up' at your age."

"Yeah, but you know what they say—as you get older the pickings get slimmer, but the people sure don't." Dinah sat now and put her head down on the table.

"Who said that?"

"My friend Connie," Dinah now looked up at him, her face open, almost beseeching.

"He says he loves me, but . . ."

Roy sat across from her and leaned forward, his face earnest. "It doesn't matter if he loves you, it matters how he treats you," he said. "Hey, husbands that kill their wives love them. Some parents that beat their kids love them. Love is secondary. It's how you're treated."

Dinah nodded miserably. "Yeah," she said. "My father loved me and I never saw him. He might as well not have loved me. So, I guess I confuse love with absence. Which is perfect. I can have an entire relationship with nothing going on from the other side. When nothing becomes enough, anything more becomes unsettling. Rudy is, on some level, as attached to me as I am to him, only he's more attached to his idea of how he should be treated, and obviously, I'm not." She sighed and shook her head sadly. "But I still don't get how he could treat me this way."

"Probably 'cause you let him," he said. "Hey, if you understood why he acted the way he did—what would that do? I mean, if he killed you, would it make any difference why? As if, if, it were because of some deficiency of yours, it would be okay. Is it ever okay to hurt someone? Is there ever a just cause? If the reason was some conflict in him that you didn't cause—well, there's a reason, but probably not a just cause."

"My father says that I should pick someone out of my head, rather than my heart, because my emotional wiring's all fucked up."

Roy shook his head. "Naw, 'cause then what if you're like Garrison Keillor and you don't know someone is right for you until decades later?"

"Do I look like Garrison Keillor to you?" she said. "Besides, do you really think that this is the love of Garrison Keillor's life or just some twilight affair?"

"What I always was afraid would happen is that," began Roy seriously, "if I married someone for less than the right reasons, then the day after the wedding, I'd probably meet the love of my life. I mean, we can't give up the search."

"But you *have* to at some point," fretted Dinah.

"No, you don't. I don't believe that. People win the lottery."

"*Three* people win the lottery."

"Hey, if you like being beaten, you should—"

Dinah interrupted. "I don't like being beaten so much as starved." Her eyes filled with tears and she looked down.

Roy sat back and said gently, "Hey, it's like Steely Dan says, 'Any major dude with half a heart will surely tell you my friend/Any minor world that falls apart will come together again.' "

Dinah wiped her eyes and put her elbows on the table, her chin supported by both hands. She looked at Roy curiously. "Are you happy?"

Roy smiled. "Among other things, yes. Happy is one of the assortment of things that I am at any given moment. And you will be again, too. You don't have to believe me right now, but it's true."

Dinah smiled. "You're a very nice man."

"Sure," said Roy. "Exactly the type you don't go for."

"Well," she said, "maybe when I'm feeling better and you don't have two relationships going on at once . . ." She shrugged. "Who knows?" she smiled. "Who knows what?—well, who maybe, but not what."

"I beg pardon?"

"Nothing."

"Let me ask you something," he said. "If you meet an A-minus guy who doesn't like you and a B-plus guy who does, who do you like?"

"The A-minus," she answered simply. "What about you?"

"Me?" He sipped his juice, shrugging. "I use the B-plus till I can get the A-minus."

NORTH OF THE BOTTOM LINE

▬▬▬

Rose stands gravely at Blaine's bedside. Thin tubes trail down from bags filled with pale liquids and lie buried in his arms. The TV is on in the high corner of the room, showing a basketball game with no sound. The Knicks, Blaine's favorite team, are losing. His eyes, though, are closed now, unaware of this impending loss, unaware of Rose standing helplessly at his bedside, watching his breath rise and fall, rise and fall, rolling like a gentle tide. A nurse takes his pulse, then checks the green line on the black board monitoring his vitals. She looks bored, efficient. In the distance, one faintly hears doctors being paged and carts of food rolling slowly by.

"How is he?" Rose asks the nurse hesitantly.

"Are you a relation of the patient?"

Rose straightens slightly. "His wife," she says, meeting the nurse's steady gaze. "His ex-wife," she admits as if coerced.

The nurse regards her severely, smoothing her white starched skirt as she does so. Something in Rose's demeanor, though, allows her to soften slightly and reply. "His condition is critical," she informs Rose crisply. "Quite honestly, I don't know what's kept him going this long." Rose's eyes fill with tears as she looks from the nurse to Blaine's pale, sleeping face, his wispy blond hair standing out lightly from his head, his forehead curving nobly above his sickly face. The nurse checks her chart and starts out of the room. "Visiting hours are over in ten minutes, miss," she says, striding out into the hall, leaving the door ajar.

Rose begins to cry in earnest now. Her shoulders tremble with the effort of emotion, ragged breaths shake her body like an angry parent. "Blaine," she cries softly, "Blaine."

Gingerly she sits on the bed next to him, her strawberry-blond hair draped over one shoulder, falling halfway down her back. Her hand seeks his, clutches it and kisses it. Seeing his wedding ring makes her cry even harder. Blaine stirs and his eyelids flutter slightly, trying to focus on the commotion occurring over his head. His eyes finally adjust, registering a sickly disbelief. "Rosie?" he says hoarsely, "Is that you, Rose?" The effort of speech proves too great for him and he begins coughing, a frightening cough from deep within him. Rose first looks startled and then alarmed.

"Don't talk—oh, I'm sorry . . . I thought . . ." Her crying recommences, making a sort of duet of crying and coughing.

Blaine's cough subsides first. "I'm glad you came," he says weakly. "I've . . . missed you."

Rose sniffs loudly, looking at Blaine's ghostly hand, which she grips fiercely in her own, hot tears falling on his knuckles. "Remember that time I made you dessert? Something with bananas, and I chopped the bananas on one of the wooden kitchen surfaces?" Here she stops to wipe her nose, which has started to run, to drip. "And in the morning, you looked at me all stern and you said, 'You didn't chop the bananas *here*, did you? Oh, God, look at this!' And there were these little knife slices in the wood. I felt just awful, awful and stupid. You said, 'You should've used a chopping block,' and I said, 'Can't you sand it or something?' and you laughed this creepy laugh and I said, 'I'm sorry, I thought 'cause it was wood, it was all right.' And you said, 'This is not your area.' "

At this Rose begins sobbing anew. Fresh, hacking sobs. Blaine looks confused and tired.

"You came to my deathbed to tell me this?"

Rose leans over to Blaine's bedside and gets herself two Kleenex with one hand without releasing Blaine's with the other. She blows her nose loudly. Blaine averts his eyes politely. "I just came to say I was sorry . . . sorry about the grooves in the wood, about leaving the sunroof open that time. Sorry that it didn't work out with us."

Blaine sighs and coughs slightly in the process. An elevator sounds from somewhere down the hall. "Rose . . ." he begins softly, squeezing her hand with all the strength he has left. Rose hiccups and mops her eyes. "Rose . . ."

"Sorry that I thought that love was a rare thing that should be fought for, but to you, it was a commodity that you trade in when it no longer services you properly."

Blaine begins coughing and coughing and coughing as though he will never stop. Only death will allow him to catch his breath. Catch it and never throw it back. Rose stands in panic and goes to the head of Blaine's bed and attempts to slap him on the back. Blaine frantically shakes his head no.

"Couldn't you raise your arms over your head—do you want some water?" To all this, Blaine shakes his hacking head no. Rose stands by ashen, clenching and unclenching her fist. "Oh, God," she murmurs, "not only couldn't I make you happy, now I've killed you." Blaine starts to laugh now along with the coughing and gradually both subside and he grows quiet. Rose stands

266

beside him apologetically. Blaine's face looks ghastly now, glowing with perspiration. "You know, one of the things I'm looking forward to most about dying?" he says weakly. Rose shakes her head obediently no. "I won't have to talk about relationships anymore."

Rose's eyes fill with tears once more and she bows her golden, strawberry head. "Don't die, Blaine," she pleads. "Or, if you do, haunt me. You've haunted me in life—why not just continue?"

Blaine smiles a faint smile and closes his eyes. "I'll meet you on the snowy moors someday in the afterlife of bad relationships," he says weakly. "You and me and George and Martha and Heathcliff and Cathy. Out there at Pedington Crag. Driving each other insane for all eternity." He opens his eyes briefly and regards her listlessly, then closes them again. Faint, sad piano music begins to play from somewhere. "Remember kissing fever," he says in a half-whisper.

Rose sits beside him ever so carefully and takes up his hand again. "Yes," she says, looking at his face fiercely, as though she might burn it into her brain.

"Well, maybe that's what I'm dying of. Kissing fever."

"Kissing me," she says. The music grows stronger, more haunting, driving toward the imminent commercial.

"You couldn't get rid of me even when I was gone," he whispers with his eyes closed. "What makes you think you can do it now?"

A woman appears at the door. A beautiful, dark-haired, surprised-looking woman. "Blaine?" she says in a shocked voice. She holds the hand of a little girl with one hand and a homemade pie in the other.

Rose's head whirls around, her blond hair flying behind her back as she meets the gaze of the woman. "Leslie," says Rose.

The two women look at each other for a long, dramatic beat as the music surges and the shot holds.

"Cut," Dinah's voice said from the producer's booth at the back of the sound stage.

"Cut," echoed Nick, the director on the floor. Melissa and Josh, the two actors playing Rose and Blaine, looked expectantly past the camera to Nick, who was listening to Dinah over his headset. "Okay," he said, nodding, "I'll tell them." Nick moved onto the set and up to the two actors. "The ladies feel the scene is fine, that the two of you are terrific," he said soothingly. "So why don't we move on to the kitchen?"

Dinah sat in the control booth with Connie. They were smoking and staring at the empty monitor above their heads. With Rudy gone, Dinah's love shone on, lit like a little pilot light, its white-hot spotlight on an empty stage. She became an effect without a cause. Dinah and her lost cause. She flapped her wings, a hummingbird trapped in a shoebox. She learned to accept the situation without believing it or understanding it. Oh, believing it because when she looked out of her face, he wasn't there, and understanding because she spoke English; but, finally, it couldn't possibly have happened. So she polished up her effect and stole back into a world of lost causes, hoping to find one to fit her effect, carrying around her love for Rudy like an unopened, ragged letter.

Connie leaned over and slapped Dinah gently on the back. "Wanna order in Thai food?"

Dinah frowned and shrugged. "Sure," she said, exhaling a haze of smoke. "Something with peanut-butter sauce and very little nutritional value. Toy food."

Connie got up and went over to the phone on the table near the door, dialing the number of Tommy

Tang's. She ordered. "Chinese chicken salad for two and four double orders of chicken satay. Two diet Cokes and extra fortune cookies. Yeah. Great. Sorkin and Kaufman. Second floor, NBC—yes, great, you remember, no problem, thanks." Connie replaced the receiver and looked at Dinah with a pained expression on her face. "Do you have any aspirin?" she said, whining slightly as she crossed back to her chair and sat next to Dinah; the chair squeaked loudly.

Dinah reached down and got her purse. "I doubt it," she said, rummaging through its cluttered depths. "But then, I tend to doubt everything."

Connie put her arms down on the panel in front of her and put her head down on her arms. "I'm having my period. Well, maybe not *my* period, but *someone's*," she moaned. "I've gone through a maxi pad *and* . . ."

Dinah handed Connie a bottle of Advil. "Connie, please, no graphic descriptions of your menstrual process."

Connie took the Advil gratefully and swallowed them without water.

"Roy Delaney on line two for you, Dinah," a male voice announced over the intercom. Dinah and Connie exchanged glances with raised eyebrows. Dinah crossed to the phone, pressed in the flashing light and lifted the receiver.

"Well, as I live, breathe and produce soap operas," she said, smiling. "If it isn't the long-lost Roy Delaney."

"I may be lost," Roy's boyish voice assured her, "but I don't know how long I am. Who have you been talking to? I think I'm just kind of average. If you want a man that's well-endowed, then maybe . . ."

Dinah interrupted. "Having a man with an enormous penis has never been an overwhelming goal of mine," she drawled. "He might as well be a great billiards player. Big penis, great billiards player . . . they're

269

not even low on my list of what I look for in a man. They're more in the 'What to Avoid in the Quest for a Pleasant Mate' category."

"How've you been?" Roy interrupted earnestly. "You sound . . . similar."

Dinah laughed, looked at Connie, then down and away. "That can't be too good," she said almost shyly. "We bonded during an awkward period." There was an almost imperceptible pause.

"Have you spoken to Rudy?"

"Not for nine months," she said. "He called a couple of times, but . . ." She drifted off.

"It's great about him winning the Tony."

"Uh-huh," she said absently, "a play about the end of the world." Dinah picked invisible lint from her sleeve.

"Is he still with Lindsay?"

"No," she said victoriously. "I hear from his sister that that's over. She's gone back to her job. I hear he's with someone else now, though. Someone with a career as big as mine who doesn't live in New York. So much for his objections to me. Are you still with . . . everybody?" She lit another cigarette and inhaled deeply, waiting curiously for his reply.

"Not really, no," he said vaguely. "So I thought that since I'm relatively available and if you're relatively also, we could . . . I could treat you that way you like. We could make plans and I could show up late. Aren't you the girl who's aroused by disappointment?"

Dinah laughed. "What are you doing out here?"

"They're making my movie," he said, "so I'm haunting the set."

"I see," she said. "A ghost writer."

"Exactly," he said, "so . . ."

"Well," she said, "I guess we've tried it apart long enough."

"Part of my strategy in wooing you," he said. "Keep you waiting."

"I wondered what I was doing."

"Now you know."

"It seems like I've spent over half my life waiting for some guy. And now it turns out that I'm doing it even when I'm unaware of it."

"It's like that commercial," Roy said. " 'I'm cleaning my oven.' "

"Well . . ." she said, putting her cigarette out and moving the receiver from one hand to the other, "I guess our lives have finally worked out."

"What a relief, huh?"

"Who is this, again?"

"Does it matter?"

"I guess not."

"I'll pick you up at eight."

"Meaning ten."

"That's for me to know and you to get all worked up over."

"This is so beautiful."

"You don't know the half of it."

"No, no," she assured him ironically. "I *do* know the half of it. I know the half of it better than anyone. I know the half of it by heart."

"Well, you know what they say," he began.

"What?"

"I'll tell you later," he vowed. "But I can promise you this, you'll be disappointed."

"Oh, baby," she said, "you *know* what I like."

"I'm not touching you," he said in a singsong voice, hanging up the phone. Dinah replaced the receiver and looked at Connie.

"He doesn't know where I live," she marveled. Connie shook her head through a cloud of smoke as the door opened and the delivery boy stood laden with two bags

of pungent toy food. Through the open doorway, a faraway radio played. . . .

> Love brings such misery and pain;
> I know I'll never be the same since I fell
>   for you.
> Well it's too bad and it's too sad but I'm
>   in love with you.
> Oh, you love me then you snub me, oh,
>   what can I do?
> I'm still in love with you.
> I, I guess I'll never see the light,
> I get the blues most ev'ry night since I fell
>   for you,
>   since I fell for you.

Connie and Dinah unpacked the bags of food and
poured the contents of the paper boxes onto their plates.
Steam rose invitingly from the food. Dinah twisted open
a beer from the refrigerator, as an alternative antidote
beverage to her Diet Cola. Connie hungrily licked some
stray sauce from her fingertips. "Is the world getting
smaller," she mused, "or am I getting fatter?—Be careful
how you answer."

Dinah swigged her beer, her eyes meeting Connie's
as she lowered the bottle and swallowed. "This reminds
me of that time I had déjà vu," she said, wiping her
mouth with the back of her hand.

"Good answer," said Connie appreciatively, biting
into her chicken satay. "Safe, but good," she continued
with her mouth full so she could be barely understood.
The phone rang and Dinah's eyes briefly met Connie's
and looked away in embarrassment. She crossed to the
phone and answered.

"It's me," the voice said on the other end. "Are we still on for dessert?"

"Yes," said Dinah, her back to Connie, her eyes on the floor.

"Great," said Dinah and replaced the receiver. She said, "Just don't make fun of me, Con, promise me that."

"Make fun of you?" Connie laughed. "Dinah, everyone should have an affair with a younger man before they're too much older. Hey, he's gorgeous, he's smitten and he's partly in character. What more could you ask for without paying too high a price?"

"I hate feeling like I'm some sort of adventure for him."

"Hey, it's not as though you have to buy him his first pair of long pants and help him with his homework. It's only a five-year difference, right?"

"But where could it possibly lead?"

"Oh, Dinah, just enjoy yourself. And, failing that, enjoy him. It might easily run aground, but in the meantime, enjoy the ride."

Dinah finished off her beer, faced Connie like a good soldier and saluted. "Heil, Hipsters," she said and strode majestically from the booth.

Dinah had found herself buying lingerie as though for some phantom trousseau. Flimsy, diaphanous nightgowns, corsets with push-up bras, garter belts and black stockings. Storming the fortress of femininity as it were, as she hoped it would be. Well, if she was going to be this barren career chick, then she'd also be this not-so-secret slave to someone's idea of love.

The shine of plausibility that had formerly gone off all her affairs now shone out of her eyes. The personality she was poured spilled out of these eyes, her hands, her mouth—got itself all over everything. It promised something. Come warm yourself by the fire of my personality.

Dinah took her polished effect and carried it around. A love letter to her long-lost causes from their prospective effect.

His flat warm hand on the small of her back—but it's not Rudy's now, is it? No, not his at all, but a new hand. It couldn't be Rudy's. His power had been in establishing uncertainty. This man is almost certain. He raises the curtain of certainty. His is a bluer eye, a lighter, more hesitant touch. Furtive. Fraught. Keeping her guessing, but she keeps guessing right. Rudy, who had loved her in a leaving way, her accessory to a delusion, who had cut off his nose to spite her face, whom she no longer needed not to have anymore. Rudy was gone.

In his place was Josh, whom she lay with in his dressing room, the actor whom she had made in Rudy's image, the actor who played Blaine MacDonald. Dinah wearing the robe that Josh professed to hate, Josh wearing nothing but his shorts, his cabana-boy shorts and his hospital identification bracelet from the show. Fugitives from an informed world.

He looked perplexed, out of his element and into hers. She ruffled his hair gently. "What's the matter, cat got your brain? Soap star feeling sudsy?"

He brushed her hand aside, flustered, embarrassed. "Don't you ever change your mind about who you are?" he asked. "I mean, don't you modify it?"

Dinah shifted and looked to the ceiling for her reply. "I guess," she said finally. "Don't you?"

"Yeah," he said. "I do and that's what scares me. More about you than me. I mean, what's to stop you from . . ." He trailed off and pursed his lips.

Dinah drew him closer to her. "What's to stop me from what?"

Josh shrugged. "Anything—going back to Rudy— anything. I mean, all that was so recent."

Dinah interrupted. "What's to stop you from going out with someone your own age?"

"You," he said simply.

She smiled. "So, until we know where we stand, let's continue lying down."

They kissed. That sweet "X" of embracing, of interfacing. This ripe, dark peach. As she entered into the kiss, she wondered if Roy would call her later, pick her up, be in her life, wade a little farther in . . . matter . . . would her mind let him matter?

She breathed into Josh's blond forgiving hair. "Here's what I like," she whispered. He smiled into her neck. "Ready?" she said, their catechism beginning. "No touching really crucial body parts until absolutely necessary. Give me ever so little when it's almost too late. I'm your creature, your little monster Frankensex."

Josh's finger lightly traced the top of her thigh.

"All warm with waiting," she continued sedately.

"If less is more, there's no end to you."

Dinah smiled, closed her eyes and turned toward him where they now lay side by side on the couch. His warm flat hand found the small of her back.

"What I like," she whispered. "No, not what, who."

Not so much in love, but in lingerie, in emotional escrow. Not so much of the world but in it. In it all the same. A seminal backup singer.

Maybe it was years of portraying Rudy that made him so right to play this part. Or maybe he was just born to it. But, whatever the reason, he was her boy, her most recent beau.

Josh's hand lightly stroked her back; the first two fingers of his right hand traced the length of her spine over her cotton blouse. "I hate that you know I like you," he said miserably.

"Why?" she asked, kissing him on the chin, pressing her body into him, feeling always like a voyeur.

"Oh because," he began, "I don't know. Normally I do things, you know, where I don't let them—women—know that I like them. But with you—well, all of a sudden it's too late for you to not know that I like you." He shifted a little underneath Dinah, who raised herself up and looked at him. Josh avoided her gaze, saying, "I feel like I should cross the room and protect myself."

"Why shouldn't *I* cross the room?" asked Dinah. "Why shouldn't I cross the room to protect myself?"

Josh looked up at her now, her head framed in overhead light. " 'Cause you can protect yourself from here," he explained, his index finger on her bottom lip. "You can be across the room from here."

Dinah's eyes softened and she half smiled. "You're so . . ." She ran a hand through his fair hair thoughtfully. "You're so *enjoyable*," she said.

"Mmmmmm," murmured Josh. "Hmmmm." He shook his head slowly.

"What?" said Dinah.

"Nothing," he said.

"What?"

"Nothing," he said, pulling her closer, his arms around her back, squeezing her to him. "I was just afraid you would say something like that."

"Like what?"

"Never mind."

"Why do you think I'm doing this?" she asked rhetorically.

Josh hesitated for a moment and then said flatly, "Research."

Dinah pulled her head back sharply, as though it had been caught in the cookie jar. She laughed, abashed and exasperated. "That's me," she said, coloring. "A guinea pig offered up to the great experiment of what it is to be romantically human."

With Josh, she felt that she had been given a stay of

276

execution, a governor's pardon. An affair that was more a haven than her usual hive. When her mind moved to make him a mouse in the enemy workshop of her head, she held it at bay. Maybe he had pretended to be her version of Rudy for so long that it had come true, he had come true, come home. With his handsome, impassive face and his turned-away way of talking, his goyish inscrutability. She had traded in one brand of indifference for another and had been in some way healed in the swap. Josh reached up over her head and turned off the light, returning to her and kissing her in earnest, pulling her shirt up over her head and throwing it across the room.

Dinah held her breath in anticipation. There was something so emotional in Josh's embrace. As if they were coupling in a bomb shelter, the sound of enemy planes overhead. Passionately, tenderly together as though each time was the last. Afterward she could never quite remember what he looked like. An entity. A benign loving entity, breathing with her in the dark, the danger now past. The air raid over.

"How much longer to run through?" she asked breathlessly.

Josh grinned as he put his hands up her skirt, precariously near her privates. "Not quite long enough," he said. "Your favorite."

Dinah took a little sharp intake of breath and put the back of one hand to her forehead. "It didn't take you long to get my number," she said, smiling now, her head slightly tilted back, her eyes closed.

"Yeah," Josh said smiling, his mouth on her neck, then so near an ear.

"Now, if you could get the other six, you could call me," said Dinah. "We could have phone sex. But until then . . ."

Josh kissed her deeply now, briefly. "We'll just have to do it in person," he said as he began descending her body, starting high on her torso and working his way slowly down with his mouth, breathing, kissing. Dinah resisted, arching her back.

"What is in person?" she asked dreamily, beginning to take her mind away, beginning her imminent foray into obedience. "What is that?"

Josh paused somewhere to the right of a breast. "You're soaking in it," he said before recommencing kissing her, again on the breast, taking it into his mouth, breathing in, breathing out. An expert in her field.

Dinah's head lolled to one side expectantly. Putting her other hand over her head, the one from her forehead now found her mouth; she bit her first finger. Touch— that old, lumbering moth—fumbled against her flame. She sighed, her other hand resting gently on his head. Luxuriating in the warm bath of *I want to be with you.* This man wants to be with her. And for the time being, she can find no fault with him for that. From outside the door and down the hall, she heard a garbled male voice announce something, page someone. Josh descended. Dinah's eyes opened, briefly focused, then closed. Pick someone and make it work. "Entity," she whispered over the top of Josh's blond head, golden like Lindsay's. His mouth moved gently down her side, teasing. She shivered, her mind wandered, went down a dreamy road. What was happening? Which man was this? Or is it all one thing? Roy? No. Rudy? Hmmm.

———

She was in a car with Rudy; he was driving. It was a beautiful day. Sunshine sparkled in the trees. Her hand rested on his between the two of them in the front seat as they sped along the road and over a hill. There were no Band-Aids on her thumbs and she wore a golden wedding band. The sky darkened as their car stopped at a toll booth. A river roared somewhere below. Dinah counted out $39.50 and handed it to her father in the toll booth, not thinking it strange to find him there, noticing only that the booth was on the wrong side. Not on the driver's side but on the passenger's; not on the left, but on the right. As the car drove slowly across the bridge, Rudy's hand slipped out of Dinah's and she looked out of the window at the river rushing beneath the bridge.

The car passed over the bridge and onto land again and they were driving through the woods. Driving through the dark woods. Suddenly, the car swerved out of control toward the trees. Dinah looked over and found Rudy gone now, no one driving the car. She grabbed the wheel, avoiding a tree, got in the driver's seat, wondering where Rudy had gone, how she would ever find the main road. She drove through the trees lit only by her headlights along the bumpy path, lost. In the Amazon, lost. Up ahead, she noticed a tall tree in a clearing. As she came closer, she saw a man standing beneath it. A black man. Dinah drove up to him, stopped, and the man got into the car. He told her that his name was Shakespeare, that he'd been waiting there for her for a long time. Long before the sky had filled with numbers he had seen her among them and was prepared to wait forever. He guided her to the main road, the sky was clearer there, the road seemed to stretch on forever. Dinah and Shakespeare headed for the horizon, staring straight ahead. The sun shone red and low in the sky. Across it were scrawled the words "Heart's Desire."

The relationship Rudy and Dinah had together now went on without them, leaving them behind. The missed boat, the jumped ship, the wayward bus. The bus that went farther and farther along the road, kicking up a lot of dust, heading toward the sun. And the dust would then settle on their subsequent mates, causing Dinah's eyes to water, Rudy to sneeze.

Giving away the company they once covetously

kept. Yep, even so and odder still, the thing they were together couldn't entirely come apart. It existed out there somewhere, a distant, yet undeniable fact. Former, but no less formidable—the Ceylon of sweethearts, of love. Change the maps, alter the charts, you'll still in some ways steer by this star. Navigate safely through those past-infested waters; they continue to lap somewhere at your back. Far from home, however broken, the thing they'd been together now mutated and took new form. The great damp and dusty beast, Ceylon, once the fierce terror of the track, now grazed, swaybacked and toothless —a faded specter of his glory days.

Because, after all, nothing is ever really over. Just over there.

The female human being, given a certain unseemly interpretation of her childhood, specific to the absence of the male parent, will tend to fixate on unavailable males in her maturity, and yearn for them mournfully until her death. Some recover by mating with friends and learning to "love" them. The rest remain fairly successful in daytime television.

ACKNOWLEDGMENTS

I would like to thank my mother for being such a good sport about what people think apropos of what I write and from whom all good things stem; my sometime roommate and full-time brother Todd; my father for "that Jewish thing"; my friend and by strange coincidence my agent and evil twin Elvis, Kevin Huvane, who thicked me into thin. For my editor, Trish Lande, who cheered me along as only someone under thirty could do, and my editor-in-chief, Michael Korda, who cheered me along as only someone over thirty could do. For my publisher, Charles Hayward, who told me to take my time and if that wasn't sufficient, he would give me some of his. For my Buddhist lawyer and boon companion, Michael Gendler—there are no words (there are, however, a couple of tattoos). For my confidante, Gloria Crayton, who keeps me company and slightly overweight. For my assistant, Cindy Lee Rogers, who keeps me sheltered from the hectic nuances of a hostile world and provides me with an unrealistic view of what is actually going on; my researcher, Bonnie Wells, who helped me explore the world of mating animals and fight the good fight of computer printout. My tree surgeon and Eastern religions expert Harper Simon; my crop duster and dermatologist Arnold Klein; my ace agent Owen Laster; financial advisor Les Kaufman; my alter ego and alter kecker Merle Obelesque, haberdasher (East Coast) Daniel Melnick, haberdasher (West Coast) Buck Henry; my pit crew: Richard

Dreyfuss, J. D. Souther, Dave Sandborn, Dr. Michael Gould, Ed Moses, Charles Wessler, and Julian Ford. My paramedics: Penny Marshall, Barbara Hershey, Beverly D'Angelo, Seven MacDonald, Betty Bacall, and Anjelica Huston for their flagging support. And for my tribe of good friends and magic people: Bruce Wagner, Meg Wolitzer, Chana Ben Dov, Beatriz Foster, Chaik and Melissa Chassay North, Jack "froggy" Winter, Arlene Sorkin, Mary Douglas French, Rosalie Swedlin, Maggie Schmidt, Sidney Prince, David Geffen, Rightbrained Steven, Anne Howard Bailey, Mary Wynn, Malcolm Ford, Shelly Wanger, Hannah Dunne, Chloe Malle, May Quigley, Mike Nichols, David O'Connor, John Calley, Jim Borelli, Romanelli, The Scotts, The Idles, The Ostins, Andrea, Howard, Reigo, Poodlecut, Linda, Bob, Dana, Lucas, Begley, Don Henley, Albert, CAF, Sean, Carin, Ilene, and Mister Snickles. And to Gavin de Becker without whom I could not have written these acknowledgments and to Bryan who wishes I hadn't.